WELL DRESSED TO DIE

(INCLUDING BONUS SHORT STORIES)

THE CHARLETON HOUSE MYSTERIES

KATE P ADAMS

Copyright © Kate P Adams 2023

The right of Kate P Adams to be identified as the author of this work has been asserted by her in accordance with the Copyright, Designs and Patents Act 1988.

All rights reserved. No part of this publication may be reproduced, transmitted, or stored in a retrieval system, in any form or by any means, without permission in writing from the author, nor be otherwise circulated in any form of binding or cover other than that in which it is published and without similar condition being imposed on the subsequent purchaser.

All characters in this publication, other than those clearly in the public domain, are fictitious and any resemblance to real people, alive or dead, is purely coincidental.

Cover design by Dar Albert

ALSO BY KATE P ADAMS

THE CHARLETON HOUSE MYSTERIES

Death by Dark Roast

A Killer Wedding

Sleep Like the Dead

A Deadly Ride

Mulled Wine and Murder

A Tragic Act

A Capital Crime

Tales from Charleton House

Well Dressed to Die

THE JOYCE AND GINGER MYSTERIES

Murder En Suite

Murder in the Wings

In memory of my father.
We agreed that you can never have too many books.

1

'I decided I should tone things down a little, I don't want to pull all the attention away from the Duchess.'

I looked in the rear-view mirror at my colleague, Joyce Brocklehurst. She was wearing a very smart pair of black trousers, but the knee-length animal-print jacket and matching stiletto heels could never be described as 'toned down'. Her signature blonde bouffant was reaching for the skies as usual and her gold hoop earrings swayed as she talked.

I looked across at Mark in the passenger seat, who shrugged his shoulders.

'She looks perfectly demure to me, I was thinking of signing her up at the nearest convent.'

'Careful, Mark Boxer, or I'll strangle you with your seat belt.'

He smirked, but I noticed he took hold of the black strip of fabric where it sat close to his neck, just in case it was more than a threat.

I drove along the estate road, slowing down for sheep who had ventured onto the tarmac and knew they had the upper hand… or hoof. Off to one side and glowing in the evening sun was Charleton House, a grand baroque building that loomed over the surrounding estate. Palace-like in its sumptuous setting, a display of aristocratic privilege, it had been the family home of the Fitzwilliam-Scotts for 500 years. And, in a manner of speaking, it was my office.

The modern-day Fitzwilliam-Scotts, the 12th Duke and Duchess of Ravensbury, welcomed the public into their house, and every year over half a million people explored the grand rooms, admired the exquisite paintings, wandered the gardens, and demanded coffee and cake. My job as head of catering expanded far beyond running the three cafés, but there were days when I felt as if scones and chocolate croissants were the centre of my universe.

This evening, however, I and my colleagues Joyce, who managed the gift shops, and Mark, a tour guide who regularly held the visitors to Charleton in the palm of his hand with his extensive knowledge of the house's history, had been invited to join the Duchess on one of her trips to support the local community. Tomorrow, the village of Castledale would celebrate the tradition of well dressing, an ancient custom that gave thanks for a reliable water source. Many of the wells – or springs – no longer existed, but the custom of decorating them, or the place they had come to the surface, with images made from flower petals and other natural materials had thrived in Derbyshire in particular. The Duchess was going to see the final stages of the process and congratulate the villagers involved.

I'd shown interest when the Duchess had mentioned this in a meeting. Although I'd grown up in Derbyshire, I didn't know much about the custom and thought it would make a fascinating Friday night out. Mark's reasons for coming were a lack of anything decent on the TV and the hope that I'd buy him dinner in the pub first. Joyce was probably hoping she'd meet a man. It hardly seemed to me like prime man-hunting territory, but Joyce could sniff out a vulnerable male at a hundred paces.

He didn't even need to be single.

2

*A*fter having dinner at a local pub we made our way to the Castledale village hall, which was a hive of activity. There was a palpable air of anticipation among the workers who hoped to exchange a few words with the Duchess. The large stone building at the centre of the Derbyshire village hummed with the voices of women and children, and a couple of men, all of whom were leaning over great slabs of clay, gently pressing flower petals, twigs, mosses, seeds and other bits and pieces found in nature into the soft material.

Over time, pictures emerged. The most common were biblical scenes, but Winnie the Pooh and a dinosaur got a look-in too. A table in the corner held a tea urn and plates of homemade cakes.

The Duchess of Ravensbury was being shown around and introduced to the team members by a rather smug-looking man who, we soon learned, had been roped in at the last minute as the chair of the well-dressing committee had failed to arrive. I imagined, as we followed in the wake of the Duchess, that we made a strange sight: a woman somewhat north of sixty dressed like an escapee from the nearest zoo, a six-foot-tall, stick-thin man with a waxed and curled moustache and a watch chain hanging from his waistcoat pocket like a Victorian dandy, and me. Five foot nothing on a good day, and only if the wind is blowing in the right direction.

'As you can see, they have a wooden base that takes the shape of the final display. The wood has been soaked and the clay has been prepared by mixing it with water – we call that puddling. You see, we need to ensure that the clay is damp enough that it will hold all the materials, and stay damp for the duration of the display being in place, but not so wet that it slips off the wooden board when placed in an upright position.' The man waved his arms around, giving a demonstration of the actions required at each stage of the process.

'A full-sized paper outline of the final image will be laid over the clay. Next, we use the pricking technique – an implement such as a cocktail stick will be poked through to make an impression and you're left with lines of small dots. Following that, we mark the outline with dark material, commonly wood – twigs, branches, that sort of thing. After that, we fill in the outline. We will start with more durable items such as leaves and stones, and the delicate items such as petals will be placed as late as possible.'

I knew that the Duchess had been a regular at well-dressing events for years and was familiar with exactly how the displays were made. She'd probably assisted on a few occasions, but her host Barry Rushton seemed to be enjoying the sound of his own voice. As he rattled on, the Duchess exchanged a few words with members of the team without him appearing to notice. It was like waiting for a wind-up toy to run out of steam.

I hung back, watching the ease with which the Duchess engaged in small talk. She was a tall, handsome woman with a warmth and wit that inspired loyalty and affection. Wearing a pastel-coloured dress ideal for the warm May evening, the flower-petal pattern a perfect choice, she chatted to an older couple. The man was showing the woman how to make sure the petals wouldn't fall out, and the three of them were laughing. The couple appeared to be telling her a story that left the Duchess smiling and congratulating them.

Recently, I had been avoiding spending too much time in the company of the Duke and Duchess, except where my work made it necessary. We had always got on very well, but last year I had ended up solving a mystery that resulted in their younger son going to prison. It wasn't my fault that he'd broken the law, but I was sure my presence was a constant reminder, so I had tried to stay out of their way. However, things were beginning to defrost between us and I felt that an evening like this one, surrounded by lots of people and with a central focus to distract us, would be unlikely to result in any awkwardness.

'Ah, Ginger, lovely to see you. Thank you so much, Mr Rushton, that's all been extremely interesting.' With a smile that could have brought an end to wars, the Duchess gracefully halted Barry Rushton's verbal deluge and turned her attention elsewhere. 'Ginger, how are you?'

'Your Grace, lovely to see you again. I don't know where Cora could 'ave got to, this is most unlike her.'

'Not to worry, these things happen. It's good to see you involved for another year.'

'You try and stop me.' Ginger cackled, her eyes crinkling as she laughed. 'Chances are that when my time comes, I'll snuff it face first into one of these things.' I watched Barry cringe. He looked about to step in, until the Duchess roared with laughter.

'Well do it on a night I'm not here, if you don't mind, although it would seem rather fitting to go that way. How long have you been doing this now?'

'Forty-five years, started off side by side with my old mum.'

'I'm so pleased your family is keeping the tradition going. Joyce, you'll like this.' The Duchess pointed at the picture that

Ginger was painstakingly recreating in dried petals and tree bark. The body of a tiger was almost complete. I had to stifle a laugh as Joyce realised that she was on the receiving end of the Duchess's sense of humour.

'Don't you start. Ginger's spent the last couple of weeks making jokes about using my wardrobe as research.'

'You know one another?' asked the Duchess, understandably surprised to discover that the rather garishly dressed clothing-obsessed Joyce was friends with a woman wearing a plain smock that had smears of clay all over it and whose hair was partly pinned up with a pencil, the remaining tendrils in a state of disorder.

'We sure do,' replied Ginger. 'Done some travelling together as well. After sharing a hotel room with her, I could tell you stories that would make your toes curl.' She gave the Duchess a knowing look, and then laughed at the pained expression on Joyce's face. 'You not going to come and have a look, old girl? You did inspire it after all.'

Joyce rolled her eyes, then cautiously tottered her way over to the leaf- and petal-littered table. I knew she'd be worried about getting clay and mud on her pristine outfit.

'Here, you have a go.' Ginger thrust a handful of twigs towards Joyce, who stared at them briefly. Then, aware of the Duchess's gaze, she leant over the dressing and made a start. Ginger joined in next to her and as Joyce's mood thawed, they started to chat. The Duchess moved off and Mark called my name.

'Soph, Soph, over here. You'll like this one.' He was standing with a woman who was creating an image of swooping birds, and introduced her as Emily Dockery. 'Check out the coffee beans. I'd be careful, Emily. Sophie might steal a handful to suck on.'

Emily laughed. 'Might not be a bad idea, I'd get this done in half the time. My back's killing me. I don't know how some of this lot have been doing it all these years.'

'Ya love it really,' Ginger bellowed across the room. Joyce looked up, eyes wide, and glanced at the Duchess, who was examining a growing picture of Winnie the Pooh and telling the children making it how clever they were. If she'd heard Ginger's impression of a foghorn, she didn't let on.

Emily looked at me and raised an eyebrow. 'She's got ears like a bat.'

'How did you get into it?' I asked.

'My mum's been doing it for a couple of years.' She nodded in the direction of a woman who appeared to be very focused on her work. 'I grew up here, but we moved away for a time after my dad passed away. Then Mum moved back and I used to visit her. Eventually, I decided I'd move here too. Our neighbour suggested we get involved with the well dressing. It's a great way to make new friends.'

She leant over and added a coffee bean to finish creating the word 'Swallow'. The picture showed a number of swallows swooping over gently rolling Derbyshire hills.

'Swallow Well,' Emily explained. 'Imaginatively named because it's on Swallow Lane! There is an actual well still in place.'

On the other side of the room, the Duchess was looking at the work of a woman who appeared to be 100 if she was a day.

'That's Betty Natchbull,' Emily told us. 'She's been that shade of red since it was clear Cora wasn't going to show up. She's furious and you don't mess with Betty.'

'Who is Cora anyway?' asked Mark as he nibbled on a coffee bean before screwing up his face, and tossing it in the general direction of a bin.

'Cora Parrish, she's the current chair. Took over the role two years ago and she's been pretty good so far. She works at a university in Sheffield and the trains are notoriously bad, so she's probably stuck between stations without a phone signal.'

'And Barry?' The man in question didn't look happy.

'He's the treasurer, been doing this for years. He was furious when Cora got the job, he's been coveting the role of chair for ages. He quickly volunteered to welcome the Duchess when there was no sign of Cora. I say volunteered, but I think he would have kneecapped anyone who tried to stop him. I suspect he thought this evening was his chance to hobnob with nobility, but that hasn't gone to plan.'

As we spoke, Barry was trailing behind the Duchess; he'd given up trying to guide her around the room.

'Did you see the article on us in the local paper yesterday?' Emily asked. I nodded, recalling a large photograph of Cora standing next to one of the partially completed well dressings. 'I half expected him to go around buying every copy and make an enormous bonfire. He was in a dreadful mood all last night. He's going to give himself a heart attack if he's not careful.'

Mark nudged me and I followed his eyes over to Joyce. Her jacket carefully hung over the back of the chair and the sleeves on her low-cut, faux-diamond-encrusted top rolled up, she was leaning over the board next to Ginger and they were chatting away as though they'd been working on the well dressing together for weeks.

'She should be careful,' said Mark, concern in his voice.

'It's only cotton,' I reassured him. 'If she gets anything on that top, it'll wash out.'

'That wasn't what I meant. She bends over any further, there's going to be a pair of indentations that Ginger hadn't planned for.' He wasn't wrong. Joyce had a cleavage that could bring traffic to a halt and right now it looked like it was keen to play its part in the evening's activity.

Emily laughed. 'I expected tonight to be a dull affair of forelock-tugging to the Duchess. You lot can come again.'

'I'm not sure Barry would second that request.' Mark pointed at the corner of the room, where a very annoyed looking Barry had got himself a cup of tea and was stuffing a piece of cake into his mouth. He was glancing back and forth between the Duchess, who was happily showing herself around the tables and chatting to whoever she found at each one, and the loudly guffawing partnership of Ginger and Joyce. He and Betty might not have been having much fun, but everyone else was having a blast.

3

'I just don't get it,' muttered Mark as we walked back to my car. 'Did they not have enough toys when they were children? Were they sent up chimneys and forced to earn their keep?'

'What are you going on about?' demanded Joyce. She was walking slightly ahead of us, her heels tap-tap-tapping down the middle of the quiet country lane. 'They're artists, dedicated to a centuries-old tradition.'

Mark looked over at me with a curious expression on his face. I knew what he was trying to communicate. Joyce would ordinarily have described something like the well dressing as a poxy little local distraction that bunged up the traffic and got in her way.

'I'll never understand you and Ginger,' said Mark. 'She seems like such a sensible, level-headed person. What have you done to make her want to spend time with you? Do you drug her?'

'I, Mark Boxer, will never understand *you*.' There was a pause. 'That's it, I'll never understand you.'

I ignored the bickering that continued between the pair and

looked out across the countryside. The sun was well below the tree line as we made our way towards the small car park, a five-minute walk from the centre of the village. I could have parked on the main street, but I'd decided that this would force me to get at least a little bit of exercise. When I first started work at Charleton House, I had taken to walking the two miles from my cottage, but that burst of enthusiasm had soon worn off and I couldn't remember the last time I had worn my hiking boots. My ever-tightening clothing was a daily reminder of my expanding waistline and I could no longer blame Christmas, which had been my excuse until well into April when it was superseded by Easter Eggs.

The shadows that had been cast by the tall stone walls on either side of the lane were losing their definition, and the colours in Joyce's jacket had become variations on the theme of grey.

'Oh, for heaven's sake!' Joyce exclaimed. 'Some people! The human race is the most lazy, despicable…'

'Careful there, you'll burst a blood vessel. What's irritated madam now?' Mark spoke the final few words in a mock posh tone.

'That! Louts, these people who think they can drive around the countryside and dump bags of rubbish or unwanted furniture.' She waved her finger insistently at a dark shape on the side of the road. It did look as though someone had abandoned a roll of carpet.

'That's Swallow Well,' I informed them. 'The one that Emily was making a dressing for.' When she'd told us, the name had sounded familiar, I now realised because we'd parked down Swallow Lane.

The simple stone well had a roughly carved base with low walls set into a grassy bank. Clear water pooled to about ten inches deep, and the roll of carpet or pile of clothing had been dumped on the edge.

'Let's gather it up and throw it in the back of my car. I'll put it in that skip in the gardeners' yard up at the house.'

'No, you won't,' said Mark, sounding unusually serious. 'You'll be calling the police. That's a body.'

Humped uncomfortably over the low wall, the body was face down in the shallow water. Floating hair radiated out from the head. A bright orange scarf fluttered around the neck. Everything was still and quiet.

Mark took out his phone and turned on its torch mode.

'Well, we now know why Cora Parrish didn't turn up,' I said.

'She couldn't swim?' asked Mark. Joyce thumped him, hard. 'How do you know it's Cora?' he asked me.

'The newspaper article yesterday had a photo of her. I can't see her face, but I'm sure it's her.'

Joyce had taken Mark's phone from him and was studying the body. 'That jacket wasn't cheap, I recognise the brand.'

'Oh, so judging her wardrobe is okay, but a bit of gallows humour isn't?'

'Stop bickering,' I demanded. 'Mark, call the police. I hope Joe didn't have any plans for his Friday night.'

4

'So, this is how you spend your Friday evenings?' Detective Constable Joe Greene didn't look at all surprised to see us. But then the three of us had developed a bit of a reputation for associating with the dead as well as the living.

'It's Cora Parrish,' I told him as he walked over to the body.

'One step ahead of us as ever, Sophie.' He was serious, focused on the task at hand, but there was no malice in his voice. I was fond of Joe, and I knew he felt the same way about me. There had been a time when we might have started dating, but I'd concluded he was more like a brother. I had finally stopped questioning that decision and was genuinely happy for him and Ellie, his girlfriend.

'So, what were you three doing out here in the dark?'

'We had dinner at the pub back in the village,' I told him, 'and then joined the Duchess at the well-dressing preparations. We were just walking back to the car when we found her. Cora Parrish, chair of the Castledale well-dressing committee, hadn't turned up to meet the Duchess.'

'I'm going to assume she wasn't here when you arrived, so what time did you leave the car?'

I looked over at Joyce, hoping she'd clocked the time.

'Five-thirty. I wanted to check that Sophie didn't need to pay in the car park, but it's free from five pm, so we were okay. And no, officer, we did not walk past a dead body because of an overwhelming urge for fish and chips. Although I wouldn't put it past either of these two, I certainly put the life of another before the needs of my stomach.'

'I bet you wouldn't say the same thing if we waved a bottle of Veuve Clicquot in front of you.'

'Mark!' Joe sounded stern, but then he could get away with reprimanding his brother-in-law. 'Leave the lady alone.' I watched the dark outline of Joyce stand a little straighter in response to Joe's supportive comment. 'Any idea why she'd be down here? Where does she live? Do you know?' He seemed to be facing me, so I answered.

'No idea, unless she'd parked in the car park too. There are some houses further down the lane.' I pointed the way we had been heading.

Another police car drove slowly towards us, its lights blinding us.

'Alright, I know where to find you all, so I reckon the boss won't mind me letting you go. Someone will come and take statements from you later. Will you be at home or in the pub? No, don't answer that, we'll find you in the Black Swan.'

None of us bothered to feign indignation at his response. He knew us far too well.

We had indeed driven straight to the Black Swan, the picture-postcard pub that we considered our local, which was conveniently located over the road from my front door. But after the adrenalin had drained from our systems and the medicinal 'stiff drink' had worked its magic, we were all tired and ready to head home. It was there that Detective Sergeant Colette Harnby found me after a text to check I was okay with talking to her so late. I assumed Joe had been sent off to explore other lines of enquiry.

I didn't mind the late visit. I was tired, but the evening's events were still buzzing around my head and I was unable to settle. She'd just have to interview me in my pyjamas.

Harnby was seated in an armchair with a mug of black coffee, as immaculately dressed as ever in a dark suit, her bobbed hair neat and formal. When we'd first met, we had been wary of one another, but had warmed to each other's company. I was back amongst a pile of blankets at one end of the sofa. Pumpkin, my rotund and judgmental tabby cat, was sitting in front of the unlit fire watching us both, her head turning from side to side as we took it in turns to speak, reminding me of an umpire at Wimbledon. She'd been suspicious of Harnby since the DS had arrived; this was their first encounter and Pumpkin was clearly reserving judgement.

'Joe said you recognised the victim. Did you know her at all?'

'No, but her photo was in a newspaper article yesterday. So anything I know is from that. I do remember that it said something about her being involved with art – a university lecturer of some kind.'

'Do you still have the article?'

'If Pumpkin hasn't destroyed the newspaper, probably.' Pumpkin enjoyed lying on the part of the newspaper I was trying to read. She also had a tendency to start shredding it, which I thought was more of a dog thing, but then Pumpkin was large enough to resemble a dog from certain angles.

I fetched the newspaper from the recycling bin in the kitchen and returned to find Pumpkin staring at Harnby whilst she took a drink of coffee. Harnby reached out to stroke her, but Pumpkin dodged her fingers. She wasn't skittish; it was a slow, considered 'no you don't, I've not made up my mind yet' movement.

Harnby gave up on befriending Pumpkin and found the page

with the interview on it. After a couple of minutes of quietly reading, she spoke.

'Art history. She worked at the Sheffield Hallam University.'

'Someone did say that she worked in Sheffield and was probably stuck on a train somewhere. That line is a nightmare for cancellations and delays.' The rolling stock was ancient and deserved the nickname Nodding Donkey for the rough ride. Many was the time I'd got off rubbing my neck, convinced I had whiplash.

Having finally made a decision, Pumpkin walked towards Harnby and sat by her feet, staring at me. I laughed and pointed at her.

'You have yourself a bodyguard,' I told Harnby. This time, Pumpkin didn't move away as Harnby reached down to stroke her.

'We'll talk to everyone who was at the village hall this evening, but did you notice anything unusual?'

'No, nothing. Some snivelling little bloke, the treasurer, took over in Cora's absence. I got the feeling he was actually pleased she hadn't arrived so he could have his moment of glory. A few people commented on how surprised they were that she was late for the visit of the Duchess, but that was it.'

Harnby nodded. 'At least we can narrow down the time of death from the point at which you walked past the well on the way to the pub.'

'Have you confirmed that it was murder and she didn't just fall and lose consciousness?'

'That's one train of thought, but it's unlikely. There were… hang on, Sophie, I know what you're up to.'

I allowed a faint smile to cross my lips. I'd been so close.

'I was just…'

'Yeah, yeah, you were *just* alright. You were *just* seeing if you could trip me up and I'd give something away. I feel like it's a complete waste of my breath, but I'll say it anyway: let us do our job. We're pretty good at it, when you give us a chance. Thanks for the coffee, and if you think of anything else, give me a call.'

She rose from the armchair and Pumpkin immediately leapt into the warm seat. 'Blimey, you'd be in my grave as fast.'

'It means she likes you, she's keeping it warm in case you come back.'

Pumpkin looked up at Harnby with an expression that could only be called adoration. It was one I was rarely on the receiving end of, and the way she decided who she liked and disliked appeared to be entirely arbitrary. Harnby gave one of Pumpkin's ears a rub.

'Well, I'm afraid that's unlikely to happen soon, Pumpkin. I have a murder to solve, unless your mother gets in there before me and does her Sherlock impression, which she's not going to do, *is she?*' Harnby looked at me out of the corner of her eye and I pretended I'd seen something on the ceiling.

She sighed and I heard the fight leave her. 'Just call me if you learn anything, I'll let myself out.'

I listened to the sound of the front door closing and thought about Harnby's parting comment. I had been involved in a number of her cases and my curiosity was already running dozens of questions through my head. But this time, I was cautious. I knew that I had risked my job by getting involved with the case that had put the youngest member of the Fitzwilliam-Scott family in prison. Luckily, not for murder, as the killer had been another of the Duke and Duchess's employees, but the whole thing had been messy and I had sworn to myself that I wouldn't get involved in that sort of thing again.

But, an inner tempter reminded me, Cora didn't have any links to Charleton House. The Duchess's presence at the Castledale village hall on the night of Cora's death was a coincidence.

No, I still needed to steer clear, like Harnby said. I should let the police do their job. But I had so many questions, and there would be no harm in finding out a bit more about Cora.

I leant over and gave Pumpkin a kiss on the top of her head. I knew she hated it, but that made me want to do it even more.

'Goodnight, girl. I'll probably find it hard enough to sleep tonight as it is, so if you could chase mice quietly, I'd be very grateful.'

5

*B*eing at work on a Saturday morning was not unusual, but being asked to meet with the Duchess on a weekend was. I made sure the three cafés were up and running and my staff were all set for the barrage of Bank Holiday visitors that were expected, and then made my way to her office.

I had once been told to imagine Charleton House being split into three. A third was open to the public, a third was office and storage space, and a third remained the private home of the Duke and Duchess of Ravensbury, who preferred to be called simply 'Duke' or 'Duchess' by those who worked on the estate, rather than the more formal 'Your Grace'. A visit to the house was guaranteed to be interesting for the thousands of visitors who came every year. The Duke's ancestors had been close to royalty and prime ministers, and a few black sheep guaranteed there were plenty of stories to be told, none of which he actively attempted to hide. I had a good relationship with them both, even though they weren't shy in airing their opinions, and the cafés looked the way they did because of their tastes, not mine. But the day-to-day running was generally left in my hands.

The Duchess was sitting at her desk opening mail when I

arrived. Their fearsome PA Gloria never worked weekends, and her absence made my visit considerably less stressful.

'Sophie, come in, please take a seat. I never seem to get through my mail. Gloria vets most of it for me, of course, so it could be worse, but I do like to have a quick look through Saturday's delivery, make her job a little easier on Monday morning.

'Now, how are you? I believe things took rather a dramatic turn last night.' She still held the ornate silver letter opener in her hands. It seemed a little improper to discuss murder with a knife being turned over and over by the person asking the questions, but it was the Duchess, and I wasn't about to ask her to put it down.

'Fortunately, there wasn't a lot to see. Cora was just lying in Swallow Well. She wasn't there when we arrived, so the police know roughly when she was killed.'

'So, they've confirmed it was murder?'

'Oh, er, no. Not in so many words, but I think that's the path they're exploring.' I kicked myself for letting my mouth run away with me. DS Harnby had done no such thing, although I was pretty sure she had almost let slip her belief that it was murder last night.

'How awful, the poor woman. I hope her husband has family nearby who can support him. I always enjoyed her talks, she was so knowledgeable.' The Duchess's eyes rested on the windows and she seemed to be giving the whole sad affair some thought before focusing back on me. 'I'm sorry, Sophie, I didn't ask you here in order to grill you. How are you? That's what I want to know. I'm aware this isn't your first body, but it must have been a shock. You weren't alone, though? Joyce and Mark were with you?'

'Yes, we were all returning to the car. I'm fine. I'm glad to be working, though, it's a distraction.'

'And a Bank Holiday, so a busy weekend that should do more than simply distract you. You have a good team, Sophie, so if you do need to go home, don't hesitate. What about Joyce and Mark, are they working too? If they are, tell them the same thing.'

She picked up another envelope and ran the blade quickly along the top. I thanked her for her concern, and then stood up to leave.

'Oh and, Sophie?' Her strong features were still and she looked deadly serious as she leaned a little further over the desk. 'I know you've been a great deal of help with past incidents – embarrassingly so for the local police, I imagine – and it's not my role to warn you off. You're a very capable woman who can make her own decisions, but I do wonder how safe it is for you to be getting involved. Perhaps it's time you left this sort of thing to the police.'

The Duchess was someone I never wanted to lie to. Luckily, she saved me the need.

'You don't have to answer. Just think about it, please.' Her tone was one of steely concern, but I did wonder if I detected a little hint of warning in there.

'I will, thank you.'

I heard the top of another envelope rip as I closed the door behind me.

6

The Library Café could, under different circumstances, be called gloomy and suffer from its lack of natural light. But the deep leather armchairs and bookshelf-covered walls made it feel like a place of respite from the hordes of visitors and challenges of running a house with over 300 rooms.

I was grabbing my third coffee of the day in a lull between customers, and mulling over the changes I needed to make to the café menus before we kicked off the official summer season. Glancing up, I watched a small child as he stood on his mother's knee and reached for the shelving behind her head. The sound of a number of large hardback books crashing to the floor quickly distracted her from trying to rescue the carrot sticks that a second child was waving in the air and tossing onto the floor. I watched as my Library Café supervisor Tina retrieved the books, gave the mother a sympathetic smile and asked if she wanted another cup of tea.

'I attended one of Cora Parrish's talks last year.' Tina had returned to the counter and was preparing a pot of tea for the mother juggling her children. 'It started off being about a local artist, Wright somebody – the Duke owns a couple of his paintings. But during the Q&A, she started to talk about a big forgery scam. It was fascinating. Did you know that there were some forgers up the road from here who were making statues in their garden shed? They said they were more than 3,000 years old and they sold for hundreds of thousands of pounds. Ended up in museums and galleries as well. It's amazing what people get up to in their sheds. Cora stayed afterwards to answer any other questions, she was really generous with her time.'

I watched as Tina went back and chatted to the child who was keen to share her carrot sticks with everyone. The Duchess had also made a reference to enjoying Cora's talks, but I had never heard of her until very recently. If she was linked to Charleton House in any way, then I *really* should steer clear of the investigation.

I was dragged from my mental wanderings by the sound of a hand being slammed onto the counter. As soon as I saw the ruby-red nail polish and matching plastic bangles on the wrist, I knew whose it was. Joyce had opted for an outfit that guaranteed she was unlikely to go unnoticed, and I imagined more than a few husbands whose wives had given them a firm jab in the side and suggested that they pick their jaw up off the floor as Joyce had passed them on her way here. Her tight red skirt looked as if it had been spray-painted on and the outline of her knickers showed that… well, that she was indeed wearing some. The simple soft pale-cream sweater appeared, at first glance, to indicate that Joyce hadn't entirely abandoned a sense of modesty. That was until your eyes took in the multiple strands of large red beads and followed them down to the neckline, which appeared to be determined to head as far south as possible. I had no idea what she wore on her feet, but I guessed it wasn't a pair of brogues.

She eyed my mug of coffee. 'I'll have one of those if you don't mind, and something delicious and naughty to go with it. One of those chocolate eclairs will do the trick. I need all the energy I can muster today, the shops are heaving. That being said, you and I are going to make an early exit, as soon as things start to quieten down a bit. No point being in charge if you can't delegate from time to time.'

Or all the time, I thought, feeling rather guilty about the occasions I had abandoned my cafés to the staff in order to root out another killer.

'Where are we going? Has a new champagne bar opened up somewhere?'

'I wish. No, we're going to Ginger's. After last night's grim discovery, and once you lightweights had headed home from the pub, I paid her a visit. She made a few comments that I think are worth some of our precious time, so you and I are heading round there to get the local gossip. I also promised to take her some jewellery I never wear anymore that will liven up her outfits a little.'

To the status of clown – but I kept that thought to myself.

'We'll drive over together. See you in the car park at four. It's looking like a top-off kind of a day.' The customer next to her overheard and the poor man's eyes were out on stalks.

'Top of her car, she has a convertible,' I clarified. He didn't move, so Joyce clicked her fingers in front of his face.

'Get your mind out of the gutter, man. Sophie, I think he needs a black coffee.'

He turned to follow her retreating figure as she clacked and jangled her way towards the door. It seemed that every coffee came with a side order of entertainment in this place.

7

Seconds later Joyce returned, being dragged by Mark. He had hold of her arm, and I was assuming that it was only her well-hidden but genuine affection for the man that was preventing her from ripping his arm off at the shoulder.

'I have to talk to you both. Sophie, where can we talk?' He scanned the room with desperate eyes. The café was busy, but a family were just getting up from a table in the far corner. 'There, I'll grab that table. Sophie, you get our drinks, and Joyce and I will go and sit down.' He spoke in hurried breathless tones. It crossed my mind that he was on drugs, but the only thing he was likely to put into his system, other than alcohol, was his occasional use of snuff, which was more for show than anything.

Joyce shrugged and followed him to the table where they leapt into the seats the minute the customers' bottoms had risen. I made Mark a coffee. He wasn't getting a cake; the added sugar high might make his head explode.

'So, what's wrong?' I asked as I sat down. 'He told you yet, Joyce?'

'Not a thing, he's just sat here looking like he's seen a ghost, or been propositioned by the Duchess, or seen himself naked in a mirror.'

At that, he focused and screwed up his forehead. 'I am sat right in front of you. No, nothing like that.' He glanced around again.

'Oh, for crying out loud! Are you in trouble?' Joyce exclaimed.

'No, no, but I can't quite believe it and I don't think I'm meant to tell anyone yet. So this can go no further until it's all finalised…'

'Please, Mark, breathe,' I begged him. 'I've done the training, but never had to actually carry out CPR. Have a drink.'

'Mark…' Joyce gave him a firm look, her patience running out.

'Okay, but you have to keep this to yourself, no one must know…' He paused dramatically, and then with hands in the air and eyes wide, he continued. 'I'm going to be on television! I'm going to have my own show. Well, not quite a show, but I get my own segment every Friday on the *Derbyshire Life* section of the local news. I have ten minutes to talk about a piece of local history. After six weeks, they'll assess the response. TV… me… amazing!'

'What fool gave you that job? And how did you get through the audition without people laughing you out of the room?' I gave Joyce a look that I hoped she would interpret as *be nice.*

'I didn't audition. Well, not knowingly, anyway. It turns out that the producer came on one of my tours and he liked what he saw. He then arranged to come on another with some colleagues – not telling me, of course. Then they came to do an interview with the Duchess, who apparently said some very nice things about me, and the next thing is they arranged a meeting with me. I thought they just wanted some help with research, or possibly to interview me on camera. I've done quite a lot of that. But no! They want me to do six weeks of ten-minute segments. This could lead to my own series. Before you know it, I'll be on

Celebrity Great British Bake Off and doing one-off specials to mark significant dates in the calendar. I'll write a book, and then I'll have to do a lecture tour.'

'Alright, Lucy Worsley, calm yourself. First things first, what are you going to wear?'

He looked at Joyce with horror in his eyes. 'Heavens, you're right. I'll have to think very carefully about the effects of the camera, the lighting, where we're filming, what I'm talking about. The choice of colours, the cut of the suit, all of that will be important. Thank you, Joyce. I need to go, I have important decisions to make.'

He dashed out of the café as if his pants were on fire.

'God help the viewers of *Derbyshire Life*,' muttered Joyce as she drained her coffee. 'God help us all.'

8

'Now then, Joyce said you wanted to know about Barry.'

'Yes, and I'd like to know more about Cora. You've been working with her for a while, can you think of any reason why someone might want to kill her?'

Ginger took a slow drink of tea and got herself comfortable in her large squishy armchair.

'I've nothing but good things to say about her, but I know not everyone warmed to her when she arrived, ooh, a couple of years ago. She grew up round here, so I guess she was returning home. She was always polite, professional. Some might say she could be a little bit standoffish. You know, she'd come for a drink on special occasions, but didn't make a habit of it, unlike the rest of us. But I thought she was nice enough. She could be charming and was wonderful with the press and very good at fundraising, and she was passionate about continuing the tradition of well dressing.

'Now Barry, who you met last night, he went to school with her and says she wasn't quite so charming back then. A bully, he reckons, says she made him suffer for years. But then he did want to take over the role of chair when the opportunity arose and she got in there first, so that might just be sour grapes. Did you see his face when Cora didn't turn up? He was over the moon, it was his chance to hobnob with the high and mighty.

'Cora's good at organising the group, too. We've never been so organised. But Barry hasn't let it go, reckons she's got a mean streak. I've never seen it, though.'

'Do you think Barry hated her enough to want to kill her?' I asked.

'Now you're askin'. I don't really know, but I find it hard to imagine. I mean, it was schoolyard name-calling, as far as I know. I can't imagine that being enough to turn him into a killer, but then they do say that it can change you, being the victim of that kind of thing. If he's carried it with him all this time, maybe it's warped 'im.'

I had some understanding of what he might have gone through. I'd been bullied too at school. Nothing horrendous, just low-level taunting on and off. I was once told I had an enormous nose and the teacher joined in. It's not true, but at that age, I wasn't aware of how ridiculous the statement was. All I knew was that it hurt, it *really* hurt. A couple of days later, the name-caller and I were friends again. And so it went, the ebb and flow of children's cruelty.

But if it didn't change, if you were picked on time and time again, maybe it never left you.

'What else do you know about Cora? I noticed a wedding ring.'

'Hugh, that's her husband, he's an architect. Don't see much of him, he seems to spend his time between here and London. They have a big house down Swallow Lane where you found her.'

'So she was killed near home. We arrived with time to go to the pub for dinner, not long after five. What time were you all due to meet?'

Ginger shrugged. 'Different times throughout the day. The

night before the dressings go up is always a long one so everyone gets there as soon as they can. Some are there all day, some for a couple of hours. People leave to get some dinner if they've not brought any, pop out to pick up kids, that sort of thing, so there's a lot of to-ing and fro-ing.

'Cora had said she'd be there in the middle of the afternoon, certainly plenty of time before the Duchess was due. I'm sure she said she had a lecture in the morning, but would get to the village hall as quickly as she could. We all just assumed she was delayed at the university, and then got stuck on a train. I reckon Barry hoped the train had derailed.'

'Can you think of anyone else who might have had reason to hate her? Is there much competition between villages and the well dressings?'

'No, it's not a competitive thing. A bit of healthy rivalry maybe, but that's it, even between the teams here in Castledale. We all know how much hard work goes into the finished dressing so we'd never criticise anyone else's work, no matter what we thought.'

'That's a point, where is all your hard work?' asked Joyce. 'I don't see any of those displays. We didn't drive past any on the way here, either. Have the police put a stop to it?'

'Boards, Joyce, not displays. No, not entirely. The one that was meant to be placed at Swallow Well will have to go somewhere else. Poor Emily, she put a lot of hard work into that, but the others will go up tomorrow. We'd never cancel, that's not what Cora would have wanted, and the petals will survive a couple of days. We can do some fettling in the morning if things need repairing.'

After Joyce had dropped me back home, I stared at myself in the mirror. Following the ride with the top down, I looked as if I'd been dragged through a hedge backwards again and again and again, which was saying something. The closest I got to a beauty regime was trying to tame my silvery grey hair into an intentionally dishevelled style, but no matter what I did after Joyce had driven off, nothing would make it look anything other than utterly out of control.

I gave up. I wasn't going anywhere anyway.

'It's just you and me tonight, Pumpkin. You don't mind the fright wig, do you?' I was fairly sure that if I could read cats' minds, she'd be telling me that she couldn't see much difference from my usual appearance.

I picked her up and carried her through to the kitchen, where I put her down on the table. It was against the rules, but she ignored the rules at the best of times. A big, modern bright-red fridge dominated the room from its corner; I'd paired it with a matching espresso machine and the two items were my pride and joy. I was testing my espresso maker to the limits, but the fridge was largely a work of art in my mind, and the few jars and plates of leftover food didn't even begin to fill the thing.

I was staring into its depths wondering if there would be more choice in the freezer when Mark's name and a message came up on my phone.

'*I hear you've been investigating without me, I'm hurt and offended.*'

Great, Joyce must have had reason to message him and told him that Ginger had been filling us in.

'*Never, I was preparing the ground for you,*' was my response. There was silence, so I tried again. '*Fancy going to see the well dressings tomorrow? It's my day off. Bound to sniff out something of interest. I'll buy you lunch.*' If that didn't appease him, nothing would.

'*Great, early morning tour finishes at 10 then I have rest of day off. Pick me up from CH. Xxx*'

I looked over at Pumpkin. 'He's like you, offer him food and all is well with the world.'

9

As promised, I'd picked Mark up at ten and we'd driven to Castledale. The roads approaching the village had lines of cars parked bumper to bumper all the way in. Castledale was known for having some of the best well dressings in Derbyshire and had been practising the custom longer than most villages in the area. The team must have been up early as the boards were all in place and the streets were already beginning to fill with people ambling between them and taking pictures.

There were six wells here in Castledale, although the beautiful swallow dressing that Emily Dockery and her team had been working on had been relocated next to an old coach house that was now open as a café. Swallow Well itself was still closed off as a crime scene, but the unadorned structure down the lane was getting almost as much attention as the beautiful boards themselves, as natural curiosity in the ghoulish pulled people as far as the police tape would allow them to take a look at the last thing Cora had ever seen. Flowers had been placed along the wall and created their own display, only this time it was one of sadness and shock, rather than thanks and celebration.

The good weather hadn't quite held, but at least it was dry.

My favourite roasters, Signal Box Coffee, had parked their sweet cherry-red VW campervan in the car park of the village hall and there was already a queue for the mobile coffee shop. They had been on the sidelines of a murder I had been caught up in at a Charleton House food festival and I had remained friends with the owners ever since. I handed Mark some money and sent him off. There was no way I was missing out on this chance for my favourite dark roasted brew.

I admired the dinosaur dressing that had been made by children from Castledale Primary School, the layers of green leaves representing wonderful leathery scales. Further along, past the church with its squat tower, a well had been dressed with an image of Jesus feeding the five thousand. In a cloak made of red petals, He handed a fish to a group of women. The picture was framed by ornate fleur-de-lis picked out in purples and pinks. The shallow half-moon well of water that the dressing was standing behind had a border of moss along the stones, and people were kept back behind an old rusty chain that I was itching to polish.

Mark appeared beside me and handed me a takeout cup of coffee. I breathed in the familiar rich aroma.

'They recognised me and wouldn't take the money.'

'That was good of them… where is it?'

'What?'

'The money.'

'Oh yeah,' he looked sheepish, 'sorry, forgot that bit. He looks like my Uncle Gerry.'

'Who does?' I looked around the crowd.

'Him, Jesus. The beard is the exact same colour.'

'Was his beard made out of tree bark as well?'

Mark grimaced. 'Might as well have been, he never looked after it. You could always tell when he'd eaten just before he came round because bits of food were stuck in it.' He shuddered at the thought. 'Isn't that Barry?' He nodded to a space just beyond the crowd where Barry Rushton was being interviewed by a TV crew. He looked as though he was being strangled in a stiff, tight collar and tie, but he was clearly loving the attention. He beamed at the camera with his shoulders back and his chest stuck out.

'I can't bear to watch him, he looks ridiculous.' I looped an arm though Mark's and pulled him away. 'Come on, let's look at another dressing.'

We strolled down the centre of the road amongst the slowly growing groups of people – families with children, elderly couples, groups of hikers who had added the event to their day's walk. Well dressing was such a well-known local tradition and for many in the area, it was an essential trip out.

The day was starting to warm up, but I wouldn't be removing my jacket any time soon. Still, it was nice to be out in the fresh air and learning more about a part of the local history that I had ignored as a teenager. I was determined to understand more about the area I'd grown up in and which I had returned to, possibly to make my forever home.

'Eh up, they've found us.' Mark used his coffee cup to point ahead where DC Joe Greene and DS Colette Harnby were walking in our direction. Despite the strong evidence of spring having settled in for the duration, Harnby was still wearing a long dark coat over her navy blue suit. Joe was in a plain grey suit. They couldn't have been more obvious if there was a neon sign above their heads, announcing their role as police officers. Plenty of people turned to look as they passed by, attracting almost as much attention as the well dressings.

'Working undercover these days, I see,' was Mark's greeting to the pair. Harnby chose to ignore him, Joe playfully glared at him. 'At least no cars will get broken into with you two around.'

'Working on the basis that the killer often returns to the scene?' I asked them. I had to agree with Mark – subtlety wasn't their strong point.

'We've been back to see Cora's husband and we're off to carry out a few more interviews. I hope you're here *only* for the well dressings?' I doubted that Harnby expected an answer.

'Have you spoken to Barry?' I asked.

'Barry Rushton? Of course, we interviewed him first thing yesterday morning. Why?' Joe eyed me suspiciously. 'What do you know that we don't, but you are about to tell us before we charge you for withholding evidence?'

I put my hands up in the air. 'Nothing, nothing. His animosity towards Cora is public knowledge, I imagine everyone was telling you about him.'

'We know all about his frustration at Cora getting the role of chair and he willingly admits to it.' I noticed that Harnby didn't say anything about the school history between the two, but I chose to assume she just didn't want to give away all their information. She had accused me of withholding information in the past, so I knew to tread carefully. 'Now, we have a murder to solve. Enjoy the day.' Harnby continued to watch me as she walked past, but as she finally turned her head away, I spotted a smile appearing.

'Talking of Barry,' Mark muttered, 'he's just gone in the pub. I reckon it's time for a very early lunch.'

10

The Bull's Head was a well-kept old pub that faced directly onto the road. Its whitewashed exterior walls made it easy to spot, and come June there would be a lovely display of roses around the door. Inside, the landlord had done a reasonable job of maintaining a sense of a traditional country pub while giving it a modern refurbishment, but it wasn't quite to my liking. The wood detailing was all a bit too pale, the furniture looked too new and the artwork like inexpensive prints bought from the internet. But the low ceilings and wooden beams went some way to ensuring it had a little atmosphere.

Barry was at the bar, speaking much louder than was necessary and greeting everyone as if they should have been honoured to be recognised by him. But it suddenly hit me what a thin veil this all was. There was a very slight nervousness in his voice – hardly noticeable, but it was there. He finally had a chance to be in the limelight, but now he was, he didn't quite know how to behave. I felt sorry for him, but only briefly.

Mark had found a menu and sat at a table near the bar. I pulled up a chair next to him and watched Barry. It took a while, but eventually he caught my eye. It happened twice more before he seemed to place me.

'You were with the Duchess the other night. Work for her, do you?'

'We do,' I replied. 'It must have been quite an honour to be able to show her around.'

He picked his half pint up off the bar and walked over. 'It was indeed, fine lady. I was privileged to share my considerable knowledge with her, she seemed very impressed.'

That wasn't quite how I remembered the interaction. I heard Mark snort a little and kicked him under the table.

'A shame that it was under such terrible circumstances.'

'Aye, but of course, we didn't know that at the time. And I was the obvious choice to take over.'

'So I guess Cora's death was a bit of a boon to you,' Mark said.

'It was... hang on, what are you suggesting?' Barry's collar looked as though it was about to cut off some key blood supply.

'Nothing at all,' I said quickly. 'We're deeply impressed with the way you stepped in at such short notice, aren't we, Mark?'

Mark nodded, a little too enthusiastically.

'Barry, why don't you join us?' I asked softly. 'I imagine you've been on your feet all morning, and you'll have had a late night. Mark can get you another half to make that a pint.' Barry seemed to like that idea. 'Mark, order me some chips while you're at it.'

While Mark went up to the bar, I turned to Barry. 'Have you lived in Castledale for long?' I asked, starting with something easy.

'All my life, never left and never will. I'll be buried in the churchyard just up the road.'

'So you went to school here?'

'I did. My folks ran the corner shop. It's still there, but it's not in the family anymore.' He loosened his tie and undid the top button. It had been painful to look at, so I felt as if I'd been released from its confines at the same time.

'You must know everyone round here, then, and remember all those who left, like Cora. Did you go to school with her?'

He stiffened a little. 'I did.'

'It must have been nice to reconnect when she returned.' He didn't answer, opting to take a drink instead. 'I've heard she wasn't all that popular when she was at school, or at least made herself quite unpopular.'

'I can't really remember, it was a long time ago.' He glanced around the pub, and then focused back on his glass.

'I remember my schooldays. They were pretty good most of the time, but I did get bullied. Not the happiest of memories. Was Cora involved in that sort of thing?'

A flicker of recognition crossed Barry's face, but he didn't answer. I had the distinct feeling that he was weighing up what to say.

Mark had returned and caught my comment. 'Ha, *you* got bullied? Imagine how much stick I got. It didn't take much imagination to pick on the gay kid.'

Barry looked up at me, then over at Mark. 'Yes, she was a bully, and I seemed to be on the receiving end of most of it.'

'She must have made your life miserable.' I was trying to remain sympathetic, but I still hadn't found much to like about the man.

'She did, she was a nasty piece of work. It didn't matter what I did, she always managed to poke fun at me. I couldn't wait to get out of school and into a job.' It seemed we'd opened the floodgates and he was keen to talk once he got going.

'You stayed, though? In the village, I mean.'

'Yes, why shouldn't I? She went off to university and I only saw her when she visited her parents. She used to pretend she didn't recognise me, ignored me.'

'You can't have been very happy when she returned for good,' said Mark. Barry just grunted and took another drink. 'And then, when she got involved with the well-dressing committee, you couldn't escape her after that.'

'I'd been doing this for twenty years! It was mine, then she swans in and takes over. It was all about her.' He chugged the final mouthful of beer in his glass and immediately reached for the half pint Mark had bought him. It looked as if he was trying to stop himself from saying anything else.

'That must have been pretty frustrating, especially when she was going to be the one who got to show the Duchess around, take the credit.'

'Ha!' Droplets of beer flew across the table at me and I pulled back. 'She loved that, couldn't stop talking about it. She already took every opportunity to tell us about the talks she'd done up at the house. "His Grace said this, His Grace said that".' He spat out the words.

'You sound pretty mad at her,' said Mark lazily.

'Of course I'm mad at her.' Barry's voice had risen enough to turn heads.

'Mad enough to kill her?' Mark asked in the same low-key tone. Barry slammed his glass down and stormed out of the door.

I stared at Mark. 'Thanks, that was subtle.'

He calmly took a long drink. 'Yeah, but he answered my question.' He winked at me, but a bowl of chips was placed in front of me before I could think of a comeback.

11

'Wow, he's a man with a grudge,' said Mark as we walked towards the car.

'Maybe he's entitled to be, if she gave him a really hard time.'

'True, but still, it must be exhausting being that angry all the time. Maybe he found an outlet for it the other night.' As we continued walking, Mark pulled a royal blue handkerchief out of the pocket of his waistcoat and studied it.

'What are you doing?'

'Seeing what colour it is in natural light. I thought it was cobalt when I chose it this morning, but out here it looks more of a Persian blue.' He rolled up the leg of his jeans to reveal a pair of socks that to my eye were a perfect match for the handkerchief. 'No,' he shook his head, 'completely different.'

'I'm sure Joyce would help you with your TV wardrobe.'

He looked at me with horror. 'No words, I have no words.'

We walked on in silence, until I decided to tell Mark what was on my mind.

'I don't think I should be doing this. I could have lost my job last time.'

'Looking into Cora's murder? Why not? This has nothing to

do with Charleton House. Anyway, the Duke and Duchess couldn't have fired you. You weren't the one who committed a crime, you didn't kill anyone.'

'No, but my sniffing around in London last year resulted in their son being jailed.'

'That was his own stupid fault. He's always been the black sheep of the family. He was going to get into trouble at some point, it was only a matter of time. Anyway, it's not like he was put away for murder, it was basically traffic offences. With his connections, being detained at His Majesty's pleasure is barely going to put a dint on his future prospects. That's one of the ways the British class system still operates. He'll be fine, and he'll have no end of stories to tell over dinners when he gets out, which will probably happen early following good behaviour and a wink in the direction of a useful judge.'

I stopped abruptly. 'I'm surprised to hear you say that sort of thing about the Fitzwilliam-Scott family. You're an unofficial one-man PR department when it comes to them.'

He shrugged. 'We all love a bit of scandal. My tours wouldn't be half as interesting if the people I talked about had behaved themselves all the time. I'm very careful when I'm referring to the Duke and Duchess and their immediate relatives, living or dead, but Lord Oliver Fitzwilliam-Scott will give tour guides of the future plenty to talk about.'

He offered me his arm, I looped mine through it and we started walking again.

'You'd have had a solid unfair dismissal case if they had tried to get rid of you. Anyway, they're good people. They've not given you too much of a hard time, have they?'

'I haven't given them the chance. I've avoided them as much as possible, which for almost nine months has been quite a challenge, but I do think they've been cooler with me.'

Mark stopped and turned to face me. 'They can't stop you

doing this, and as far as we know, this case has zero links to the Duke and Duchess.'

'Cora has given talks at the house.'

'Only two that I can find, and yes, I checked. She doesn't have any kind of relationship with the Duke and Duchess and she was killed miles away from the estate. If you want to dig around, then you carry on. I know you're itching to. You've looked distracted ever since we found her body, so I know it's all you're thinking about.'

'I suppose.'

'Suppose nothing. Come on, let's go back to mine. Bill hasn't seen you for ages and I want help choosing some cufflinks.'

'Alright, but that's it. If you ask me to choose underwear that matches, I'm straight out the door.'

'As if I would. But now you mention it…'

'I'm sorry about the mess. Good luck finding a seat that doesn't have an item of clothing strewn across it.' Bill, Mark's husband, gathered up a pile of brightly coloured shirts and hung them on the back of the door.

'Hey, I was starting to lay them out for each episode.'

'Why can't you at least keep them upstairs? Use the guest bedroom.'

'The lighting is better in here. Back in a minute.' As Mark disappeared up the stairs, Bill and I caught up on day-to-day life. His job as a teacher, a million miles away from his previous career as a professional rugby player, guaranteed he had plenty of amusing stories to tell.

'…when his mother came in, she swore that he'd never do such a thing. I told her I'd personally watched him throw the chair out of the window and I wasn't aware of any poltergeists in the school, but I could always give the Ghostbusters a call.'

'How did she take that?'

'Not well, she threatened to have me sacked. Not that she'd get very far. I mentioned it to the Head to give him advance warning that she might be on the blower to him, and he just called them another pair of Mary and Josephs. It seems he's very familiar with that particular set of parents.'

I gave him a quizzical look.

'Mary and Josephs? It's what we call parents who behave like their child is the son, or daughter, of God.'

'Ahhh yes, we have some of those who come to the café.' It was hard to imagine any parent daring to stand up to Bill. He still had the big, strong build of a rugby player, and the broken nose to match. He had more of a belly than he did back when he played the sport professionally, or so he'd told me, but beyond that, he looked as though he kept himself fit.

I waited until Mark reappeared before asking Bill, 'So, how does it feel to be married to a celebrity?'

'It's going to be tough – paparazzi on the doorstep, people asking for autographs while we're in restaurants, the complete loss of privacy. But I'll do everything in my power to support him, and then when he decides he wants to become Prime Minister…'

'Are you done, darling?' Mark asked with a definite tinge of sarcasm.

Bill winked. 'I'll put the kettle on.'

'Right, you can help me with this, then we can get back to the murder.' Mark held a leather box out to me like he was carrying a crown before flipping the lid open to reveal neat rows of cufflinks.

'What murder's this? You going to be donning your deerstalker again, Soph?' called Bill from the kitchen.

'Cora Parrish,' Mark shouted back. 'The woman whose body we found at that well on Friday night.'

Bill reappeared. 'Oh yeah, I meant to say to you, Delia was talking about that.'

'Delia?' queried Mark.

'You know, the cleaner, the one who always gives us a bottle of brandy for Christmas and it goes straight in the cupboard next to the previous year's bottle. She waters the plants in my classroom, which is a good job cos I never do. Well, I ran into her at the supermarket this morning and she was telling me that she cleans for them, Cora and her husband. She'd been at their house only that morning. She was quite shocked by it all, although it didn't stop her wondering if Hugh would still want her to clean for him or if she'd lose her job.'

'Well, well, well, it's a small world!' declared Mark before looking at me. 'It's a sign. Bill, any chance you've got her phone number? I think Sophie might be on the lookout for a cleaner.'

12

'I'm still not sure about this,' I said, looking at the house with the pink door and the cheerful flowers in pots on either side. Delia had invited us straight over when we'd phoned and Mark had dragged me out to pay her a visit.

'We're just going to have a chat with her. We don't have to do anything else after that if you don't want to.' Mark paused, and then looked at me. 'What did you do with her?'

'Who? What?'

'My friend Sophie, the woman who would risk the wrath of the local constabulary in the name of justice. The woman who would pick up the scent of evil after a murder had been committed and follow it until she stood at the feet of a killer. Whoever you are, whatever planet you've come from, I want my friend back.'

I swatted him. 'Get out. Let's go and talk to Delia.'

Delia was a small woman, smaller even than me, if that was possible. I'm guessing she was in her late sixties, but she bustled around with the energy of someone half her age.

'Come in, come in, you're Bill's fella, aren't you. Lovely to meet you, come on in, make yourself at home. Hello, dear, you must be Sophie.'

The house was as spotless as I expected. The rooms were warm and cosy, photos of family members adorning the walls. It looked as if Delia had a lot of grandchildren.

'You make yourselves at home, I put the kettle on when I saw you pull up, so I won't be a moment.' I watched as Mark picked a bit of invisible fluff off his waistcoat. He'd been preening himself even more than usual since his announcement.

'Right then, tea, coffee, a jug of milk, brown and white sugar and some chocolate digestives. I'll let you help yourselves as you know what you like and how you like it. As the actress said to the bishop.' She roared with laughter. 'Oh, I am sorry, I've never met either of you before, but Bill's told me so much, I feel like I know you, Mark, and Bill and I are always saying things like that to each other.

'Now then, you want to chat with me about poor Cora? Really I'm bound by a sort of unspoken confidentiality with regards to my clients. But if Bill trusts you, then so do I. Now, how can I help?'

I let Mark take the lead, he had the connection with her.

'Cora and Hugh, what are they like? Were they like, I mean.'

Delia took an enormous bite of a biscuit and wasn't in the least bit embarrassed about making us wait while she crunched her way through it. No food shame. I liked her.

'Oh my, they were very interesting. She was into all that art, and he does something with buildings... architect, that's it. The house is beautiful. It had been a vicarage. Lots of big windows and a beautiful garden. They were both very nice to me. Businesslike, though, you know what I mean? Not very chatty, but always polite and they paid me well.'

She had almost finished her biscuit and I swear she hadn't dropped a single crumb. I felt guilty about the pile that was growing on my lap.

'Were they happy?' I asked.

'Depends how you define happiness, doesn't it? He was working away quite a lot, travelled up and down from London, but they were one of those passionate couples.'

I was a bit worried where this was going. Maybe she'd walked in on something.

'I heard them have a couple of blazing rows, and they didn't seem to care that I was in the house. By the time I finished, they'd have made up and were happily having a cup of tea in the kitchen.' She shook her head. 'I couldn't cope with that kind of relationship, too stressful. My Frank – he's in the greenhouse out back – we know each other's likes and dislikes, we balance each other out. Haven't had a cross word in forty years.'

'Did you hear what the arguments were about? Were they very serious?'

A thoughtful expression settled on Delia's face.

'Well, on occasion I did.' She paused again, whether for effect or because she was still deciding whether or not to tell us, I couldn't be sure. Then she leaned forward in her seat. 'They moved to Castledale about two years ago from London. It looked to me like they were maybe considering their future retirement, or wanted to escape the rat race. She grew up near here, did Cora. Not in Castledale, but a few miles away. Maybe she wanted to *come home*, so to speak. But whatever reason they chose here isn't quite as interesting as why they moved in the first place.'

She took a drink of her tea and a bite of her biscuit while keeping her eyes on mine. She knew how to build atmosphere, like all great storytellers.

'They were having a row one day, and Cora was complaining about how much time he spent away. Hugh was saying it was her fault they were out here in the middle of nowhere, which is not true. Castledale isn't that remote. Anyway, she said it was his fault because he'd made the rules, then what they were sayin' all got very complicated. After overhearing a few more arguments, I was eventually able to put it all together. It seems that Cora had an affair. They decided to remain together, but Hugh insisted that they move so they didn't have to risk coming across whoever the bloke was she slept with. It sounds a bit like it was meant to be some kind of punishment for her. Not bad as punishments go, though, beautiful big house in the countryside. And she's got, sorry had, a very good job at a university.

'But like they say, fancy houses and the like don't buy you happiness. There must be a lot of people like that. You know, life looks perfect, but behind those walls it's a different story.'

I digested the information. An affair, a husband who made the couple uproot their lives from London.

'So, he was still very angry.' I hadn't meant it as a question, but Delia replied anyway.

'Oh yes. Moving up here didn't solve their problems, not really, not from what I saw.'

'You said they would make up quickly, but do you think they really did? That the issue would be forgotten? Or do you think it was simmering away between the fights?' Mark asked.

'Ooh, now you're asking. It's a good question that 'n all. He did have this very calm, warm voice when he was talking normally to me. Wasted on him a bit cos he always looked very stern, which could be confusing.' She picked up her third digestive and started munching away. 'Don't get me wrong, he could have a good time. I've seen him at some of their parties. They didn't throw big ones, just dinner parties or small garden parties, that sort of thing. They have… had such a lovely house and the garden is beautiful, so it was the perfect place to entertain people. I helped out a couple of times, walked around with a tray of food, tidied up.

'Anyway, he had people over the night that Cora died. It wasn't my usual day to clean, but I did some extra hours so the house was all set, and then went to the school. Only half a dozen guests, I think. The caterer was pulling up as I left.

Wouldn't that be nice, to have someone come and cook when you had people over? Very sensible if you can afford it. Now then, would anyone like another biscuit? I have more in the cupboard.'

'So, we have an unfaithful wife and an angry husband, whose home happens to be a short walk from where the victim's body was found,' Mark summarised. 'Aagh!'

'Sorry, I didn't see that. It's like driving off road, there are so many bloody potholes.'

'Yes, well the top of my head is closer to the roof than yours, so take it easy, will you.' I grinned at him. 'That was not a challenge, Sophie Lockwood.'

'Your summary is correct. Although it seems that Hugh had a house full of witnesses as to his whereabouts. But even if he didn't, it seems a bit obvious to me, although killers are typically known by their victims. Besides which, if Hugh went from the house, killed her, then went back to the house without any of his guests noticing – highly unlikely, by the way – any evidence would be easy enough to find, and Harnby and Joe will be looking at him as a possible suspect.'

'That's assuming they know about Hugh's motive.'

'Are you calling your brother-in-law a dozy PC Plod who can't find out something we discovered in five minutes?' Mark assumed a mock look of deep concentration. 'I'll tell him.'

Mark laughed. 'It's nothing I haven't called him before. I still think Hugh should go on our list, though. If nothing else, it gives us an insight into Cora's life and personality.'

'Agreed. Now, what next?'

'I knew it!' Mark punched the air. 'There was no way you could resist trying to find Cora's killer.'

'But if there are any signs that this has a link to Charleton House, then I'm walking away. I can live with her having done a couple of talks at the house, but if it turns out to be more than that...'

'It's not, I promise.'

'Okay, home. Bill will be expecting you back for dinner and I have a cat who will be sat at the window with a sign saying *help me, I'm being neglected.*'

'You should make her catch her own meals.'

'She does that as well.'

'That explains her size. You should feed her lettuce.'

It was no wonder to me that Pumpkin wasn't fond of Mark. But he wasn't wrong, and I drove home musing over the possibility of putting her on a diet.

13

*B*efore my team had even opened the door of the Library Café to our Monday morning visitors, Mark had taken over a table, spreading his books everywhere, including the chairs around it.

'Have you got enough room there or do you need me to pull another table over? The customers can balance their plates on their knees.'

Mark didn't look up. 'No, I'm good, thanks.'

'I was being sarcastic.'

'Yes please, that would be great.'

'I could get you a slice of lizard snot cake with an extra squirt of badger milk cream.'

'Thanks, I'm starving.'

'Earth calling Mark, Earth calling Mark.'

One half of his moustache had been twisted into a narrow straight line from where he'd been absentmindedly playing with it. The other half had maintained its perfect curl.

I tapped my knuckles on the table. 'What are you working on?'

'Hmm?' He finally looked up.

'What are you working on? It must be fascinating.'

He looked pained. 'I don't know what I'm going to do. I have to come up with six themes, one for each of the segments I'm filming. So far I've narrowed it down to twenty-five, but I keep finding new things that I want to talk about. I've no idea how I'm going to make my mind up.'

He flicked through some of the piles of paper to demonstrate how much stuff he had. 'There are myths like the Bakewell Witches, lots of food-related history. I could talk about the drowned village of Derwent, but I can't miss out the Cromford Mills and Hardwick Hall. The list goes on and on.'

'Well, look at it this way. If you get more than the six episodes, you'll have a ready-made list to work on. Or… you could use all these ideas to write a book.'

'Are you suggesting that I might not get more than six? That's not a very… ooh hang on, you're right, I did say that a book would be next. A lot of the chapters are right here before me. I could be on the cover looking all intellectual next to the ruin of a building that overlooks the glorious windswept Derbyshire scenery. I could do signings here in the Charleton House shop. Joyce would love that, I'd sell loads of copies. She could have a life-size cardboard cut-out of me holding the book standing in the corner.'

'Did you say a life-size cutout of yourself?' The sound of Joe's voice over my shoulder made me jump. 'It's a while until Halloween, but I like to see that you're planning ahead.' I knew that Joe would want me to get him a coffee, but not before I'd given Mark a warning.

'Please don't suggest that to Joyce, her reply will hurt your feelings. Either that or she'll get one and you'll spend the rest of your days finding it in weird places, or with knives stuck in it. One way or another, that idea will haunt you if you say a word to her.'

'Wise words…' I heard Joe add as I walked off.

. . .

'Come on, then,' I said as both Mark and I stared at Joe sipping his coffee.

'I came here for a break, not an interrogation. You know I can't tell you anything about an ongoing investigation.'

'We were there,' said Mark. 'We're part of that investigation.'

Joe ignored that.

'It must have been tough, telling Hugh his wife had been killed,' I said.

'Very, it always is. I'm not actually the one that tells them, it's Harnby, but still it's a difficult conversation. This time, we had to break up a party Hugh was holding.'

'A party?' I exclaimed.

'Well, not so much a party, more drinks with mates. Colleagues, he actually said. At least he had company.'

'And witnesses to his whereabouts,' I added.

'Yes, five witnesses who can all… hang on a minute, I know what you're doing.' The familiar warm, cheeky boyish grin appeared on his face. 'Sophie Lockwood, you are digging, that's what you're doing. You're digging for clues so you can do your own investigation.'

I held my hands up in surrender. 'It never even crossed my mind.'

'You lie like a rug.'

I feigned shock. 'Okay, but can you at least confirm that she died by drowning at the scene?'

'You really are thinking like a police detective. Why don't you pack it in here and join the force? You may as well.'

'And bring an end to a limitless supply of free coffee and cake?' huffed Mark. 'Don't you dare suggest such a thing. You can have her on a temporary basis, a sort of consultant.'

'Erm, excuse me, I am here, and you're starting to sound like my pimp.'

'Do you need one?' Mark raised an eyebrow and I made a mental note to withhold any more free cake for the rest of the week.

'You're both exhausting. Do you know that?' sighed Joe. 'Alright, I can confirm that Cora died by drowning at the well in which you found her. That do you? Cos you're not getting anything else from me.'

Once Joe had finished his coffee and I'd given him a free chocolate brownie, because apparently I owed him, he went back to work.

Mark tutted. 'He's just at the start of a murder enquiry and yet he's swanning around here getting free coffee and cake. And to think the police claim they are understaffed.'

'He was working. Whether it was his idea or Harnby's, he was round here seeing if we'd found out anything. They're not daft.'

'I noticed you didn't say anything about Hugh and Cora's rocky relationship.'

'No, I feel a bit bad about that, but they probably know already, and if they don't, they will before long.' I took my glasses off and gave them a clean on the apron I was wearing. 'You know, I hate to say this, and I don't want to say it too often, but you were right.'

That made Mark look up from his notebook so quickly, I thought he might get whiplash.

'Do go on.'

'Looking into Cora's death. It's like my brain is itchy from wanting to find out what happened, and actively working on it is like scratching it. It feels good.'

'She's back!' he declared, raising his mug in the air.

14

J was helping Joyce by laying out a table of hardback books in a large room that was part of the stables complex. White walls reflected the evening light onto the beautiful wooden floor, and through the floor-to-ceiling windows we could see early arrivals milling in the cobbled courtyard. During the day, children would be in here, taking part in activities run by the education department. The rest of the time it was an events space.

Joyce was briefing a member of her team. 'They can get a book here, pay for it, and then join the queue to get it signed. Once they hand over the money, you need to write the name they want the book dedicated to on a Post-it note *very* clearly. Double-check with the customer that the name is spelt correctly, and then stick it on this page of the book. We're expecting a full house and many will buy more than one.' She sounded like a rather stern headmistress – in other words, terrifying. But her staff knew her well, and they both feared and loved her. Their loyalty was spoken of in hushed tones and some joked that Joyce had put a curse on them.

The piles of books, *Beyond the Paint: The Story of Britain's*

Greatest Art Forger, were being prepared for a reading by the author, Ryan Lavender. Joyce came across to the table I was working at, picked up a copy and turned it over to the photograph of the author on the back.

'I'm told he's good looking, but I can't see it myself,' she said. He was rather attractive in an intellectual kind of a way: slim with tortoiseshell glasses, jeans and a blazer. 'A role model for Mark, I imagine.'

'How so?'

'TV series, book, lecture tour. Although he wears the young male academics' uniform of jeans and a blazer, as opposed to Mark's dandy with that ridiculous pocket watch. In fact, I'm surprised that he isn't here, fawning.'

'He's giving a private tour, otherwise I'm sure he would be.'

'No he isn't.' Joyce nodded in the direction of the door where Mark had just appeared. He waved and walked over.

'What happened to your tour?' I asked.

'Cancelled. We go to a lot of effort to pull it all together at the last minute, and then we get a phone call ten minutes after the start time to tell us they won't be coming. We'll still charge them, but my guess is they have enough money not to care. So, instead of wasting the delights of this magnificent building on some banking bigwig who is probably showing off to his young mistress, while they're both likely to be on their phones the whole time, I am being paid to come here and support a media colleague.'

I bit back a smirk.

'Media colleague?' Joyce asked, not hiding her amusement.

'Absolutely. I'm not sure there'll be anything I can pick up from his presentation skills, but I can get an idea of how these events operate.'

Joyce had the answer for him. 'How they operate is a bunch of rabid housewives hang on every word, some clever clogs tries to ask a difficult question in the hope of proving he's brighter than the speaker, and then we take all their money off them. Easy.'

Mark picked up a copy of the book and walked off to find a seat, calling, 'I'll pay you tomorrow,' over his shoulder.

'With interest,' Joyce called back before turning to me. 'Look, I should be done here by nine o'clock, then Ginger has invited me to the pub. Some of the dressers are meeting for a drink. You should come with us – we'll be at the Black Swan, so you don't have much of an excuse. You can go home, feed that fat cat of yours, and then join us and dig for more information about Cora.'

'Pumpkin is not fat. She is big boned.'

'You told me she got stuck in the cat flap.'

'Yeah alright, but keep that to yourself. She'd be mortified if she knew I'd told anyone.'

Joyce rolled her eyes. 'Now, go on, get that other box of books emptied. You might as well make yourself useful.'

15

*I*t being a Bank Holiday, the Black Swan was busier than on a typical Monday night. There was no need for the fire to be lit on such a warm spring evening and I half expected to find the well-dressing team in the beer garden, but I was alerted by the familiar guffaw of Ginger Salt and the sight of Joyce's hair towering above the bar.

'How did the lecture go?' I asked after I had wiggled my way past a couple of blokes waiting to order and squeezed in next to Joyce.

'As I predicted. We had to deal with the barrage of love-struck women queuing to get their book signed. I left the team with the stragglers. They're more than capable of performing a rugby tackle on anyone who tries to climb across the table to get more than just a signature.'

'Is he *that* popular?'

'I might be exaggerating a little. I assume you want one of these.' She handed me a glass of what looked like gin and tonic.

'Thanks. Which one did you choose?' She looked blankly at me. 'The gin. He has over seventy, which one did you opt for?'

The blank look remained. 'How do I know? I asked for a gin

and tonic, my guess is the glass contains precisely that. Need any more information?'

'Stone Circle Gin.' The head of Steve, the landlord, appeared from below the bar. 'I guessed she was ordering for you so I thought I'd go with a new arrival. It's a bit flinty, which I know you're not a fan of, but I reckon they go heavy enough on the juniper to balance it out.'

'Cheers, Steve, glad someone's switched on.' I noticed Joyce freeze momentarily, then give me a look that also deserved the description of flinty before walking off with her tray of drinks.

'Sophie!' Ginger wrapped me in a hug that almost crushed my ribs. 'Glad you could join us. You remember Emily and her mum Lydia? Betty and Barry are engaged in a battle over who gets to have the keys to the village hall, so we won't hear from them for a while.'

Lydia smiled and shook my hand. 'I hope you enjoyed seeing how we work on Friday evening,' she said, her eyes giving me a very clear once-over.

'Lovely to see you again.' Emily reached over for a hug that took me by surprise. 'Ginger said you found Cora's body, that must have been a hell of a shock. Are you alright?' There was genuine concern in her voice and she kept a hand resting gently on my arm.

'I'm fine, Joyce and Mark were with me and we realised very quickly that she was dead. It must have come as a shock to the group, too.'

Emily sighed. 'It certainly was. We did start to worry as the hours went by, but we know that there are sections of that train line where you can't get a phone signal for love nor money. I was sure she had a good reason to be late, but I didn't expect that. It's certainly kept Barry quiet. He spent all night moaning about her lack of commitment and her true colours emerging, then looked rather shamefaced when we heard the news, as he should. It's been quite peaceful ever since.'

She glanced over at Barry and Betty, who had their heads together and scowls on their faces.

'Did you know Cora well?' I asked.

'Not really. She was nice to chat to when we were working on the boards, but she didn't socialise with us very much. I don't think she had the time. She was incredibly organised, though, and basically doubled as chair and secretary, so this year went smoother than ever, until the end.' Emily stared into her glass for a few moments and I decided it was wise to change the subject. Her mum was chatting to Steve across the bar, so I asked if they knew each other.

'That's always happening, she used to be his teacher. She can't get him to stop calling her Mrs Dockery.'

'You said you followed your mum and moved back to Derbyshire. Was that just family ties or did something else bring you here?'

'I decided on a career change and got a place on a master's degree in Sheffield. Mum said I could live with her. I really liked the idea, Mum and I get on well and I'd often thought about moving back here. Everything seemed to fall into place. What about you, been here long?'

I smiled. 'Nearly four years. Like you, I moved home. Not into my mum's, but she's not far away. I'd been in London for a long time and when the job came up at Charleton House, I couldn't resist.' I didn't need to tell her about the failed engagement after I walked in on my fiancé in bed with someone else and also discovered he'd been stealing money from the restaurant we both worked at.

I glanced over at Joyce and Ginger. They were chatting with Lydia and a woman who had just arrived.

'It's a pretty big week for Mum, she's retiring from her teaching job.' Emily had spotted where I was looking. 'After Dad died, she took a break, but then threw herself back into it. I think it was that which got her through. We moved to Kent, but she never really settled there. We'd gone to be near family, but this was always our home. I was actually pleased when she moved back here.'

'I'm sorry to hear about your dad, was that recent?'

'No, I was just a kid. It's all a long time ago.' Emily smiled fondly. 'He was a teacher too, geography.'

I smiled back. 'I'll never forget what an oxbow lake is.'

Emily laughed. 'A lot of people say that.'

'So, tell me about your master's,' I said.

'Medieval history, I'm interested in migration in the ancient world…'

I listened with fascination. It was nice to be talking about something other than cupcakes or murder for a while.

Pumpkin was making biscuits on my lap. Well, actually I think she was subjecting me to torture under the guise of typical cat behaviour. I made a mental note to cut her nails in the near future, I was starting to feel like a pin cushion.

I was sprawled out on my leather sofa, a rather indulgent purchase that Joyce had helped me choose. I say choose, but actually she declared that it was right for my little workers' cottage, and when Joyce declares, it's hard to argue that it is anything other than the law. She was right, though, it was perfect: classy and comfortable, and easy to get cat hair off, unlike my clothes. There were days when I left the house at risk of being mistaken for a miniature yeti.

I'd enjoyed my evening chatting to Emily. We'd discussed what we liked about Derbyshire, and our shared love of cats – or subservience to, depending on how you look at it – and we'd bonded over a couple of helpings of chocolate pudding. We'd ended the night promising to get together for coffee.

My phone started ringing and Pumpkin leapt off. I gave my

legs a wiggle; I'd been getting cramp, as well as a course of feline acupuncture. Mark's face appeared on the screen.

'OMG, I can't believe I'm being phoned by a celebrity.'

'Oh, give over.'

'Will you give me a signed photograph?'

'Pack it in, Lockwood.'

'Oh, come on, you can't expect Joyce and me not to milk this for all it's worth and make your life a living hell for as long as humanly possible. You'd do the same.'

'True, but I like to think I'd do it with Wildean cutting remarks that go on to get quoted throughout history.'

'I'm sorry I'm not as poetic as you. To what do I owe this pleasure?' Pumpkin had returned and was sitting on the back of the sofa, staring at me. I'd lifted my laptop onto my knee and she didn't look happy at losing a potential nap location.

'You know, we really should get new chairs for events. After ninety minutes, my rear end had gone numb. I still haven't got all my feeling back in it yet, and you have to change the wine you serve. The Pinot Grigio was like vinegar.'

'I didn't provide the catering, Lavender's team used their own. And how dare you suggest that I'd serve second-rate wine.'

'Oh, well that's alright, then.'

'So, aside from the chairs and the wine, Mrs Lincoln, how was the play?'

Mark laughed. 'Ooh, a cultural reference, I am impressed. It wasn't bad. He's actually an interesting chap who knows his stuff. I was expecting to write him off as a celebrity first, historian second, but that would have been unfair. He just knows how to market himself. We had quite an interesting chat afterwards.'

'Mmm.'

'Are you listening?'

'What? Yes, yes, of course. Sorry, I was just pulling up some of the latest news stories about Cora.'

I ran my eyes over one report. The journalist had covered all the usual things – her involvement with the well-dressing festival, that she was found minutes from her house, that she worked at a university and specialised in…

'Mark, you didn't happen to get Ryan Lavender's number, did you, or have a way of contacting him?'

'It wouldn't be hard to track him down, why?'

'I'm wondering if he can help. I didn't think about it until just now, but Cora has done a lot of work around art forgery. Hang on…' I pulled up her page on the university website. 'Yes, I was reading this the other day. She lectured in art history and theory, but she had other interests and had presented at a number of symposiums on forgery. Some were simple "histories of art forgery" kinds of thing, others got a bit more complicated and talked about "authenticity" and "perceptual discrimination". It's all gobbledegook to me, but sounds impressive. Maybe Ryan has heard of her, or knows a bit more about some of the subjects she was looking into. I think it might be worth asking.'

'You might have hit on something there. I shall endeavour to seek him out in the morning. I'm sure he'll remember me from this evening's event.'

'No one could possibly forget you, Mark.'

'I'll take that as the compliment I'm sure it wasn't intended to be. Goodnight, my dear. See you upon the morrow.'

16

I'm not sure why I bother to set an alarm. Having an eighteen-pound cat leap on you does a pretty good job of waking you up, no matter how deep your slumber, and this morning was no exception. It made me think again about the possibility of putting her on some kind of diet.

I lay in bed for a little while, listening to Pumpkin purr directly into my ear and grimacing each time she tested the sharpness of her claws on the back of my neck. If I'm honest, it's a nice way to start the day, her bulk is rather comforting.

She yowled in protest as I got up, and then attempted to kill me as she weaved a path right in front of my feet until I reached the bottom of the stairs. I didn't need the last thing I saw before my death to be the blur of an overweight tabby cat with eyes that could laser a hole in a wall.

'BLOODY HELL, PUMPKIN... MOVE... PUMPKIN... I swear I'm going to... SHIFT...' would be my final words. Not exactly poetic or full of meaningful advice for the next generation.

When I finally left the house, I felt that I'd only narrowly got away with my life.

. . .

I started my Tuesday in the Stables Café, set in the 18th-century stable block. Visitors didn't need a ticket to the Charleton House grounds to reach the small café, so it was popular with dog walkers, cyclists, hikers and others exploring the 40,000-acre estate. On a warm sunny morning, it was a lovely way to start the day.

My team opened this café earlier than the others, as we didn't need to wait until the house was open. We would pin the doors back and allow the scents of spring to drift in and mingle with those of coffee and the freshly baked pastries and cakes that had just been delivered. Sparrows danced around on the backs of empty chairs and edged as close as they dared to the first customers of the day. I never minded their presence, it was a reminder for people to put their rubbish in the bin. Which, of course, they often didn't, but that wasn't the birds' fault. We humans were the grubby ones.

It was the kind of morning that put a spring in your step, and I took my time chatting to the staff and enjoying the coffee they had handed me as soon as I walked in – I had them well trained. Everyone was in a good mood – the customers smiled, the staff laughed and joked.

'Look,' Martin, the café supervisor, called me over to the door. 'Up there.' A sparrowhawk sat on the roof of the building opposite, casually surveying the scene below him. I wondered if he knew that he lived in one of the most beautiful parts of the country, how lucky he was to be hunting in the grounds of a magnificent estate, rather than perched on the top of a concrete car park in the centre of a city. I remained watching him until he flew off, and then I attempted to drag my mind back into work mode.

After doing a final check with Martin and handing out dog biscuits to all the four-legged customers sitting in the courtyard, I wandered back to the house, well aware that soon I was going to have to turn my thoughts from the calm beauty of the morning to the ugly subject of murder.

I spent the rest of the morning in my cramped little office, looking up as much as I could on Cora Parrish, but the only information I could find online was related to her work. I wondered if she had been involved in a high-profile forgery case, identifying an art criminal who was now out to get her, but if she had, there was no mention of it in the press that I could find. Besides which, I didn't see any evidence that she was actively involved in forgery cases, or even knew how to identify one. She seemed to me like a successful academic who had made a move back to the part of the country where she had been born and bred. Once here, she had raised the hackles of Barry Rushton, and Cora and Hugh hadn't been able to leave their personal problems behind them.

I felt as if I just didn't know enough about her. Maybe she had other friends in the village, or other interests. I typed in her name again, but this time I added in the names of various towns and villages in the local area. Finally, something came up. Cora was on the judging panel of a local art show held in Buxton.

'Knock-knock.' Mark leant louchely against the door frame. 'I'd ask if I could come in, but you'd have to leave to make that possible. I guess I could sit on the desk with my legs crossed. You do know that the size of your office is directly related to your status within the organisation?'

'You share your office, so you'd have to divide it between all of you. And if I remember correctly, they moved someone else in there last month, drastically reducing the space you could lay claim to.'

'Oh yeah, well it was worth a try. Working, or detecting?' He indicated towards the computer monitor with the takeout coffee cup in his hand. I assumed he had already charmed one of my staff into giving him a free coffee.

'Take a guess.'

'Find anything useful?'

'Perhaps. It turns out that Cora was on the judging panel for a local art competition, so it might be worth talking to a couple of the organisers.' He nodded. 'And you?'

He pulled out his pocket watch and flicked it open with a well-practised motion. 'I'm meeting the Duchess in the café. I'm leading a VIP tour for her tomorrow and she wants to brief me on the guests and their interests.'

'I'll stay in here, then.'

'You can't keep avoiding everything except the most essential of meetings with her or the Duke. This can't go on forever.'

'I went to the well-dressing evening with her.'

'That's only one thing, you need to stop hiding.'

'Really? You just watch and learn, I was amazing at hide and seek when I was a child.'

He gave an exaggerated sigh, tutted and left. 'If anyone asks,' I heard him declare loudly as he walked through the kitchen, 'Sophie is not here, she is definitely not in her office and she is absolutely not on her computer, avoiding the Duke and Duchess and anything resembling work.'

I wondered how long it would take until he actually drove me to murder.

17

I always felt guilty taking time out from the day job to do something utterly unrelated, like investigate a murder, but I knew I was leaving the cafés in the safe hands of my very competent team. Plus, my guilt hadn't actually stopped me before.

The art competition that Cora had been involved with was being run in association with the Buxton Pavilion, where a gallery was housed in the Victorian cast-iron and glass structure. I spent a little time browsing the paintings, ceramics, jewellery, photography and more showcasing the work of talented local artists. I didn't buy anything this time, but I could have easily pulled out my credit card.

I caught the eye of a woman who had just finished selling a painting of the nearby Opera House to a customer.

'Can I help you?' A little notice on the desk said *Artist on duty: Helen Atkins, ceramicist.*

'I wanted to talk to someone about the Pavilion Annual Art Competition.'

'I'm afraid the entry deadline has passed.' She was petite, wearing a tight pair of jeans and what looked like a hand-crocheted cardigan in all sorts of shades of blue. It looked pretty and not fussy, warm too in the cool of the pavilion.

'Oh no, I didn't want to enter.' She looked bemused. 'How heated is the competition? Do those who don't get accepted get very angry?'

I saw the flicker of a smile. 'What have you heard? You're not the press, are you?'

'Heavens, no.'

'Good.' She grinned. 'Are you talking about Betty, by any chance? This is only the second time in nine years her work didn't progress through, and it's been two years in a row. I thought she was going to shatter all the glass in the building when she marched in here the other day.'

'Was her anger aimed at anyone in particular, or was she just generally annoyed?'

Helen paused, looking at me intently. 'Has this got anything to do with Cora Parrish's murder? Only I've just had the police around asking the same question.'

'Really? Wow! Yes, sort of. I just wondered who might have had it in for Cora, she was such a nice person.'

'Are you a friend of hers?' I hesitated a bit too long and her smile disappeared. 'You *are* the press!'

'No, no, I'm not, honestly. I'm one of the people who found her body. I know I should leave it to the police, but I'm curious. I want to know who would do that to someone.'

Helen's expression softened a little, but I clearly wasn't out of the woods.

'That must have been really awful, I'm sorry you experienced that. But I don't understand what you think you can do. The police are clearly hard at work and you really should leave this to the professionals. I can't tell you anything about the entrants to the competition and I shouldn't have made that comment about Betty. I want to see the person who did this to Cora caught, too, but I can't help. Sorry.'

She walked back to her desk where another customer was waiting to be helped. I had been hoping to tease a bit more information out of her, even if it was just some general stuff about Cora and what she was like, but I clearly wasn't going to get anything else from Helen.

I walked out into the sunshine, but not until I'd bought an ice cream in the café. Enjoying the flavours of rum and raisin, I made my way slowly back to the car via the Pavilion gardens. I meandered around a small manmade lake, past cascades and over footbridges that spanned the narrow River Wye.

I was crunching on the cone and licking ice cream off my fingers when I heard a familiar voice.

'Sophie Lockwood, stop right there.' I turned slowly to face Detective Constable Joe Greene.

'Morning, Detective. Nice day for it.' I smiled. He looked uncomfortably hot in his suit and tie, and I considered offering to buy him an ice cream.

'Hmm, I'm wondering what it's a nice day for.' He raised a single eyebrow and peered at me. 'Why do I think you might be up to no good?'

'You're a detective. You're inherently suspicious.'

'I am, but when you're around, my radar starts to get all squirrely.'

'Well, I can assure you, I paid for this ice cream. You will receive no reports of theft. Well, you might, but it wasn't me.'

'That's not what I'm talking about and you know it.' I tried to look as blank as possible and kept on crunching my way through the wafer cone. 'I thought I saw you come out of the Pavilion, but I could have been wrong. I hope you weren't anywhere near the art gallery.'

'Joe, I know I've got under your feet in the past, but maybe I was just there to buy some artwork for my house.' I felt bad for lying to him.

'Unlikely. It took you over three years to get a decent sofa and that wouldn't have happened if Joyce hadn't strong-armed you into a shopping trip. I've also just been in there asking questions and the longer I do this job, the less I believe in coincidences.'

My shoulders fell as I gave up the act.

'Alright, but she didn't say anything. She said she couldn't give me any information and to leave it to the professionals.'

'She sounds like a very wise woman and I suggest you take her advice. Shouldn't you be at work?'

'Yes, I should, but you know my lot, they won't even notice I've gone. If anything, they'll be glad to have a break from me breathing down their necks.'

'I'd rather that than you breathing down mine. Go on, go back to work.'

I gave him a mock salute.

The car was hot and stuffy and I quickly wound down the windows. I started the engine, and then turned it off again when my phone rang and a photograph of Mark appeared on the screen. I put him on speakerphone and closed my eyes.

'Tina wants to know where you are. The kitchen is on fire, you've run out of coffee and the Duchess choked on a chunk of week-old flapjack.'

'Tina is the best café supervisor on the planet and could deal with all of those problems with both hands tied behind her back. Better luck next time. What do you want?'

'Lovely to speak to you too. I was phoning with good news. The eminent Ryan Lavender is going to meet us for coffee and cake tomorrow, in the Garden Café. You can pull out all the stops and we'll charm him with fine glassware and scintillating conversation.'

'We want to know if he had come across Cora, not ask him to marry us. Why all the fuss?'

'Because he could be a useful contact for me, and anyway, we already know he'd come across Cora. Well, I know, but I haven't told you that bit yet.'

'That's great news. I have some news too. You know the art competition that Cora was going to be judging?'

'Go on.'

'Well, the woman at the art gallery said she couldn't give me any information and to leave it to the police, but not before she'd let slip that someone called Betty had entered and had thrown a fit when her work was rejected for the second year running. I'm wondering if it's the same Betty who is part of the well-dressing group.'

'She looks like the kind of woman who'd throw a fit, she has a face like she's sucking a lemon.'

'Agreed. We'll find time to go and see her later in the week. And one other thing.'

'Oh yes?' Mark sounded intrigued.

'If you ever suggest we sell week-old flapjack again, I'll bar you from all of the cafés.'

18

I heard a yowl from the kitchen and Pumpkin came thundering out.

'What's going on in there?' I called. Mark walked into the sitting room and shrugged his shoulders. I gave Pumpkin a stroke. She was wet and annoyed, and stalked off. 'Why is she wet?' I asked Mark with suspicion in my voice.

'I couldn't find a tea towel, I figured she'd do.'

'Mark, you rotten sod.' I passed him the basket of garlic bread. 'Eat some of that and play nice.'

'Sorry, Soph, I'll leave him at home next time.' Bill shook his head as though Mark was an embarrassing child. I'd invited them both over for dinner – nothing fancy, just a quick meal that I threw together midweek when I didn't have the energy to go to great lengths in the kitchen, but felt too guilty to heat up a microwave meal. Pasta with tinned tuna and peas. It doesn't sound like much, but if you get the best tinned tuna, the right pasta and some good-quality Parmesan cheese, it's a fabulous quick and easy meal. Toss in a ton of garlic bread and you're set.

I handed Bill a beer.

'I had a kid ask me if I had beer in my mug this afternoon,' he said. 'I told him no and he replied, "*Well, you should cos my dad says it takes the edge off*".'

'He sounds like a wise one. I thought about teaching,' I told him.

'What happened?'

'Nothing. I thought about it, decided that I didn't like getting up that early when I was a child and I still wouldn't like it, so went into hospitality and spent most of my time working evenings.'

'And what about now? You have to start fairly early to get the cafés ready, go to meetings.'

I responded by nodding in the direction of Pumpkin who had just sauntered back in. 'Meet my alarm clock.'

Bill laughed. 'Well, you're not alone. I had a pupil who told me he wanted to be a teacher and asked what you had to do to become one. When I told him that you had to go to university, he thought about it for a minute, then declared he was going to be a footballer instead.'

'Good move,' said Mark, in between growling at Pumpkin and baring his teeth.

'Why have you got it in for my sweet girl?' I asked. 'She's done nothing to hurt you.'

'Not yet, but she's thinking about it, I can tell. She's planning my death.'

'I know it's not all cats, you fell head over heels with Penny the Persian when you met her in London.'

Mark growled at Pumpkin again. She was looking at him like he was an idiot, a view I agreed with.

'She wasn't inherently evil.'

'Neither is Pumpkin.' I wasn't quite so sure of that, but I wasn't going to let Mark know.

'Has Mark never told you?' Bill asked me, reaching out to scratch Pumpkin's head. He took her by surprise and she pulled away before running out of the room. Mark now growled at Bill, who laughed. 'Oh, for heaven's sake, I'll tell her.' Mark scowled, crossed his arms and slumped into the sofa. 'Mark here had a run-in with a tabby kitten when he was a spotty youth.'

'It wasn't a kitten, it was full sized, huge.'

Bill looked at me and shook his head. 'Kitten. Mark walked into a room, the kitten jumped off a shelf and landed on his shoulder, digging its claws in to hold on. Mark was traumatised and ever since has hated tabbies. He's convinced there's a secret tabby society and they're all plotting to get him.'

'They are. You're forgetting the one that bit me a couple of years ago when we visited your cousin. Took me years to get over that, I'm still not. If you'd seen the blood after that tabby took a chunk out of me, it looked like a murder scene.'

'It did not. Yes, you bled, but it soon stopped.'

'Not until it had stained my favourite silk shirt, I had to throw it out. And the cut got infected, I nearly lost my finger.'

'Alright, I get it.' I looked at Mark with mock sympathy. 'You basically hold a deep-seated and wildly unfair prejudice against tabby cats, judging them all because of two unfortunate incidents. I thought you were better than that, Mark Boxer, I really did.'

Bill grinned.

'I hate you both,' said Mark as he stood up. 'I'm going to get more pasta. If you two want any, you can get it yourselves.' I laughed. It was easy and fun to wind up Mark and I didn't feel an ounce of guilt. He did it to me often enough.

Bill's face took on a serious look. 'Mark said that talking to Delia was useful.'

I nodded. 'It was. Cora's sounded like quite a…' I paused, wondering which word was most suitable '…dramatic, uneasy household.'

'I couldn't handle that kind of drama,' said Mark as he walked back in, our teasing apparently forgotten. 'I get that it works for some people, and that the making up bit can be great, if you know what I mean, but still, it must be exhausting.' He looked over at Bill. 'Don't say a word.'

Bill raised his hands in surrender. 'I wasn't going to say anything.'

'It does seem like the kind of relationship where an argument could get out of hand and she ends up dead in the lane. Maybe they fought, she stormed out and he chased her, drowning her in the well,' I suggested.

'But she was meant to be at the village hall,' Mark reminded me.

'Yes, but she could have gone home first. Had the row before Hugh's guests arrived.' I stopped and thought. 'No, Delia said the caterer pulled up as she left, so that doesn't work. What if Hugh's guests arrived, she came back from Sheffield and they had an argument in private. She left, Hugh followed her, killed her and went back to the party. She drowned so there wouldn't be any blood on him. If his clothes were wet, he could dash upstairs and get changed.'

'But the guests would have noticed that he was wearing a different outfit,' Bill said. I had to admit this idea was going nowhere, but still something about it was tugging at me.

'Okay, so we'd need to talk to the caterer and the guests to be able to build a case against Hugh, and I can't see much chance of that happening. Joe and Harnby would kill us. Barry clearly holds a grudge. If Cora made his life hell at school, then moved back to the area later in life and took the position of chair from under his nose, then maybe it all became too much. I wonder what their relationship was like when they were working on the well dressings, maybe she was still bullying him in some way.

'Then we have Betty. If she is the same woman as Helen at the Buxton gallery mentioned, she could have held a grudge against Cora for not getting through to the final round of the art competition. It's all a bit woolly and Miss Marple-like, though.'

'Perhaps Ryan Lavender will be able to throw some light on her work reputation,' said Mark hopefully.

'Yes, and I'd like to get a better feel for her personality. Maybe we should talk to Ginger and Emily again. They're both pretty switched on and spent time with her. They can probably help us build a picture.'

'I'm not surprised Joe gets concerned about you two,' said Bill. 'You're one step away from putting pictures and maps on the wall and connecting them with pieces of string. It's not so long ago that you were wary of getting involved, Sophie, and now you're stuck in like your life depended on it.'

He was right. I couldn't help it. I had promised myself that I would stay away from this kind of thing, but murder had a habit of refusing to stay away from me. Besides which, I had been there when Cora's body was discovered. I thought about her lying at the well, her head in the water. Someone had done that to her, and I really wanted to know who.

19

I hadn't planned to spend my Wednesday morning phoning every member of staff not currently scheduled to work on the weekend to ask them if they could come in. We were getting a bit thin on the ground and at this rate, not only would I be working, but I'd need to clone myself. One of my team was getting married and, of course, everyone had wanted to go.

I was putting the phone down after leaving yet another begging voicemail when Tina popped her head round the door.

'Panic over. I've managed to get a couple of staff from the catering company you used the other week for that wedding, so you can still have your weekend off.'

'Thank God. You're a star. I owe you big time.'

'No, you don't. But next time, write yourself a to-do list so you don't forget things like getting more staff when we need them.' She was right, I'd known about the wedding for months and kept putting off sorting out the staffing. Tina was so competent that she often put me to shame, and this time she had jumped into action when we realised that I'd forgotten to do such an important job.

I was more than happy to come in, but Tina wouldn't hear of it. 'I know what your diary is like for the next couple of months. If you don't get this weekend off now, you won't have another chance for weeks.' I really didn't mind working weekends as I got to focus on the cafés and the customers. With a lot of the staff at Charleton House only working Monday to Friday, it meant the phone didn't ring and emails weren't flying into my inbox on the other two days. But I had plans to meet my mum on Saturday.

'They're coming in tomorrow for a couple of hours to learn the ropes. Can I leave that with you, Chelsea?' Tina looked over towards the café's assistant supervisor who was restocking the fridge with sandwiches and soft drinks.

'Of course. I'll make sure they receive *all* the training.' Tina smiled at her, a conspiratorial look passing between the two women.

'Great, I'll give them a call, tell them they might be here all afternoon and all night, however long it takes for them to make the perfect cup of coffee for their new boss who is rather… hmmm, *particular* about her favourite hot beverage.' Tina eyed me as she reached the end of the sentence.

'Good word, particular,' I told her. 'Because I know you were thinking of some others, all of which might get you fired.'

'Unlikely. I know too much about you, Sophie.' She grinned and left me standing at the espresso machine, which I'd been polishing the whole time she'd been talking. I liked a good cup of coffee, and I treated the espresso machine like it was a Porsche and I was a petrol-head. So what?

'Am I really that bad?' I asked Chelsea. She glanced at me, then turned back to her work.

'No comment.' Her voice was gently teasing. I stopped polishing.

'Really? Am I that bad?'

Chelsea also stopped what she was doing. 'Tina really does give all new staff a course on how to make your coffee just the way you like it. She instils the fear of God into them. She calls it *Sophie's Perfect Latte* or *How to Keep Your Job*, tells them this is the final hurdle. It doesn't matter how well they do the rest of the tasks, their employment here is dependent on this last test. She can be very stern about it too.'

'Are you kidding?' I screeched unintentionally, surprising myself at the sound that came out of my mouth.

'It's true! Even now, it can take some of us a couple of attempts before we think we've got it right and are prepared to bring a coffee to you. I really hope I can teach these new ones how to do it or we might all lose our jobs.'

'Well then, we better find out. When you've finished that, you can make me a coffee.'

Chelsea laughed. 'I walked into that one.'

'Don't worry, Chelsea,' called Tina from the kitchen. 'One day, I'll tell you everything I know about her, and then you too will have the knowledge and be able to take back power.'

'I swear, I'm going to fire you both,' I muttered, and gave the espresso machine a final polish.

'We're not very busy and we do actually have enough staff today.' The sound of Tina's voice brought me back into focus.

'Hmm, what?' I'd been staring into space for so long, my computer monitor had gone into sleep mode.

'We have enough staff if you want to head out and, you know, talk to people.' So, she knew what I was up to. 'We all know what you're doing, we have seen this before.' She must have read my mind. Yep, Tina was a smart one. I stood up, stretched my back out and grabbed my car keys.

'I don't know what I would do without you. Please don't respond to that, my fragile ego couldn't take it.'

Tina laughed. 'You are the glue that keeps this well-oiled

machine together, and you sign off our timesheets so we need you around in order to get paid.'

'I'm glad I make such a valuable contribution. If you need me, call. I'm off to talk to a man about a dog. Well actually, a grumpy old woman.'

'You're seeing Joyce?' That made me howl with laughter as I left the office.

Betty Natchbull lived on the outskirts of Castledale in a large detached house, although the sign said *Highview Cottage*. It was set up above the village so certainly had a view, but it wasn't what the word *cottage* brought to mind. It had to have at least five bedrooms and well over two acres of grounds. Carved in the stone above the door was the year 1831. It was well maintained, and the window frames looked to have been freshly painted, the grass perfectly manicured.

The door was opened by a woman considerably younger than Betty. She was dressed in jeans and a simple long-sleeved t-shirt. Betty's daughter, perhaps?

'Hello.'

'I was wondering if it was possible to speak to Betty. She's not expecting me.'

'Who is it?' A familiar shout came down the hallway. The strident voice echoed off the marble floor in the small entrance lobby. The woman gave me a questioning look.

'Sophie Lockwood, I work at Charleton House. I was with the Duchess on Friday night, at the well-dressing evening.'

'Did she say she knows the Duchess? Bring her in.' There was nothing wrong with Betty's hearing.

I was led down the pristine hallway. Painted in various shades of cream, it reflected the light. A neat row of paintings lined the full length of both walls. At the far end, I stepped into an enormous conservatory that had neatly laid-out bamboo furniture to one side, and Betty standing at an easel surrounded by the paraphernalia of an artists' studio on the other. She clearly took all this very seriously.

She stepped out from behind her latest creation and eyed me up and down.

'I remember you. You can go now, Fiona. I'll see you in the morning.' Betty actually looked at her with something resembling affection, and the woman departed. 'Now, what is it you want?'

'I wanted to talk to you about Cora.' I was suddenly very nervous. I hadn't actually thought about how I would navigate this conversation, and Betty was intimidating. *I seem to be surrounded by intimidating older women*, I thought as she put down her paintbrush and inspected me.

'Sit,' she instructed. 'I'll decide whether or not to offer you a drink in a moment.' This was starting to feel like a mistake. 'So, what is it about Cora that interests you so much? Can the woman not rest in peace?'

'Well, she was murdered, so it wasn't a particularly peaceful end.'

'True enough. So, what do you want to know and why? And don't waste my time with lies.'

By now, I was wishing I had brought Joyce with me as my bodyguard. I decided that honesty was the best policy, too afraid to find out what might happen if Betty discovered I was lying.

'Come on, girl, I haven't got all day.'

20

After I had explained my connection to Cora's murder, Betty sat back in her seat. She had demanded we both sit on the bamboo chairs on the other side of the large conservatory.

'And you want to talk to me because?'

'As you knew her, you might know someone who had a grudge against her.'

Betty stood and walked slowly across the room. 'I need a cup of tea.' I assumed I was meant to follow.

Once I had been directed to sit at an enormous wooden table in a large, fussy kitchen, and Betty had made herself a cup of tea and me a mug of awful instant coffee, she sat down opposite me.

'Cora Parrish. Ambitious, hard-working, officious, impatient, arrogant. I've been well dressing for over fifty years and she treated me like I'd been there less time than her. There are some extremely experienced and knowledgeable people in that group and she paid little heed to what they could bring.'

'And that group of people includes you.'

'Of course that includes me, I just said I've been doing it for over fifty years.'

'That must have made a lot of people very angry.'

'Extremely.'

'I believe she had a link to another part of your life as well.' Betty looked at me sternly over the rim of her teacup, but said nothing. 'She was a judge for the Pavilion Annual Art Competition in Buxton, which you had entered.'

Betty appeared to be considering how to respond. There was something a little too still and considered about her, it was unnerving. When she spoke, it was with a forced calm.

'I have absolutely no doubt that she was using the judging as an opportunity to put me in my place. Let me know that a new regime had now been established.'

'You've been entering for...'

'Nine years. Until now, I have been in the final of at least one category every year that I have entered.'

'Except one.'

'Yes, alright, there was last year, but I had just had my hip replaced and I was not on top form. That was not my fault. There is only one person who has won as many categories as I have, Harriet bloody Smedley, and if she wins anything this year, she will have overtaken me.' I noticed that Betty had kept hold of her teacup with both hands the whole time we had been talking, and it was currently hovering mere millimetres above the saucer. The woman was like a coiled spring, I was worried she'd have a heart attack in front of me.

'I believe you were extremely angry that you didn't have any artwork in the final show.'

'What does that mean?'

'You went to the Pavilion to complain, rather loudly.'

That annoyed her. 'If you had been in my shoes, you would have reacted in the same way. I am a highly respected artist. If I had discovered my talent earlier in life, I could have had a very long and well-rewarded career.'

I decided to redirect the conversation. 'Can you think of anyone who might have wanted to kill Cora?'

After a brief pause, Betty finally put her teacup down.

'I don't mix with killers.'

'The most unlikely people can be pushed too far.'

'Perhaps in the world you inhabit.'

I was exhausted, this was like trying to get blood out of a stone. Betty was a woman who seemed to have had plenty of practice at talking a lot, but saying very little. There was something unfeeling and cold about her. I wondered if this was what it was like to sit in front of the matriarch of a criminal gang. I just hoped I wouldn't be followed in the car and driven off the road, only to be pulled out of my vehicle and shot.

We looked at one another in silence for what felt like eternity. This was getting me nowhere. I wondered if she had been any more forthcoming with the police, assuming they had spoken to her. Surely they had questioned all the members of the well-dressing group?

'Thank you for your time, Betty. I don't want to take up any more of it.' She rose from her seat and escorted me to the door, seeing me off with a very curt *goodbye.*

I pulled over at the side of a country road. A long line of cows was staring at me over the fence as I retrieved my phone from the bottom of my bag and called Mark.

'Are you free?' I asked, not giving him a chance to say anything.

'Until three o'clock.'

'Good. Meet me by the main gates, I'm coming to pick you up.'

'Where are we...' but I'd hung up before I could hear any more.

21

'I hope we can get lunch after this. I had my eye on a steak and kidney pie.'

Mark was fastening his seatbelt as I pulled away from the main gates of Charleton House, doing my best not to hit any of the visitors who seemed to lose all sense of spatial awareness once they entered the grounds.

'Good choice. They were made fresh this morning. They go pretty fast, though, so there might not be any left when we get back.'

'Oh great! Well, wherever we're going better be worth it.'

'We're off to visit a grieving widower. We'll get some flowers on the way.'

'Hugh? We're going to visit Hugh?'

'We certainly are. It's about time we paid our respects and gave him a chance to talk about his darling wife whose story we are now, sadly, a part of.'

Mark nodded. I spent the next couple of miles filling him in on my visit to Betty.

'She was so guarded, it was difficult to tell whether that was just her way or if she was hiding something. She certainly didn't like Cora and had her reasons for disliking her. She also lost her rag over the judging of the artwork, so we know that she can be pushed over the edge.'

'It's one thing to be angry for not getting to the final of a local art competition and another to be pushed so far over the edge that you kill someone. Plus, did she have the opportunity?'

'We know that many of the well-dressing group were coming and going that day.' I pondered everything I knew about Cora's death so far. It wasn't much. 'Maybe I'm losing my touch, but I'm just not getting a grip on any of this. I'm out of practice.'

'That's your own fault for being so afraid of the Duke and Duchess. If you'd just got on with things as normal, you would have stumbled over a dead body or two long before now, and you'd be so well-practised that you'd have identified Cora's killer by the end of the weekend.'

'This isn't a hobby I want to excel at. I'm not like Betty, trying to win a competition.'

'Really? You're not competing against yourself?'

I was able to stop the conversation getting any more philosophical by pulling up outside a flower shop in the centre of Castledale. I handed Mark a twenty-pound note.

'Go on, you've got good taste.' Flattery always works well on Mark and he leapt out of the car, returning a few minutes later with a small but elegant bouquet of flowers.

'Right, let's hope he's in,' I declared as I pulled away. 'If not, those flowers will look great in my kitchen.'

The car wheels crunched up the gravel driveway and I parked next to a large stone urn that was surrounded by out-of-control jasmine. The scent was wonderful and I took a deep breath as we walked up the wide steps to a rather grand crisp-white front door.

As I rang the bell, I looked at the front of the house. While

Betty's 'cottage' was impressive, this house was both large and graceful. It was very well cared for, but there was a softness about this building that was missing at Highview Cottage.

I could see movement at the end of the corridor through the glass in the door and eventually a tall, slim man came into view. As he opened the door, I could see the severe look that Delia had described, and I couldn't help but compare it to Betty's. I had a feeling that this was just the way Hugh looked, while Betty was actively viewing the world with suspicion.

'Can I help you?' He glanced between us both.

'Hugh Parrish?'

'Yes.'

'I'm Sophie Lockwood and this is Mark Boxer. We're sorry to call on you out of the blue like this. You see, we and another friend were the people who found your wife… found Cora.'

He stared at me, presumably processing the information I had just given him.

'We wanted to pay our condolences.' Mark held the flowers out towards him and Hugh took them, still looking a little bewildered.

'Come in, please.' Delia had been right, he had a warm, soft voice that didn't match his distracted, serious expression. He was dressed in light-brown trousers and a white shirt that had sharp creases down the arms where it had been ironed. Walking with a very upright posture, he led the way into the kitchen. This one had a warmth to it which came from careful design and use of colour. So much consideration had gone into Cora and Hugh's home, it belonged in an interior design magazine. But there was no radio playing, the house was quiet and still.

'We're very sorry for your loss,' said Mark. It wasn't often I saw him standing with someone equally tall and skinny. We must have made a slightly odd sight, as if they were a different species and I was an alien from another planet.

'Thank you. It's very good of you to call by. So… so, you found her, you say.' He looked away as he said it.

'Yes. We were walking back to the car park.'

'She was lying in the well?'

'Yes.'

An awkward silence developed.

'That's a beautiful painting,' I said, wanting to shift the atmosphere, even just a little.

'What? Oh yes, Cora's father painted it. It's round here somewhere.' The painting was of a rocky gully or chasm. Light bounced off the silvery rocks, the green of trees, ferns and moss making the picture look soft and inviting.

'I believe that Cora was involved in the art world.'

'Yes, yes, she was. She lectured in art history.'

'So, not a dangerous profession.' I said it without thinking.

'No. A random attack. It must have been.'

'Is that the view the police are taking?'

Hugh had started to fill the kettle with water. I wasn't sure if he hadn't heard or chose not to answer my question.

'Would you like a cup? I was never going to get much work done today, although I have been trying.'

'That would be lovely, thank you.' And just like that, Hugh seemed a little more relaxed. The sound of the water boiling, the mugs being brought out of the cupboard, the motion of normal household activity warmed the room, and I wondered if we might now be able to find out more about Cora. But Mark spoke before I was able to ask a question.

'It might be too painful, but would you like to tell us about Cora?' I was so used to his sarcasm and teasing humour that hearing such a sympathetic tone from Mark was a bit of a surprise. I knew he was a kind, sweet man, but he wouldn't have wanted me to tell anyone.

Hugh leaned back against the counter and sighed, but it did seem to be a sigh of relief. He went on to describe an ambitious, determined woman who did everything with passion and energy. The more he talked, the more I realised that I would have liked to have met Cora, although I did find it easy to imagine that she'd made well dressers like Betty feel overwhelmed and trampled on. A stylish bull in a china shop, perhaps.

'Was she popular with her colleagues and students?'

'The week before she died, she had dinner with visiting professors one night, then another evening went for drinks with some of her students after one had won an award. She wasn't too friendly with them, she liked to keep boundaries in place, but she would stay just long enough to be polite and show that she felt it was worth celebrating.'

I looked at her father's painting. 'Did Cora paint?'

'She did, she was very good. I'll show you.' He led us through to an office. It was colder in here, the sun hadn't reached the large windows. Rows and rows of shelves were stuffed with books. An enormous old wooden desk with a wonderful leather swivel chair dominated the room. A coffee table was piled high with art books and a couple of local guides to Derbyshire.

'She did this a few years ago when we were on holiday.' A beautiful watercolour captured St Mark's Square in Venice. It looked like a summer morning, early before the crowds had descended. 'And this one the week after we moved here.' I recognised it immediately as the view of their garden and the fields beyond, the same view you could see from the kitchen. 'I was annoyed because I thought she should have been unpacking boxes, but instead she sat outside painting. I wish I hadn't said anything now. She hadn't had time to do any painting over the last couple of years. I kept encouraging her, but she was so busy.'

'I believe she was judging a local art competition?' I said.

'Yes, her second year. I told her she should be entering it, not judging it.'

'How was it going? Did it get contentious at all, artists unhappy they hadn't been chosen?'

He laughed. 'It's hardly the Royal Academy. She did say once that someone had taken the news that they hadn't progressed pretty badly.'

I guessed that was Betty. 'Was she worried about it?'

'I don't think so. She said that something could get rather awkward, but I don't know what she was referring to. Why?'

'Oh nothing, just curious. She was very talented.' I turned, stopping to admire the desk. 'I've always wanted a desk like this.'

'We've moved it between every house we've lived in. It's incredibly heavy.' I stroked the edge. The wood felt soft, almost velvet-like after decades of use. The books and paperwork on its top looked as if they hadn't been touched.

As though he had read my mind, Hugh said, 'I can't bring myself to go through all of that. I'll probably ask one of her colleagues from the university to come over and sort it out, they'll know what's important.'

My hand was resting close to a notepad. At the top of it, the word '*WHY?*' in capital letters was followed by a series of exclamation marks, and lower down '*Lud's Church*'.

'Was Cora religious?' I asked.

'No, not particularly. Although we'll hold her funeral at the local church. You're both welcome to come, especially after…'

'Thank you.'

After an awkward pause, I decided it was time to leave. 'We should go. We didn't want to disturb too much of your day, we just wanted to meet you and tell you we were sorry.'

'That's very kind of you.' After taking our mugs, he showed us out.

As we got back in the car, I thought of something and turned to Mark.

'Was anything stolen from Cora?' I couldn't believe I hadn't considered that earlier.

'I don't know, but that's something it will be easy enough to get out of Joe. It would be a bit daft if we paid all this attention to the case and it turned out she was just the victim of a mugging.'

'Just?'

'You know what I mean. If we've been looking for a murderer where a murderer never was.'

He was right, but then Joe would have told me if that was the case, a way of stopping me from paying it too much attention. I made a mental note to ask him the next time I saw him.

22

'Where are we going?' asked Mark as I drove past the turning that would take us back towards Charleton House.

'To Castledale's village hall, I want to have a look at something.' I pulled up outside the Bull's Head pub. 'Don't even think about it, you have a tour to deliver later.'

'Spoilsport. So, what are you looking for?'

'Apparently, the well dressers were coming and going, so anyone could have left, killed Cora and returned, and no one would have paid any attention.' I circled the building as I spoke. 'I can't see any CCTV, although Joe might confirm that for us.'

The front door to the hall opened out onto the main street, but there was a fire exit to the rear. I recalled seeing it open when we were there on the Friday night that Cora had died, so I knew it was well used. Outside there was a bucket of sand with cigarette butts forming a top layer. A small courtyard backed onto a stone wall and, beyond that, a field. I scanned the horizon.

'A lot of the car park where we left the car is visible from here, so I wonder if it's possible to see who is coming and going on Swallow Lane.' I pointed things out as I spoke.

'You'd need to have good eyesight.'

'Or at least not have bad eyesight. And if someone was wearing something distinctive...'

'Like a bright orange scarf.'

'Exactly like that. If you knew what you were looking for, you might be able to follow their progress down the road.'

'But to get from here to there, you'd need to go down the main street. One of the buildings there must have cameras, the pub or the post office maybe, and the police will have checked those. If someone left the hall having seen Cora, killed her, then returned, the police would have seen them on camera and they'd have had someone in custody by the end of the weekend. I haven't seen Joe drinking a celebratory pint, so I'm guessing that isn't the case.'

Mark had a good point.

'Okay, let's try this. I want you to go back onto the street, see if there is any vantage point from which you can see someone cutting across the field.'

'How will I know? It's going to be green grass behind green bushes, I won't really be able to tell. Oh, right...'

I had found a foothold on the wall and hoisted myself up. I swung a leg over and sat straddling the wall. It was a long time since I'd done anything like that.

'Alright, girl, steady on. You didn't give me a chance to avert my eyes.'

'What do you think you're going to see? A glimpse of my socks?'

'That could be quite shocking to someone with a delicate sensibility.'

'Well, if you meet someone like that, you can introduce me. Go on.'

Once Mark was out of sight, I jumped off the wall and into the field, grateful that I was rarely to be found wearing high heels, thinking of Joyce and her stilettos. They wouldn't have stopped her, she would have just aerated the field as she went.

I walked slowly across the field. The ground wasn't even and I had to watch where I put my feet. Tufts of grass hid ankle-twisting holes and there were muddy patches which hadn't quite dried out in the good weather. It took four and a half minutes to get to the wall on the other side. It felt like a lot longer, but I'd timed it with my watch.

The wall next to the lane was lower on the field side and it was easy to jump up and sit on it. Below me was a steep bank down to the lane, making it much harder to get down. I decided not to try it.

Leaning over, I could see that I was only about ten or fifteen metres from the well. At that point, a small copse of trees sheltered it, so the site of the murder wasn't visible from anywhere other than the road itself. All the same, the killer must have taken one heck of a chance; there was after all a car park just a little further down. It hadn't been busy when we parked, only four or five cars were already there, and the pub had its own car park, which had been full. Almost everyone had parked either there or in the row of spaces outside the village hall.

Nonetheless, the killer had to have been angry in order to take the risk of killing Cora here, not thinking about how easy it would have been for someone to drive past and see them. This wasn't a drawn-out event, an argument that got out of hand. This was someone who saw Cora and hurried over with the intention of doing her harm. If they were that angry, then I could only assume that their motive was personal and emotions were running extremely high.

I walked along the edge of the field as I thought it through. The well couldn't be seen from the back of the village hall as the road was on a lower level than the field, so assuming the killer had been working there, how could they have spotted Cora? As I walked towards the top of the lane, I realised that it gradually rose, and by the time I had reached the main street, the field and the road were at the same level and there was a direct view to the back of the village hall.

I stepped out onto the main street and waved at Mark as I walked towards him.

'I wondered where you'd got to,' he called.

'I'm surprised you didn't pop into the pub for a sneaky half.'

'I considered it.'

'So, could you see anything?'

'Not a dicky bird. The view of the field is blocked by that row of bushes. So anyone cutting across wouldn't appear on any cameras.'

I walked over to a bench and sat down. 'Of course, this is only relevant if the killer was part of the well-dressing group, and I'm not convinced about that.' Betty certainly had a grudge against Cora, but could she have got over that wall? She definitely wouldn't be quick enough to do so and cross the field before Cora had gone past and arrived home safely. I'd like to have seen her try, though. I imagined the angry old woman ploughing across the field, waving her fist in the air.

'What about Hugh?' asked Mark. 'What did you make of him?'

I sat in silence for a few minutes, thinking about our visit before finally replying.

'He's very hard to read. It's like his face and his voice aren't communicating. He sounded like the grieving husband who was still trying to come to terms with the death of his wife. But the emotion didn't quite meet his expression, and we know they had a tempestuous relationship. I feel really sorry for him, but I don't quite trust him.'

'He had guests, though, so we can probably assume she didn't go home first.'

'No, but maybe she messaged him to say she was walking back from the station, and he snuck out and met her on the road. They argued and he killed her. It was sheer luck that no one drove down the road then. Maybe if they had, it would have jolted him out of a rage and he wouldn't have got as far as killing her. They would have just argued and then gone back to the house, all smiles for the guests. Then she would have gone on her way to the village hall.' The station was on the edge of the village and only ten minutes' walk away from the Bull's Head, so Hugh would easily have been able to judge her whereabouts.

'I don't know how they did it,' said Mark.

'What's that?'

'Kept the relationship going after she was unfaithful. If Bill did that, it would break my heart and it would be the end of things. I'd never be able to trust him again.'

'It sounds like their trust *was* damaged, all those arguments.'

'Yes, but they still created a home together. That house is beautiful, and the garden. And they moved up here. They invested a lot, and not just money, in really giving it a go.'

'True, which makes it even harder to work out if Hugh might have been the killer. On the one hand, if he really wasn't over the betrayal, then his anger and jealousy could have erupted into murder. On the other hand, they had made a big commitment to trying to move on, which would suggest they loved each other and wanted to have a future together. Hugh could have had the opportunity and he had the motive, whether or not he did it. That could go either way.'

'Betty?' Mark asked.

'As much as I like to imagine her hurtling across that field in a fit of rage, I don't believe she could have done it.'

'Assuming the field was the route the killer took.'

I nodded. 'Now Barry, on the other hand, is a stocky little man. He might have quite a bit of speed and strength tucked away. I don't find it a stretch to imagine him clambering over that wall and barrelling across the field.'

'Barrelling? Hurtling? Do none of these people just run?'

I dug Mark in the ribs. 'Whatever you call it, I'm sure Barry could do it, and being the victim of bullying can scar people.'

'I'm really not liking Cora,' Mark declared. 'She was a bully at school, she was unfaithful, and yet she was able to just move on, hold her head high. She convinced Hugh to move back to the area she grew up in, got involved in a major local event – not just involved, but she was running the show. She was a judge for the art competition. She must have known who Barry was, yet he didn't say anything about her apologising or trying to put things right. She didn't exactly put her head down and do her penance. It sounds to me that she basically lived her life as she wanted and anyone else's feelings be damned.'

I couldn't help but agree.

23

The Charleton House Garden Café was not so much a café as a beautiful restaurant in a Baroque orangery with enormous ceiling-high windows that looked out onto the gardens. It suited a glass of champagne more than a mug of coffee. It was not yet warm enough to open up the terrace, but we were getting close and the gardeners were preparing the lime and lemon trees for relocation to the space in their terracotta pots.

Mark was already at the table when I arrived. He was polishing a knife nervously, even though it wouldn't be dirty. My staff knew I was meeting someone here and would have been running around making sure everything was spotless – they knew they'd face my wrath if it wasn't. It wasn't often I got angry, but when I did, I became one of those frighteningly calm and controlled people who make others afraid of the possible eruption. Psychopaths and serial killers, is how Joyce describes them, and me.

'Put that knife down,' I hissed. He did as he was told.

I noticed that Mark's moustache was freshly glistening and its curled ends were perfectly symmetrical. The green handkerchief that poked out of his waistcoat pocket matched his tie and no doubt his socks.

'You look like you're about to go on a first date.'

'Have I made a big mistake?'

'What are you talking about?' I sat down, my anger at Mark's implicit criticism of my staff dissipating. He looked genuinely concerned.

'Do I really belong on television?' I was too surprised to say anything. 'I know that I talk about it, and I know that I deliver superb tours and get fabulous feedback, but television...' He lowered his voice. 'Can I really pull this off?'

'Bloody hell, Mark, are you having a crisis of confidence?'

'I am human, you know.'

'I don't doubt it. Well, sometimes I do... Is this because we're about to meet Ryan Lavender? He's not a Hollywood star. Actually, if he was, I'd be even less impressed, but he's a historian who ended up on TV, like you're going to be. You're just as good as him. You were all fired up after attending his talk, he was going to be your best mate.'

Mark had obviously had the time since then for the doubts to set in. 'I don't have a PhD.'

I really was surprised. I had never seen Mark unsure like this. I'd often wished his self-confidence was catching.

'So what? I've never met someone with so much historical knowledge at their fingertips. You could write a couple of PhD theses with all the research you've done. There is no one that knows the history of Charleton House like you do. Even the Duke and Duchess call on you for information.'

He fell into a thoughtful silence and I poured us some water for something to do. One of the servers caught my eye and gave an almost imperceptible nod towards the door. Ryan had arrived.

'Mark, you're a bloody genius, and handsome to boot.' He got the point and looked up as Ryan was escorted to our table. We rose and shook hands.

'Good afternoon, Dr Lavender. Thank you for making the time to see us.' Mark sounded so wooden.

'Ryan, please.' He laughed. 'I've never got used to "Dr". My mother is forever telling people, but I tend to forget until someone else mentions it.' He turned and shook my hand. 'Sophie, I assume.' We all sat. 'What a beautiful space, a step up from the Starbucks around the corner from my office.'

'The coffee's a lot better as well, I can guarantee,' I replied, smiling. I hadn't paid much attention to Joyce's comment at the book signing, but he *was* very good looking, much better in real life than in the photo on the back of his book.

'Sophie runs the café. All three of them, actually,' said Mark, now sounding very proud.

'Really? Well, it's fabulous.'

I wondered if I was blushing, I felt like it. *Grow up,* I told myself. We ordered coffee and I asked our server to bring a selection of cakes.

'Heavens, I guess I'll have to come off the diet,' Ryan commented, smiling. I looked at him and Mark. They were both beanpoles, it would be very easy to hate them.

After a little small talk, and giving Mark a firm kick under the table when he started polishing a fork, I got to the point.

'Ryan, Mark was telling me that you knew Cora Parrish.'

'Yes, I did. Her death was very sad, and disturbing. I still find it hard to comprehend, although it had been a little while since I had actually seen her.'

'Can you tell us about her? What was her reputation like?'

Ryan looked about to speak, and then stopped himself. 'I am rather curious, what is your interest in Cora? You sound a little like a police officer.' He looked amused rather than suspicious.

'Mark and I, along with another friend, we discovered Cora's body.'

Ryan looked visibly shocked. 'Heavens, that must have been horrendous. No wonder you're interested. If you've any kind of enquiring mind, you'd want to know more after an experience like that.'

It was refreshing to hear someone respond in this way. Most people found my interest a little bit odd, to say the least.

'Well, if there's anything I can do to help, I will. So, what can I tell you about Cora? To be honest, not a huge amount, I didn't know her very well. Our paths crossed at a couple of conferences and we exchanged emails here and there. She wasn't a big figure in the field – she had a full-time job teaching art history, so most of what she did in relation to forgery was on the side. Having said that, she seemed to pop up all over the place. She gave the impression of being extremely hard working.'

'Gave the impression? What was her reputation like?' I asked. He appeared to mull over the question as he took a bite of a strawberry tart. I couldn't help but notice his long, thin fingers, and he had very neat nails. He didn't bite them, that was for sure.

Eventually, Ryan shrugged. 'Middle of the road. She wasn't a leader in her field, she didn't chair committees, but she gave a number of presentations and wrote a few articles. But, she was always there at receptions with a glass of wine in her hand. I often saw her talking to the guest speakers, and she was always in the photos of events. She just had a... a presence, I suppose you'd call it. That's why I say she gave the impression. She clearly liked to be seen places, and I think she liked the attention she was able to cultivate.'

It seemed to me she liked attention in general. A bully at school, the affections of a man other than her husband, involved in prominent local events.

'So, what *did* she do in her field?' asked Mark.

'She did have a few papers published, which were okay, but not ground-breaking. She was also interviewed a few times by the press. I don't know if you remember the William Cloveberry case a few years ago? Well, she was someone the media asked for quotes.'

Mark shook his head. 'Cloveberry? Doesn't ring bells.'

Ryan picked up the cafetière and held it in my direction.

'Would you like a top-up?' Now *that* was a cute smile.

'Please.' I heard Mark give a small, very fake-sounding cough. I looked at him. He was smiling in a way that made it clear he'd read my mind. I wasn't going to hear the end of this.

'It must have been seven or eight years ago, William Cloveberry was imprisoned for art forgery. He could copy almost anything, took orders. His work was sold as the genuine article for years and ended up in many famous museums and galleries. Even the British Museum had a number of his works, maybe still does. He has never admitted the scale of his work and identified everything out there. Cora was interviewed as someone who could make a few general comments about art forgery – how much it happens, some of the more famous cases, that sort of thing. I seem to recall that she wasn't very complimentary about William.'

'Why would she be?' asked Mark, in between licking cream off his fingers. The chocolate eclair he had been eating had lost some of its filling and Mark was struggling to maintain any kind of decorum.

'A lot of these forgers are really quite talented in their own right, they have very interesting stories and are passionate about their art. There is only so much you can say to disparage them without having to resort to criticising their personality or appearance, which is what she did. It was quite out of character for her. She can be pretty tough, but she also recognises their talent.'

'Did she slander anyone viciously enough that they might want to kill her?' I asked.

'William was pretty mad. Used some colourful language to describe her.'

'What happened to him?' Mark was reaching for a miniature

Florentine as he spoke. He could eat the whole plate and not put on a single pound, his legs were hollow.

'Got ten years in prison. I would guess he is out by now.' I glanced over at Mark. His eyes met mine.

'What?' asked Ryan. 'Do you think he could be involved? His release dates might work.'

'I'll have a look, I presume that sort of information will be online.' It would give me something to do this evening. 'What about her colleagues at the university? What is her reputation like there?'

Ryan appeared to think for a little while. 'I'm not entirely sure. I haven't heard anything, good or bad. Like I say, she wasn't that big a name in her field. I do know someone who might be able to help, Daniel Grind. He works in the art history department at Sheffield Met. He'll know her pretty well. I'll find his contact details and get them to you.'

The thought of having a valid reason for further contact with Ryan was rather appealing.

'Why don't you two exchange phone numbers?' suggested Mark, mockery in his eyes.

'Of course, here's my card.' Ryan handed me his business card and I exchanged it for one of mine.

After a little more conversation, Ryan had to leave. 'Do you need to have a ticket to the house in order to come to this café?' he asked, gazing around the room.

'Yes. Unless you're a guest of the family or here for a meeting.'

'Hmm.' He looked thoughtful. 'I'd like to bring someone here for afternoon tea, she'd love this.' I felt a sinking feeling in my chest. Was I jealous? I hated to admit it, but maybe I was. I gave myself a mini talking-to. I was very happy with my life as it was.

I said goodbye to Ryan at the entrance to the café, Mark could escort him out. It would give him a chance to quiz Ryan about his TV work, and anyway, the Duchess was heading my way.

24

'Sophie, business or pleasure?'

I was confused. The Duchess smiled.

'Ryan Lavender. Lovely young man.'

'Oh, yes. Business. Mark wanted to talk to him about his television work and they kindly invited me to join them.' The Duchess had a regal air to her, but she was actually very approachable. She was universally liked by the staff; even Mark turned into a fawning teenager when in her company and she was hardly his type.

'How are you after your unfortunate discovery last week?' She looked genuinely concerned.

'I'm fine. Not something I'll forget in a hurry, I just wish we had arrived earlier and had been able to disturb her attacker. Mark said she gave a couple of talks here.' I really didn't want the Duchess to find out about my interest in Cora's death, but I also didn't want to miss this opportunity. 'I wish I'd seen them, it sounds like they would have been very interesting.'

'Indeed, I was telling Alexander that I remembered attending one of them. It was after we had discovered that one of his Ruskins was a fake. The talk I attended was a members' event.

Alexander introduced her. I thought she was rather, how can I describe her? Bullish? No, that's not quite right. She was very certain about herself, anyway. What am I saying? Describe a man like that and you'd simply say that he was confident and it would be a positive trait.'

Her attention was diverted across the café and she waved at someone. 'Please excuse me, Sophie.'

I watched her walk across the room. A number of people turned to look as they recognised her, added to which she was a tall, statuesque figure. She made me feel like a slumped dwarf.

I pulled my shoulders back and set off towards my office. It was about time I tackled the emails that were bound to be piling up in my inbox. That is if I could get Ryan's smile out of my mind for long enough to concentrate on anything.

Ginger was bustling around my kitchen. I'd called her to see if she was prepared to talk to me about Cora and she had suggested that she come over with dinner.

'I told her about the dreadful state of your fridge.' Joyce had arrived with her. The two were joined at the hip these days. They were like Thelma and Louise without the suicide, although killing a bloke wouldn't be beyond Joyce. 'See, look at this.' Joyce had flung open the door of my fridge. Ginger peered over her shoulder.

'Margarine? Dear God, girl, you can get some of the finest butter made up the street and you've got one of those tubs of fake yellow gunk. I blooming well *can* believe that it's nothing like butter, thank you very much. A bottle of beer, that I know you don't drink, and half a can of tuna. That's for Pumpkin, I presume. For a catering professional, it's very disappointing.'

As Ginger turned to face me, I saw she was smiling and there was a crinkle at the corner of her eyes. 'Ignore Lady Macbeth here. You can have whatever you want in your fridge, luv. Joyce, stop judging the girl, we all know that your fridge contains little except champagne and various face creams. Make yourself useful and open the wine.'

Joyce strode to the other side of the kitchen to retrieve some glasses, but not until she'd harrumphed and shaken her head at me. Ginger opened drawers and cupboard doors, gradually finding plates and cutlery.

'Don't tell me,' she'd said. 'You relax, I'll find what I need.' I took her at her word and sat at the kitchen table, watching the two of them prepare our meal while looking like the oddest couple I'd ever seen.

With a plate of steaming shepherd's pie and a glass of wine each, we moved into the sitting room. Joyce perched awkwardly on the edge of the sofa, balancing the plate on her knee.

'I don't see why we can't sit at the table, much more dignified,' she complained.

'Relax, woman,' her friend demanded. 'We're having a nice casual dinner, we are… chillaxing, I believe the word is.'

'If I get any of this on my Orla Kiely skirt, I'm blaming you,' Joyce muttered. The skirt in question was covered in big, bold and simple brown and green flowers with orange centres, so a spill might just blend in. I put my plate on the coffee table and went into the kitchen, returning with something that might help.

'How about this, Joyce? It should make things easier.' I set up a small table that was the perfect height for her to eat her dinner off while she was sitting on the sofa.

'Much better. Thank you.' The woman could even make 'thank you' sound like a criticism. Ginger was watching with a look of amusement. 'What are you staring at?' Joyce demanded.

'It's a vision of the future.'

'What are you on about?'

'Give it a few years, and when Sophie and I are visiting you in the old folks' home, this is what we'll see. Only you'll be in one of those wing-backed chairs and you'll have a tartan rug over your shoulders.' She giggled to herself and tucked into her shepherd's pie.

'Ladies,' I said before Joyce had the chance to reply, 'play nice, please, and no throwing food.' Joyce curled a lip and pretended to flick her fork in the direction of Ginger. I laughed out loud.

'So…' Ginger said between mouthfuls, 'you wanted to know more about Cora? What sort of thing do you want to hear?'

'Well, the more I talk to people, the more I get the impression of someone who was very busy, achieving a lot – a full-time job, research, involved in local activities. But I'm beginning to wonder how much she actually did, or was she just projecting an image?'

Ginger continued to eat, and then put her knife and fork down. 'Very astute, Sophie, very astute. It's interesting that you say that. I always enjoyed her company, and she certainly did a lot for the profile of our well-dressing group, but I don't recall seeing her doing a lot of the heavy lifting, so to speak. Barry is a moaner, but he isn't afraid of getting his hands dirty. Betty is stronger than she looks and was helping lug the wooden frames around, even when we told her to leave it to the young folk. Cora was good at marshalling the troops, talking to the press. She was often late, not surprising with those trains, but it was a regular thing. I do recall thinking one day how odd it was that she was as clean when she left as she had been when she arrived, and now I think about it, it was because she wasn't very hands on.'

'So she was quite superficial?' I asked.

'I wouldn't go that far. I'm sure she was genuinely interested in the history of the well dressings, she was very focused on what needed doing and how we were organised. I would say that she enjoyed leading and she certainly enjoyed being the centre of attention.'

That seemed to mirror what Ryan had said about Cora.

'I'm just not getting the feeling that anyone local hated her enough to want to kill her, it all feels like little squabbles. On

Friday night, you said there was quite a lot of coming and going. So it was possible for someone to have left for a while and no one to have noticed?'

'Oh, absolutely.'

'I'm sure the police will have asked about that...'

'They did, yes.'

'Do you think it likely that some of that movement might have been forgotten? That the police don't have a full picture?'

'Oh, definitely. Besides which, we all arrived at different times and that just confuses things further. There was a real air of excitement about the Duchess's visit as well, so everyone was a bit dizzy. Talk to some of them in the run-up and they wouldn't have been able to tell you their own name.'

'Did many people use the back door?'

'Oh yes, there are a couple of smokers who went out. Some people had left boxes of supplies out there, some went out to take phone calls. What are you thinking?'

'That confirms that someone in the group could have left for a little while, killed Cora and returned. I'm not convinced that Betty could have done it, although she has a motive and you've just said she's pretty strong.'

'As an ox, but I'm not sure she could take on another person.'

'And there's Barry.'

'Not impossible, he never liked the woman. Do you think it was one of us?'

'Maybe. I need to look at a link with an art forger who she criticised in a newspaper article. He should be out of prison by now.'

'That sounds more likely,' said Joyce, who had cleared her plate and was now nursing her wine glass. 'Bad-mouthing a convicted criminal isn't a good idea.'

'You have experience of that,' asked Ginger, 'from your time as a gangster's moll?'

'I was never a gangster's moll. I had a few invites, but I turned them down.'

'That was brave of you,' Ginger said, sounding impressed.

'Actually no, it was brave of them to ask.'

Joyce gave her a knowing look and raised her glass in her direction.

'So it could have been related to Cora's work?' Ginger asked.

'It's a distinct possibility. I've found out a little about her academic interests outside of the day job, but I don't know anything about her university work.'

'You should ask Emily.'

'Why's that?' Other than the well dressings, I wasn't sure what the link would be.

'She's doing her MA at the same university Cora worked at, Sheffield Hallam. Different department, but she might be able to give you a way in, the name of someone it might be useful to talk to.'

'Brilliant! Thank you, Ginger.' If Ryan didn't get back to me with Daniel Grind's contact details, Emily could be a useful ally.

'Any time. Now, come on, let's hear more about what you've found out. Tell me about this forger, that sounds interesting.'

25

After a couple of glasses of wine, I'd pulled out my laptop and the three of us were scrunched up together on the sofa, peering at the screen. William Cloveberry, art forger, had indeed been released from prison a couple of months ago. Every picture I pulled up of him presented a scowling face, which looked like his standard expression.

'If he broke a smile, he might be reasonably handsome,' said Joyce, her priorities the same as ever. She was right, though. I hoped he never wanted to pursue a career in customer service.

It looked as if there wasn't an artist whose work he hadn't copied. He had also made Egyptian style figurines and Assyrian reliefs. Cora's criticism of him did seem personal in tone. Focusing on his lack of a formal education, she called him reckless and callous, whereas in all the other interviews about him he had come across rather well. I made a note to get a copy of the autobiography he had written in prison, which sounded fascinating.

I wondered if there had been more going on between the two of them. Was this a chance for Cora to get back at him for something?

'When was he sentenced?' asked Ginger. I scanned the page.

'In 2016, eight years ago.'

'Seven,' boomed Joyce. 'I know maths isn't your strong suit, Sophie, but for heaven's sake, that's seven years.'

'I've been drinking.'

'Then how do you account for all the free coffee and cake that makes its way to the Finance Department every month? An advance apology,' she explained to Ginger, 'for all the mistakes that everyone knows will be in her paperwork.'

Ginger looked surprised. 'Blimey, how do you cope with measurements for cake ingredients? I'm surprised that you don't have baking disasters left, right and centre.'

Joyce laughed. 'The birds at Charleton House are well fed and fat because of all the redoes she has to make. It's a good job that the majority of the cafés' baked goods come from a local bakery.'

'Have you two finished?' I asked. 'Okay, so Cloveberry went to prison seven years ago, and Cora badmouthed him very personally and publicly.' Had an academic interest and an ill-thought-out response to a journalist's question put her life in danger? 'Was there a bigger history behind her comments about William Cloveberry?'

'You think he might be the person she had an affair with?' asked Ginger, sounding incredulous. 'He's got a face like a slapped ar... sorry, he's not particularly good looking.'

Joyce laughed. 'Why have you suddenly got so demure? Maybe she wanted a bit of rough. Maybe she thought it could give her an insight into the world of forgery, research for her studies.'

Ginger nodded. 'Yes, that might be it. That cute policeman friend of yours would be able to find out.'

'You're not going to tell Joe, are you?' said Joyce, turning to me and sounding surprised. 'Don't you want to beat them to it again? Reveal the killer and make them all look daft?'

'I don't want to make the police look daft, I want to find

Cora's killer. I must admit, I do like getting there before them, but it's not a race. Well, not exactly. I could ask Joe about this. If it gives the police something to pursue and it turns out that Cloveberry did kill her, then great, case closed. If not, then I might still get there before them.'

Joyce thrust her phone into my face. 'Go on, then, call Joe.'

'It's ten o'clock at night. I can't call him now.'

'He's investigating a murder. I doubt he gets a lot of sleep at the moment, and he should be primed to leap into action at the first sign of new information.' Joyce had unlocked the phone and had her fingers hovering over the screen. 'Go on, what's his number?'

I sighed and reeled off the digits. Joyce grinned.

'What?'

'You know his number off by heart.'

'For crying out loud, that is such old news. He's dating Ellie now.'

I heard the click of him picking up his phone.

'Joe, it's Joyce. Are you dressed?' I couldn't hear his response. 'Hmm, glad to hear it. Now, we need you over here at Sophie's, we have some information for you… No, it cannot wait until the morning. You want to catch the killer, don't you?… Yes, Cora's killer… We are doing no such thing, it just… it just cropped up and now we want to assist the police like the diligent citizens we are.'

I could have sworn I heard a snort from the other end of the phone.

'Good, we'll be here. And get your skates on, I need my beauty sleep.' She hung up. 'He's on his way.'

'I don't think he had much choice.'

'Oh, he had a choice,' said Joyce as she topped up her wine glass, 'but luckily for him, he made the right one.'

. . .

Joe looked tired. He declined the offer of wine and beer, and I knew we needed to get to the point. I ran him though everything we had discovered, the timeline of events and the possibility that had taken root in our minds.

'So, you know about the affair. You *have* been sniffing around,' he said with some disapproval.

Ginger laughed. 'The affair's common knowledge, my boy. Village gossip, there is little that gets past us.'

He gave a huff. 'Alright, so let's say they did have an affair. Why would she then badmouth him in the press? Surely she wouldn't want to draw attention to any connection between the two of them?'

Ginger gave him a sympathetic smile before explaining. 'I doubt you've ever run into a woman scorned. You are a gentleman, Joe, but should that change, you might face the full wrath of a woman with a broken heart. We don't all sit and weep, some of us get our own back regardless of the consequences. It would also explain the personal dig at him, although you might want to argue that that comes from inexperience at dealing with the press. We can't find much else she's quoted as saying, but I think there might be more behind it than that.'

Joe was scrolling through the article and occasionally typing something else into the search engine. He rubbed a hand across his face.

'The case keeping you up late?' I asked.

'Kind of, and I've got my exams coming up, so I'm studying when I get home.'

'Exams? What exams?'

'My sergeant's exams. I decided it was time.'

'Good lad.' Ginger slapped him on the back and he nearly dropped my laptop. I grabbed a corner to steady it and Joe pushed it in my direction.

'Okay, I'll talk to Harnby in the morning. There's no harm in seeing where this Cloveberry bloke is.'

'So, the diligent citizens came through,' declared Joyce. Joe turned slowly to face her.

'Don't go getting any ideas. We don't need any more help.'

'But you are very grateful for the input from the diligent citizens.'

'Yes, Joyce, I'm very grateful. I think. Now, if the diligent citizens don't mind, this detective constable would quite like to become a detective sergeant, so I need to go home and study. I'll see myself out.'

Before he left the room, he turned and looked at me.

'I'll drop by the café tomorrow. I think you might need to inject the caffeine straight into my eyeballs.'

'I'll have the syringe at the ready.'

26

It was almost midnight before I managed to crowbar the two women out of the door. I couldn't understand why, despite being around twenty years younger than both of them, I was the one desperate to go to bed and they wanted to open another bottle of wine. This morning was going to be spent drinking multiple cups of coffee to wake myself up.

I leant against the counter, latte in hand.

'How is it?' asked Chelsea.

'Perfect,' I said after taking a sip.

'Phew.'

'What did you think I was going to do if it wasn't perfect?'

'None of us want to find out, but we have a back-up plan.'

'What's that?'

'We'll lock you in your office until you are too weak to do more than beg us for coffee, any kind of coffee, of any standard.'

'She's not joking,' shouted Tina from the kitchen. 'We've had practice runs. We reckon we can get you in there in six seconds. I'm determined to get it down to four.'

'Remind me to fire you all once this caffeine kicks in.' I could hear a phone ringing. 'Can someone get that?'

'It's your office phone,' called Tina. I walked slowly to the office, hoping that whoever it was would hang up before I got there, but the voicemail kicked in.

'Hi, Sophie, it's Ryan. I was…'

I grabbed the receiver. 'Hi, Ryan, sorry, I was just serving a customer. How are you?'

'Very well. Thanks again for a lovely coffee and selection of cakes yesterday.'

'My pleasure.' There was a moment of silence which was about to slip into awkward until Ryan saved it.

'I've got Dan's number for you. Daniel Grind from the Sheffield Hallam University.'

'Yes, of course.' I jotted down the number he gave me. 'Thanks so much, I appreciate it.'

'No worries. Hey, I might see you on Sunday. I've booked a table at the Garden Café, I'm bringing someone for afternoon tea. Will you be working?'

So, he wanted to see me. Maybe. But he was bringing someone. A girlfriend?

'It's actually my day off.'

'That's a shame.'

'But I often come in on my day off – you know, get a bit of work done in the office, help out the staff. So I might be here.'

'Great, well, I'll look out for you.'

'Great.' There was another pause. 'Bye.'

Could it really be his girlfriend? Maybe it was his mother, or a treat for a friend's birthday. Why did I care? I would find out on Sunday. Right now, however, I was going to call Daniel Grind. But first, I needed more coffee.

'TINA!' I bellowed. After her earlier comments, she could make it.

'Yes?'

'AAGH!' I jumped out of my skin. She was leaning in the

doorway of my office. 'What the hell, how long have you been there?'

'Long enough.' She looked at my mug. 'I'll refill that when you tell me who you might see on Sunday.'

'What? No one, just someone Mark knows.'

'And that you're hoping to know?' There was a deeply mischievous look on her face. 'I know, I know, you're going to fire me.' She turned and walked away, calling over her shoulder, 'Just let me make your coffee first.'

Mark had agreed to meet me at the railway station. He was working from home, not something he did very often, so clearly it wouldn't matter if he wasn't *actually* at home for the next few hours. First, though, I needed petrol, otherwise I wasn't going to make it much further than a couple of miles outside the Charleton Estate.

The petrol station was quiet. Only one other car was getting fuelled, and I recognised the woman at the pump. I waved.

'Fiona, right?' I asked. She replied with a warm smile.

'Yes, Fiona Hardcastle. You came to see Betty yesterday.' She replaced the nozzle on the pump. I didn't want her to go just yet.

'Fiona, can I ask you a question?'

'Sure.' She walked over to join me.

'Did you know Cora Parrish?'

She looked at me with an expression of uncertainty or curiosity, I wasn't sure which.

'Sort of, why?'

'Did Betty talk about her?'

'She did.' Fiona still sounded very uncertain about how to respond. 'Betty has talked about her death a few times, it's been a shock to everyone. Why?'

'I just want to know more about her. I found her body and...'

'Oh hell, I'm sorry, that must have been awful.'

'Thank you. Did you know her at all?' She hesitated a little too long. 'You did, didn't you?' She hesitated again before replying.

'I went to school with her. I don't have very fond memories.'

'I've heard she was a bit of a bully.'

'Bit?' Fiona responded with a downbeat laugh. 'She was deeply unpleasant. Pupils, teachers, she didn't care. If she targeted you, she made your life miserable.'

'Did you become a target?'

Fiona shook her head. 'I managed to dodge that bullet. I was a quiet child, I think I was just invisible. I never drew attention to myself, stayed out of her way.'

I thought about someone Cora had bullied. 'Barry said he had been on the receiving end of her taunts. I can't believe that you and he were at school at the same time.' Fiona looked considerably younger.

She laughed. 'It's hard to deny he hasn't aged well. It's not because I look particularly good.' She was wrong there, she had flawless skin and clearly wasn't wearing any makeup. I couldn't spot any roots either and she wasn't going grey.

'I think you look great.'

She smiled and her face lit up. 'You're very kind. My mother and grandmother had great skin, and I was fortunate enough to inherit that.'

'Do you think there was anyone from your schooldays who hated Cora enough to hold a grudge right up to now?'

'And want to kill her? You'd have a list as long as your arm. If they ever held a class reunion, it would probably turn into a celebration that she was dead. I know that sounds awful, but she really wasn't very nice and I can't imagine that anyone will be particularly sorry. No one should die the way she did, but she ruined a lot of children's schooldays.'

'She seemed to be very involved locally, and she got on well with many of those at the well-dressing group.'

Fiona nodded. 'I know. Maybe she'd improved over the years.

Barry is the only one in the group who knew her from school, and he certainly held a grudge. The others only knew her for the last couple of years and I'm sure she came across very well. Unless you were Betty, of course. It would be a shame if she was killed because of her behaviour as a child, especially if she was different now. Maybe she even regretted it. But I'm not aware of her ever talking to Barry, or anyone else, and apologising.'

I spotted the time on the clock on my dash. 'Heck, I've got to go, I'll miss my train. Thanks, Fiona.'

'Any time.'

I got back in my car and drove off. So it certainly wasn't just Barry who had been Cora's victim as a child. I wondered how many of them still lived in the area and knew that Cora had returned.

27

'I don't see why we couldn't have driven in.' Mark was nodding along with the train, and overemphasising the movements.

'Stop it, it's not that bad.'

'Really? I'm going to need medical support after this.'

'You are if you keep messing around like that. We didn't drive because I didn't want to faff around trying to find parking, and I enjoy travelling by train. The scenery is lovely, and I find it calming, depending on my company.'

The Derbyshire scenery, its gentle rolling hills, patchwork fields and cute villages, was one of the things that had made the decision to return north so easy. As we neared Sheffield, we were looking at mills and industrial estates. They weren't as pretty, that was for sure, but they were interesting. It was a sign of the city we were nearing and a reminder of its role in the country's Industrial Revolution. Sheffield was known for its history of producing steel. It was famous for its cutlery, but I now knew it for its arts and culture.

'Did you know…' I could tell from his tone of voice that Mark was about to launch into tour guide mode '…that when Queen

Victoria opened the town hall building, she did so using a remote control lock from her carriage? When she turned a key in the specially made lock, it triggered a light in the building. That was the signal for three men who were tucked away out of sight to open the gates.'

'So, how did that work? Did she have access to Wi-Fi?'

Mark looked thoughtful. 'You know, that's a very good question, I've never considered that.' He pulled out a notebook and scribbled a note. 'I will endeavour to find out and report back.'

The building we were heading for was a short walk from the station. A modern structure of glass and concrete, it had a poem by Andrew Motion adorning the full length of an exterior wall. I imagined Cora walking to and from the station on an almost daily basis. I wondered if any of the people who passed us had known Cora or missed her walking down this path, striding towards a meeting or dashing for a train.

Daniel Grind had come down from his office to meet us. He was a scruffy version of Ryan in some ways. His jeans were crumpled, the t-shirt he wore had a faded image on it and the navy blazer looked like an afterthought, an attempt to adhere to some kind of dress code. He wore fabulous bright orange-rimmed glasses which I immediately coveted.

He bought us all a coffee from the café in the lobby, and then led the way up to his small corner office. The large windows made for a bright space, but its view over a car park wasn't exactly inspiring. Colourful children's drawings covered the doors of a cupboard. A photograph of Daniel with a young child on his shoulders was pinned to a cork board.

'Excuse the mess. If you knew me, you'd realise this is actually quite tidy.' He lifted a pile of papers off a chair and dumped them on an already teetering stack on the corner of his desk. Next, he cleared a battered armchair of a mound of books. 'Please, sit.'

I noticed Mark looking rather sniffily at the armchair before slowly lowering himself into it. I made a note to call him a snob when we left.

'So, you want to talk about Cora? What would you like to know?' Daniel looked open and friendly without an ounce of suspicion, and he didn't ask why we were interested, which was a relief. I always struggled with that question.

'Please. What was she like to work with?'

'Hmm, she was a curious character. Very professional, dedicated. She had high expectations of her students, but not unreasonable. Some might say she was ambitious, which is how she came across, but that's not how she acted in practice.'

'What do you mean?' asked Mark, who looked as though he had finally relaxed in the armchair.

'Well, she never actually went for promotions or angled to be the speaker at conferences. Which was surprising for the image she projected. You know, the whole dress for success thing, network with the right people. She did all of that, but just stayed at the same level.'

'Do you think she might have been applying for things, but not telling people in case she was knocked back?' I always kept quiet when going for a new job because I didn't want any failure to be public knowledge.

Daniel shook his head. 'There's no way she could have kept that quiet here. The information would have been around the department in a shot. I do have a theory, though…'

'Please,' I encouraged him.

'She commanded real respect around here. She knew her stuff, she understood the job, the department, she knew how to make things happen and who to talk to. I don't think she ever wanted to appear like she didn't know something, to be out of her depth. She was comfortable. If she got promoted, she would be the new girl at that level. She would have to learn a lot, and very quickly.

'Cora had a lot of respect and she knew it. People weren't exactly afraid of her – well, some were – but she was someone you wanted to keep on side. I think she would have lost some of her self-confidence if she'd moved into a position where she had to regain that trust and respect.'

I liked the way Daniel thought. It was a really good interpretation and fitted what we already knew: that Cora liked to have control. Some might do that by getting more and more power with promotion after promotion, but Cora did it by knowing everything about where she was. That gave her confidence and a different kind of power and control. It also showed that the bully had her own insecurities – she didn't want to be seen as a failure.

'You said people weren't afraid of her?'

He gave the question some thought. 'No, not in the traditional way, but she very quickly became a strong, stable presence. People were wary of her, perhaps that's a better way of putting it.'

'How did the students get on with her?' Mark was now so relaxed, he was practically part of the armchair. Mind you, I doubted the seat cushion had much support in it. He was going to need help unfolding his long legs and getting up.

'Fine, as far as I know. I haven't heard of any complaints. She kept her distance. If there was a special event or celebration, she might go for one drink, but I don't think she was particularly pally with any of them.'

There was a knock. 'Come in,' called Daniel. The head of a young woman popped around the door.

'Oh, sorry to disturb, I was just wondering if I could pick my essay up off you.'

'Of course, Steph, come on in. Actually, you might be able to help with something. Steph here was a student of Cora's. Am I right in thinking that she wasn't overly friendly with you students?'

The young woman looked at Mark and me, but any curiosity was overridden by the need to answer a question from a tutor.

'She was friendly, but professional, if you know what I mean. She'd come for a drink from time to time if there was a particular reason, but that was it, she never stayed long. She came out with us a couple of weeks ago. Melanie had been accepted onto a PhD at King's and Cora bought a bottle of champagne. We liked her, you knew where you stood with her.'

Daniel handed over her essay. 'You did a really good job, we'll talk about it next week.'

Steph beamed as she looked at the top sheet. 'Great, thank you.' She smiled at us, and then left.

'Steph's incredibly bright, but that's the first essay she's handed in on time all year. That'll be the main subject of our tutorial next week.' He shook his head. 'She's going to have to sharpen up for next year. If she gets her act together, she'll be in line for a first.'

'Is there anything else I can help you with? I don't mean to rush you, but I'm delivering a lecture in half an hour, and if I'm honest with you, I haven't given it a moment's thought.' He grinned like a naughty schoolboy. '"Don't do as I do, do as I say," as my mother used to tell me.'

'Yes, just one thing. Was Cora researching anything in particular at the moment?' I asked.

'Hmm, I'm not sure what she was working on. Actually, that pile there,' he indicated towards the books he had removed from the armchair, 'they were Cora's. I said I'd return them to whichever library they came from, but I haven't had a chance to take a look at them.'

I stood up and examined the spines. 'Could we borrow them? I'll return them to the library.'

'It might not be the university library. She will have accessed a variety of collections, and not just from Sheffield,' he warned.

'That's okay. I promise you we'll get them returned.'

'Sure, saves me a job.'

I loaded myself up with the books, trying not to grin as Mark attempted to get out of his seat, looking like a contortionist in the process.

'Thanks, Daniel, we're really grateful.'

'Any time. Happy to help out a friend of Ryan's.'

We exchanged an awkward handshake as I balanced the books, and then Mark and I left him to work on his lecture.

28

'Madrid,' said Joyce.

'It should go on the list, I agree, but I'd like to go to Scotland,' replied Ginger. 'Edinburgh is a beautiful city, and just think of all the men in kilts.'

Joyce suddenly looked interested. Ginger certainly knew how to appeal to her audience.

'Hmm, that's not a bad idea. I believe the Balmoral Hotel is rather nice.'

'The Balmoral is out of our price range, dear, you're not married to a clan chief yet.'

'Give me time, and anyway, that's what money is for. We can't take it with us.'

Ginger rolled her eyes. 'We didn't all get to take ex-husbands to the cleaners.'

'No, but I did, and he thoroughly deserved it, the cheating… anyway, I'll pay.'

'You will not!' declared Ginger.

'You can pay for me,' I said as I sat down with a tray of drinks.

'There you are, Ginger, perhaps I'll go with Sophie.'

'I doubt Sophie would put up with you for the time it took

you to cross the border. I'm the only one daft enough to be your travelling companion. Make that your dogsbody.'

I listened to the two of them bicker for a few more minutes. With the hum of other conversations in the pub as a backdrop, it was a comfortable and entertaining place to be.

After returning from Sheffield, I'd given Mark a lift home from the station, and then gone back to work. It had turned into a very busy afternoon, and after I'd dropped Cora's books at home, I had turned around and come straight to the pub, where Joyce and Ginger were just finishing dinner.

They were odd friends. Joyce, with her blonde hair piled high, a full can of hairspray required to keep it in place, a collection of clothing so large that she could have dressed a small nation, and more shoes than Imelda Marcos could have dreamed of. Ginger, on the other hand, appeared to toss on the first loose-fitting outfit she could find, but she still looked fabulous, buzzing with enthusiasm about life. I could only hope that I had half their energy when I reached their age.

By the time they had finished their debate, they had settled for Edinburgh.

'You should get the sleeper train up,' I suggested. 'Travel overnight, take a hamper of food and a bottle of champagne for supper.'

'Ooh, now there's a thought.' Ginger's eyes were like saucers. 'What a brilliant idea.' She grabbed my hand. 'Thank you, Sophie. I'll get onto that tomorrow.'

Joyce looked less sure of the idea. 'I'm not sleeping on the top bunk.'

'Do they have bunks?' Ginger asked. 'Oh, never mind, if they do, then I'll go up top. I don't think you could make it up the ladder in your heels.'

'I'd take them off... oh, shut up, woman.'

Ginger giggled.

'Sophie, how was your day?' It was an obvious attempt to redirect the conversation, and it made me smile.

'Good, thank you.'

'Mark said you'd been to Sheffield, doing a bit of Miss Marple-ing. He texted me,' Joyce explained.

'We did. I don't know how useful it was, but I'm getting more of an idea of Cora.'

'You know, the more I think about her, the more I realise that I didn't really know her at all,' said Ginger. 'She didn't give much away. You don't realise it at the time, but you're the one doing all the talking. It's quite a skill.'

'It's manipulation, is what it is,' said Joyce. 'Got any more suspects, Sophie?'

'From the university? No. She hadn't worked there all that long, but she quickly got herself a good, solid reputation.'

'You should ask Emily what the students thought of her.' Ginger nodded towards the bar where Emily was standing with a group of friends.

'I did get to speak to one of Cora's students. I didn't think that Emily was taught by her.'

'She wasn't, but she might know something.'

Ginger was out of her chair before I had the chance to reply. Emily hadn't even been in the same department as Cora, so I doubted that she would know anything other than a bit of gossip, and I hadn't got the impression that Cora had been the subject of much of that.

'Grab a seat, girl,' Ginger said as she pulled a chair out for Emily, 'you might be able to help Sophie,' and then went back to the bar.

'Hi, of course.'

'Sorry, Emily, I don't want to disturb your night, and I doubt you can help anyway, but Ginger insisted…'

'Don't worry,' Emily laughed, 'she's said she'll get me a drink, which sounds like a fair deal to me.'

'I know you weren't taught by Cora, and you weren't even in the same department as her, were you?'

'No. Same building, but different department.'

'Well, I spoke to a student from her course who said that Cora didn't really have much of a reputation either way personally at the university. Didn't have much to do with the students. But she had a solid reputation as a lecturer. Is that the way you thought of her?'

'Sounds about right. Like I said, I saw her around to say hello to, but I didn't take any of her classes and had no university dealings with her.'

'What about when she went out with students for a drink, were you ever there?'

Emily shook her head. 'No, I don't think she spent much time with them. Kept her distance, and none of my friends were taught by her, either. I saw her in a bar with some of her postgrads the other week, but I was with my friends. Have you managed to find out anything interesting? Ginger said you were keen to discover who killed her.'

'I'm just curious, you know? I'm not sure she was someone I would have wanted to spend much time with if she were alive, but there doesn't seem to be that much that's interesting or unusual about her, if you discount her rather dramatic personal life.'

Emily thanked Ginger as a glass of wine appeared in front of her on the table.

'Sounds like a fair assessment. Which begs the question, was it a mugging, or a case of mistaken identity? If there's nothing about her that points in the direction of an obvious killer, then maybe she wasn't the intended target.'

That had been raised before. It had still been daylight when she was killed, so in theory it would have been obvious that it was Cora, but maybe the killer didn't know her very well, or was a hired assassin who made a mistake. But this was the small village of Castledale we were talking about. Hired assassins were the kind of thing that only happened in the movies.

'Hello, Sophie, are you still with us?' Joyce was waving her hand in front of my face.

'Sorry, I was just thinking. Thanks, Emily.'

'Not sure how I helped, but my pleasure. Thanks for the drink, Ginger. I'll give you a call about that coffee we talked about the other day, Sophie.'

'Looking forward to it.'

Emily walked back to the bar.

'So, was that helpful?' asked Ginger.

'Maybe,' I replied, wondering if this was the mystery that would have me stumped. That would please Joe and Harnby.

29

I was welcomed back from the pub by Pumpkin, who seemed pleased to see me. I was less pleased to see that she had thrown up on the kitchen floor, and to add insult to injury, she sat and watched me clear it up with a superior look on her face. I really was her servant. She then beat me to the sofa and I had to try to make myself comfortable whilst contorting my legs around her.

I pulled a blanket over my legs, and over Pumpkin, and opened up my laptop. I wanted to find out more about the art forger that Cora had spoken critically about in an interview, William Cloveberry. I reread the article that had quoted Cora, and then did some more searching. I wasn't sure that a single article badmouthing him would give him cause to kill her, unless he was a particularly angry and violent man, not the image that I would automatically attach to an art forger. I imagined a calm, level-headed person who – though not afraid of committing a crime and defrauding people of hundreds of thousands of pounds – liked to live a quiet, safe, stress-free life. Would that kind of person make their way to Derbyshire with the intention of killing a person? He might have wanted to talk to her, though, discuss what she'd said, have a frank conversation, and it had got out of hand. Maybe he had gone to visit her and she had run into him on Swallow Lane as she popped home before heading to the village hall. Perhaps her words had damaged Cloveberry's chances of starting his business again, assuming that prison hadn't put him off. It was just too much of a coincidence that Cora had died around the time that he had been released.

More hunting around found a couple of short newspaper articles, but he had hardly been major news, at least not for much more than a day. After half an hour, I had found nothing of interest.

I heard a funny squeaking sound and watched as the lump beneath the blanket next to my feet moved a little. Then Pumpkin's head appeared from under the edge with a very surprised expression. I knew what that look meant.

'You had a nightmare?' She stared back at me like she was trying to figure out where she was. 'Come on, come and have a snuggle.' She quickly made her way up onto my lap, and with her nose just under my chin, she snuggled in hard, purring. I spent a lot of my time pretty certain that she was the offspring of Satan, but I still gave her more kisses than she wanted, and having her huge bulk crushed against me like this made all the dead mice, frogs and occasional vomit cleaning worthwhile.

She rubbed the top of her head against my chin and I stroked her while reflecting on what I had found out and who might have killed Cora. I was tired and fuzzy from the gin and tonic I'd had in the pub, so I didn't get far. On the armchair, just out of reach, was the pile of books that Daniel Grind had given me. They were some of the last things that Cora had been studying.

The leather of my sofa creaked as I reached over as far as I could. This clearly made Pumpkin unhappy, based on the claws I could now feel digging into my skin and the low grumble she was emitting.

'Hang on. If I can get the books, then you can settle down while I read.'

She glared at me. I leant over the edge of the sofa a little further and Pumpkin jumped, her pointy feet pressing hard into my stomach as she leapt off, leaving me winded. At least she had made my task easier for me.

There were ten books, all with little sticky tabs that Cora must have used to mark important pages. I piled them up on the floor next to me and started flicking through them. Even if I didn't have the brain power to actively work through the puzzle of Cora's killer, my subconscious might pick up on something. Or at least, that was what I hoped.

Two hours later and I had drawn a blank. I had started off just flicking through to the tabs, but then I decided that Cora might have found something and not marked it. I didn't want to take the chance of missing anything.

After reading about brush strokes and the variety of paint ingredients, I was fighting the urge to go to sleep. This was not going to become a subject I wished to know any more about than was absolutely necessary. I actually nodded off with the last book open on my knee and woke to see that it was almost 2am. Time to go to bed, but with half a book left to skim through, I figured I'd finish it first.

Now, sleeping is one of my favourite activities, so delaying going to bed when I am already tired is not something I do lightly. But this time, it well and truly paid off. Half way through the book, and beyond the last tab that Cora had placed in it, a number of handwritten notes were tucked between the pages. I recognised the writing as Cora's, having seen some of the notes on her desk. Alongside these notes was a black-and-white photograph.

I read through the notes. It took me a while as they got quite messy at one or two points. The pages were packed with handwriting that looked as if it had been scribbled down in a rush. Cora had been either running out of time before having to be somewhere else or excited by what she had discovered.

They were regarding an unnamed artist who had forged the works of Chagall, Le Corbusier and Dubuffet, amongst others. There was a timeline and notes about court dates. It looked as if Cora had needed to dive into court records on a visit to London in order to get more information – the train ticket was being used as a bookmark. According to the notes, it was, however, possible to find information about the artist's own original work online. Although not very well known, he was a well-respected artist who created beautiful paintings of Derbyshire.

I looked at the photograph and the notes, again in Cora's handwriting, on the back. It had been taken at an art exhibition, also in London. In the photograph, I found myself staring at the artist and three other people. Two of them were not familiar to me and their names didn't ring bells. But the artist's name did, as did the image of his wife. Despite the photograph being at least thirty years old, she was most definitely familiar.

It was Castledale's very own Betty Natchbull.

30

'Well, Scotland is booked,' declared Joyce as we walked across the Library Café, coffees in hand. 'September. Perfectly timed for me to recover from the summer holiday bedlam that descends upon us here, and the chaos of the Edinburgh Festival is over. I will have to start considering my wardrobe. If Vivienne Westwood could make such a feature of tartan, then so can I.'

'You'll also need to learn the Highland fling.'

'The what?'

'It's a dance,' I told her. 'If you're going to get yourself hitched to a wealthy Scottish laird, then you'll need to hold your own at a ceilidh.'

'If I find myself a man, I won't have to hold my own anything.' She smirked over her mug. I shook my head.

'Heaven help the men of Scotland. I'm wondering if I might need to warn them, give them a head start in running for the hills.'

'Even in these heels, I'd catch them.' Joyce stuck a leg out from under the table. The navy blue stilettos were trimmed in bright pink that matched her suit, which was trimmed in navy. It was just like Joyce to make the brightest colour the feature rather than a cheerful trim. Mind you, the colour wasn't the most risqué feature.

'I take it the skirt was made last?' I asked. I had no doubt her comment was right, she could run the London marathon in a pair of stilettos and finish without a single blister.

'What do you mean?' Joyce ran a hand over the fabric. Even her fingernails coordinated, each one delicately striped in perfectly matching navy and pink.

'Well, it looks like they ran out of fabric.'

'What are you... oh, very funny. If you've got it, flaunt it, that's what I say.' And she certainly had *it*, all the way up and beyond. I felt rather dowdy in my black trousers and white shirt. I was still avoiding the shopping trip that Joyce kept promising to take me on. Actually, make that threatening to take me on.

'Speaking of well-dressed women, how is your hunt for Cora's killer going? That Victor Stewart jacket was a good one, such a shame the water would have ruined it.'

Her comment was so inappropriate, I had to laugh.

'What? His clothes don't come cheap.'

I looked up to see Joe walk in. 'I'm not investigating anything,' I muttered in a hushed tone.

'But you've been...' I kicked her under the table and looked towards the door. 'Ah, message received and understood. You are a mere café slave with poor taste in outfits. You have no interest in a recent murder whatsoever.'

'Poor taste? What are you saying? This is very smart and appropriate for...'

'A funeral.'

'Ladies, do I need to mediate a dispute?' Joe looked down on us.

'You need to arrest her for an extremely serious fashion crime,' stated Joyce in an exceptionally posh voice.

'I'll get you a coffee,' I grumbled in Joe's direction. 'You can entertain the Wicked Witch of the West.'

'That's a bit harsh.' Joyce's voice had gone up a couple of octaves.

Joe gave her the once-over. 'Only a little, and anyway, it's the North West.'

I laughed and left them to it.

'So, how goes it?' I asked Joe, trying to make my question sound as relaxed and non-specific as possible. Joyce had left us alone. Her mobile phone had rung and apparently there was some kind of tea towel crisis in one of the gift shops.

'Do you mean life, or our current investigation?' From the look on his face, I knew I'd been rumbled.

'Let's start with life.'

'Well, I don't have one. This sergeant's exam has taken over my life. Which I suppose is how it should be, but I can't wait until it's over.' He did look tired. Since he'd started dating Ellie, a member of the conservation team here at Charleton House, he'd smartened up his act decidedly. But today, his shirt looked as if it needed ironing and he had clearly put his tie on in a rush.

'You'll do fine.'

'Maybe.'

'Having a murder investigation going on at the same time can't be helping.'

'Too right.' He ran his fingers through his hair, which left it sticking up in different directions.

'I was wondering, and just wondering,' I said, trying to sound as innocent as possible, 'did you look into William Cloveberry? It does seem like a heck of a coincidence that he was released and not long afterwards, Cora is found dead.'

'You're assuming he was released.'

'He wasn't?'

'Yes, actually he was. He left prison and moved to Nottingham.'

'So, not a million miles away from here. It would have been very easy for him to get to Derbyshire, he could even have come a couple of times to scout out where Cora lived and… hang on, why are you talking to me about this without giving me a warning to keep my nose out and let you do your job?'

Joe smiled. 'Two reasons. One, I'm too bloody exhausted to argue, and two, William Cloveberry died of a heart attack two weeks after he was released from prison, so I was happy for you to talk yourself down that particular dead end.'

'That coffee is no longer on the house,' was the only response I could come up with. Joe looked into his mug.

'And if I refuse to pay?'

'You can roll up your sleeves and wash some dishes.' I decided to make the most of his tiredness. 'I have another question.' His shoulders slumped. 'Am I right in thinking that any activity beyond the Castledale village hall and over towards Swallow Lane wouldn't be caught on CCTV from the main street because of foliage, or cameras not covering the area?'

'Bloody hell, Sophie, you don't let up, do you. I'm not telling you.' He sounded like a petulant child who didn't want to share a secret.

'Well, I don't think it would. Just saying.'

'That's hardly going to be new information for us, but thanks for *just saying* anyway.'

'Ah, so I'm right.' I couldn't help but give him a triumphant grin. 'Would you like a free brownie? I think you've earned it.'

'I'm still too tired to argue. Can I have it to go?'

31

Thanks to Joe's lack of sleep and general distraction, I wasn't going to waste any more time heading down the William Cloveberry route. He'd looked like such a miserable bloke, I wouldn't have been keen to meet him anyway; he would probably have even pushed Joyce's charm skills to their limit. However, one person of interest was definitely alive and kicking: Betty Natchbull. I knew I could have told Joe about the link, and probably should have done, but he'd looked so done in, he'd only have forgotten anything I said. That was what I was telling myself, anyway.

I had nipped out for a quick visit to Highview Cottage. Assuming that Betty would be home, I was hoping I would get a glimpse at her artwork. I wondered if she was as good as her husband had been, if her not getting through to the final of the art competition had been a genuine shock, or if she had usually been able to intimidate the judges and Cora had stood up to her. Even if that wasn't a strong enough reason for Betty to want to kill Cora, it might have contributed to her anger.

I spotted Fiona's car. I wasn't sure whether her presence

would be a good or bad thing, but there was now a chance I would be met by at least one smiling face.

'Sophie, hello.' Fiona looked surprised, but pleasantly so, when she opened the door. 'I presume you want to talk to Betty?'

'Please.'

'I'll see if she's free. Well, I know she is, but let's see if she's taking visitors.' Fiona smiled conspiratorially at me. If anyone was going to know Betty's quirks, it was someone who worked for her.

She left me waiting in the hallway for a few moments before returning and signalling me to follow.

'She was a bit reluctant, but I convinced her to see you.'

Betty was sitting in the conservatory, reading a newspaper. The fabric on the cushions of the bamboo furniture made it look as if she was sitting in the midst of a jungle, the large plants placed around the space adding to the effect. I half expected a monkey to come swinging down from the ceiling. All Betty needed was a pith helmet and a net to complete the scene.

She didn't look up as I came in.

'Should I get you some drinks?' asked Fiona. Betty seemed to hesitate before replying.

'Coffee. If that suits?' She looked at me and it was clear that even if it didn't suit, that was what we were getting. I wasn't going to argue, even though I would have turned down the nasty instant stuff she had served me last time given the opportunity. If I was going to get anywhere with this woman, I was going to have to pretend that whatever Fiona served was the finest coffee I'd ever tasted.

'You'll need to wait while I finish this.' I watched as she stared at a page. Her eyes weren't moving much, I didn't think she was actually reading anything. I pulled a book out of my bag and placed it on the coffee table between us. That seemed to catch her attention. I could see her peering at the cover, and then she closed the newspaper, her curiosity getting the better of her.

'You wanted to talk to me?'

'Yes. I know you are very passionate about art, you're a talented artist yourself, and I believe your husband was an artist too.' I figured a bit of flattery would do no harm.

'He was.'

'I came across some of his work. He was also very talented and seems to have had a successful career.' I laid the photograph on the table, but kept it close to me.

'Here we are.' Fiona walked in and placed the tray on the table. A cafetière was steaming gently. *Thank God.* 'I was sure you'd want the good coffee,' she said, sounding sweetly innocent before glancing my way, her mouth twitching into a smile as she left us alone. I quickly concluded that I liked Fiona.

'Would you tell me about him? I'm keen to know more.'

'Why on earth would you want to know more about Tony? He's been gone a long time.'

'How long?' I asked.

'My husband passed fifteen years ago.' I noticed that her eyes kept flicking over to the photograph. 'He was indeed very talented. It was Tony who encouraged me to paint when we first met.'

'I believe he had a lot of exhibitions.'

'He did, yes. He was very well respected as a local artist, but he never gained the national recognition that he deserved, and would have achieved had he lived.' This was clearly a source of regret for Betty.

'Did he enter the Buxton art competition?' I remembered too late that this was a sore point.

'No, he did not. He established it, it would have been inappropriate.'

'I would have thought that if he was the founder, it might have been named after him following his death.' That seemed to do it, not that it had been my intention. Again, I had spoken without thinking.

'What is this about? I don't believe for one minute that you have come here to discuss the merits of my husband's paintings. I also know that you have been asking a lot of questions in the village. Now, tell me the real reason for your visit or leave.' She was actually a little frightening once she got going.

I turned the photograph and slid it over towards Betty.

'Yes, that is Tony and me. What of it?' There was a coldness in her question.

'I know that he had another string to his bow. He was an equally talented forger.'

'How dare you!'

'I dare because Cora had clearly done her homework. I have no doubt that if I retraced her steps, I would find the evidence that she had come across.'

Betty was turning more and more red. It wouldn't be long until I saw steam come out of her ears. It looked as if she was struggling to find the words to respond, so I stepped in.

'I am not here to focus on your husband, nor have I mentioned this to anyone else. Was Cora threatening to talk publicly about it? Was she writing an article that would expose your husband's crimes?'

'I have no idea,' Betty exploded. 'How would I know?'

'Because if she did and she told you her plans, I have no doubt that you would have wanted to keep her quiet.'

'Are you suggesting that *I* killed Cora? That's preposterous.' She burst into a forced laugh. 'Utterly ridiculous. In case you haven't noticed, I am a woman of advancing years. I have Fiona here to make my life easier, precisely because I am no longer a young woman with the strength to do something as physically strenuous as murdering another person.'

I looked at Betty. She wasn't exactly a spring chicken, but that didn't mean that she wasn't fit, or that once rage and adrenalin took over, she wasn't capable of anything. I didn't actually know how strong Cora was. It might have been that Cora fell as they argued, and then all Betty had to do was hold her face down in the water. She could even have sat on her until she drowned. It was all entirely possible.

Almost as though Betty had read my mind, she said, 'Well, I didn't. I didn't have the opportunity. I was working on my board all evening. You saw me there.'

'Not the whole time, I didn't. I was looking at the work, talking to people. Lots of the group were coming and going, almost everyone had the opportunity to leave for as long as it would take to kill Cora.'

'Well, there you are, then, everyone had the opportunity.'

'But not everyone had the motive, Betty. Not everyone's husband was about to have his past crimes exposed and his reputation, which had miraculously remained intact until this point, destroyed. Was that why you didn't push for the competition to be named after him? It would throw too much light on him? People might dig and find out what happened?'

'This is ridiculous, all of this is ridiculous.' She was starting to look like a little old lady, and if it wasn't for what I knew and had seen of her, I might have felt sorry for her. 'This conversation is over.' She stood with an ease and speed that didn't go unnoticed. 'You can leave now.'

I didn't argue, although it was a shame. The coffee was rather good.

32

As the front door was firmly closed behind me with a loud slam, I saw Fiona's car turn out of the driveway. Maybe she was running errands for Betty, or she finished work early on a Friday.

I sat in my own car for a moment, trying to think. I did actually believe that Betty had what it took to kill Cora, especially if all she'd had to do was hold her head under the water. Betty climbing the wall behind the village hall was a bit of a stretch, but I decided not to think about that. Where there's a will, and all that.

I ran through the conversation with Betty. Was there anything she had said that gave the game away? It had been nice of Fiona to make decent coffee, although whether that really was for me, or because Betty was also drinking it, I couldn't be sure. She was certainly a very attentive assistant, or housekeeper, or whatever she was.

That gave me pause for thought. Very attentive, and no doubt very efficient. I wondered how loyal she was; after all, she'd seemed to share a moment of amusement with me at Betty's expense. How long had Fiona worked for Betty? How close were they? Was Fiona loyal enough to kill for Betty, with or without Betty's knowledge?

I thrust the car into gear and set off. I had no idea why, but I had the urge to follow Fiona and find out where she was going. After she'd initially turned out of the driveway, there was only one way that Fiona could realistically have gone and I shot off in that direction.

I opened the window to let out some of the warmth that had built up in the car while it had been sitting in the sun, and turned the radio on. Tina Turner blasted out of my speakers – now there was someone I hadn't heard in a long time. I put my foot down. I knew many of these roads and could anticipate the blind and gravel-strewn corners. After playing chicken with an oncoming mail van, I overtook a tractor on a narrow stretch, the long grasses of the bank catching my mirror and the bramble bushes probably covering my car with scratches, but that was okay. They'd match all the other marks that covered my old faithful rust bucket.

I had to take a guess at a couple of junctions, but I imagined Fiona was off to the shops in Castledale. I slowed down as I drove along the main street, looking for Fiona's car parked up at the side, but it wasn't there. I was about to give up when I saw it up ahead, turning into Swallow Lane in the direction of Cora and Hugh's house.

I pulled to a stop just up the road from the house, but within sight of the driveway and front door, watching as Fiona knocked on the door and Hugh let her in. What on earth was going on? So, Fiona knew Hugh, but how well? Had they been having an affair? Had Cora found out and Hugh or Fiona had killed her? After all, Fiona hadn't been at the well-dressing session, so I wondered whether she had appeared on the police's radar.

I couldn't think of any other reason why Fiona was calling round at Hugh's. He already had a cleaner, so perhaps they were friends, a thought that took my mind straight back to the idea of them being lovers.

I picked up my phone and called Mark.

'I can't talk long,' he said the minute he answered. 'I'm with my director. He's just discussing something with the cameraman.'

'You filming already? That was quick.'

'No, no, not yet. Thank goodness, I'm not quite ready for that. No, we're just checking out a couple of locations. They like a lot of my ideas, but want to see if it all works visually.'

'Okay, well, can you ask Bill if he can ask Delia if she knows why Fiona would be visiting Hugh?'

'Who, what, where? Say that again.' I explained in a bit more detail. 'Why might Delia know?'

'Because as nice as she is, that woman keeps an eye on all the comings and goings in that house. She managed to work out why Cora and Hugh had moved back up here because she was listening in.'

'Fair enough. I'll give him a call when we're done here. He'll still be at school and Delia will be cleaning, or gossiping with him later.'

'Thank you. Good luck.'

'Keep saying that. It's all getting disturbingly real the closer the actual filming gets.'

'Don't worry, the camera will love you.'

'Oh, I know.' I laughed; that was such a Mark comment.

I looked back over to the house. Was there an even more complex picture? Were Hugh, Betty and Fiona all tied up in this together? Anger, jealousy, sex – all common motives for murder, and all were swirling around Cora's untimely death.

33

The Library Café was buzzing when I returned, with a mixture of staff who had decided to start sliding into the weekend over a coffee, and visitors who had spent the warm day walking miles around the grounds and house and were now refuelling on cake before the drive home. I loved the cafés when they were like this. I had tried to make all of them warm and friendly places, and at times like now, I really felt I had achieved my aim.

Chelsea was efficiently serving a line of customers, while Tina was making coffee and preparing toasted sandwiches accompanied by a young woman I didn't recognise.

'Sophie, this is Rachel. She's working this weekend, so I'm showing her the ropes.'

'Great, Rachel, thanks for helping out.'

She smiled. 'Happy to.'

I started to make my way to my office. 'Oh,' I stopped and turned back to Rachel, 'and ignore anything she says about me and coffee.' Rachel smiled again and looked at Tina. 'She's already given you the *how not to lose your job* training, hasn't she?'

Tina looked towards the ceiling. 'I've never noticed that crack before.'

'You're fired,' I said. Tina laughed.

'See what I mean?' she said to Rachel. 'Her latte wasn't up to scratch this morning.'

I shook my head. 'Rachel, you're promoted, you're the new supervisor.' I walked to my office, the sound of Tina laughing in the background. I grinned to myself. How my team put up with me, I didn't know.

Half an hour later, my office phone rang.

'Bloody hell, you're actually at your desk.'

'I am, Mark, and don't you start. I've got Tina giving the temp staff an overly honest assessment of me, so you can be nice.'

'Always. Look, I spoke to Bill and as luck would have it, Delia was with him having a break, although I think she'd only been at work about half an hour so she hardly deserved it. Anyway, she does know Fiona. She doesn't know if she and Hugh are getting it on, but Fiona is related to Betty, sort of. She's her step-granddaughter.'

'How does that work?'

'Betty was her husband Anthony's second wife. He had a daughter from his previous marriage and Fiona is his granddaughter,' Mark explained.

'She never said they were related.'

'Did you ask?' I didn't respond. From his tone, he knew the answer.

'So, she might have a very good reason for wanting to protect Anthony's reputation.' If I was honest, I was a bit disappointed. I liked Fiona.

'I guess so, why? Had he been a bad boy?'

'Yes, I'll fill you in later. Does she know anything at all about Fiona and Hugh? Were they friends?'

'The only thing that Delia could think of is that she's going away for three weeks next month and Hugh still wants someone to clean. It might be that Fiona has offered to do some temporary work. Apparently, it's quite well known that she does that sort of thing for Betty.'

'Sounds reasonable. Although I'm not sure she would want to clean for him if she'd just killed Cora. But then, she could take on the work as a way of having a snoop around, seeing if Cora had left any notes behind that mentioned Anthony, maybe get chatting to Hugh to see if Cora had said anything to him about her grandfather. Working at the house for a couple of weeks would give her a chance to tidy up in more ways than one.'

'You might be onto something. See you in the pub later and we can think about our next move?'

'Sure, but I'm meeting Mum for coffee in the morning, so I'm not going to stay too late.'

'We'll see about that.' He laughed as we hung up.

'Sophie,' Tina was at my office door, 'you've been paying quite a lot of attention to that recent murder in Castledale, right?'

'That's a polite way of putting it, but yes.'

'You might want to talk to Rachel. She was telling me about some of her previous experience and it turns out that she was working at Cora's home the night she was murdered.'

I was out of my chair so fast, you'd have thought it was on fire. I found Rachel restocking the cake display, and Tina took over so I could have a word.

I took her to a quiet corner of the kitchen. 'Rachel, odd question, but it's about the job you did at Hugh Parrish's a week ago.'

'Yes?' She sounded uncertain, as though she was in trouble.

'Was Hugh there the whole time?'

'Of course, it was his event. It was something to do with work.'

'So he was hosting it the whole time? He didn't go out?'

Rachel shook her head. 'No, but it was only a small dinner, just six people including Hugh. I worked it with Bonnie, the chef.'

'Did his wife, Cora, come home at any point?'

'You mean the woman who was killed?' I nodded. 'No, not that I'm aware of. I heard a couple of the guests say that they were sorry that she couldn't join them. She was doing something with flowers, a display of some kind.'

'Well dressing.'

'That's it.'

'And you're sure Hugh never left the house?'

'Not that I know of. Although he did disappear for a little while at one point. He'd asked us to hold off serving dessert, they wanted to take a break between courses, and they went into the garden with their glasses of wine. After a while, Bonnie wanted to check on timings for the rest of the evening, see if they were ready and if we should also start making coffee, but he wasn't in the garden. I went to look for him in the house. I eventually found him, but it took a while.'

'And do you know where he had been?'

'I found him coming out of his office, but he hadn't been in there when I'd first checked, so I've no idea. I had heard him talking to one of his guests about taking a call, though.'

'And how long was he gone for?' Cora had been killed just up the road from the house, so it wouldn't have taken him long to meet her, commit the crime and get back.

'I've no idea. I reckon it was about twenty minutes that I was looking for him, but I don't know about before that. Is everything alright? Oh my God, you don't think he did it, do you?' She looked genuinely horrified. 'He was really nice. And I'm sure he never actually left the house.'

'Oh, it's nothing, I was just curious.' I didn't try to explain any more to Rachel. Instead, I left her to it and wandered back to my office. It would be useful to see Mark later and talk it all through.

34

Mark was chatting to Steve, the landlord of the Black Swan, when I arrived.

'Ah, my date is here. Steve, pour this girl a gin and tonic. Make it large, cold and use some weird gin that she's likely never heard of.'

'As you wish, sir.' Steve pretended to doff a cap. 'I'll bring it over, Soph.'

Mark and I found a table in the corner, close to the unlit fireplace that dominated one of the rooms. It was certainly too warm for a fire tonight, but it looked amazing in the winter and was the perfect backdrop at Christmas.

'So, go on, then. What have you found out?'

I sat back in my chair and tried to work out all the jumbled information in my head. 'Okay, so, there's Betty, who could have killed Cora in an attempt to protect her husband's reputation. It looks like Cora had found out in one of those books she was studying that he hadn't just been a reputable artist, he had also been an accomplished forger, and I would guess she spoke to Betty about it. I'm not convinced about Betty vaulting over the wall behind the village hall, but stranger things have happened.'

'Betty, one.' Mark counted on his fingers. 'Next?'

'Fiona, granddaughter to Anthony Natchbull, same reason as Betty. Although I do wonder if there was more between her and Hugh, which would give her a second motive.'

'Two.' Mark stuck another finger in the air.

'Hugh. Could have had enough. Cora's affair upended his life, he's clearly not happy here. They often argued, perhaps he too was having an affair, maybe Cora was having another affair, but no one has said anything about that.'

'Three.'

'Oh, and Barry, I forgot about him. She made his life miserable at school and perhaps he took the opportunity to finally get revenge.'

'Four.'

'Here's your drink. Sorry, I got cornered by a regular and couldn't escape.' Steve put a glass in front of me and went straight back to the bar. I took a long, much-needed drink.

'Do you want me to order you another? Get them lined up?'

I laughed. 'Maybe. One of the problems is that almost anybody would have had the opportunity. It would have been possible to see her walking down the street from the back of the village hall, and just as possible to get to her without being seen on any CCTV, and it's a quiet lane. There were hardly any other cars in there when we used the car park. Hugh might have seen her coming down the lane, or she might have sent him a message. Plus a lot of phones have that GPS thing so you can keep an eye on where someone is.'

'Yeah, me and Bill use it. I call it *Find My Husband*.'

'So Hugh might have spotted that she was nearby, gone out, killed her, and returned to his dinner party.'

'Why didn't he plan that for a night when Cora was home?'

'I don't know. Schedules? Hugh's guests were from out of town. It was the night before the well-dressing festival, there was no way Cora would miss it.'

'But she did.'

'Cos she was dead, Mark, I think that's a pretty good excuse.'

'Hmmm, I guess it's difficult to argue with that one. Although I'm pretty sure that you wouldn't accept it as a reason for one of your staff being late to work.' Mark pointed at me with his glass. 'You'd tell them to die on their day off.'

'I think you're mistaking me for Joyce. She'd turn up at the funeral with a written warning and slip it into the coffin.' That made him laugh, hard.

We drank in comfortable silence for a few minutes. I watched the Friday-night crowd around the bar grow and the tables fill up. The Black Swan is popular with locals and tourists alike, and the guest rooms are usually fully booked throughout the summer. I felt very lucky to be able to call it my local, and even luckier that I could see it from my front door.

'Have you spoken to Joe?' I asked. 'I wonder how close they're getting to identifying the killer.'

'No idea. If he's not at work on the case, he's got his head in his books for his exams.' The silence returned and I wondered how we could find out if Fiona and Hugh were sleeping together. It would strengthen her motive, although Cora planning to spill the beans about her grandfather could be more than enough.

I saw a hand waving from over at the bar. It was Emily. Mark saw her too.

'That's a thought, what about the university?' he asked.

'What about it?'

'Might there be someone there with a motive, one of her students or colleagues?'

'I guess, but nothing has come up and I don't know how we'd get that information.'

'True.' Mark took another drink, and then remained quiet.

'You alright?'

'Knackered. I'm trying to make sure the filming doesn't impact on my job, so I've had a few late nights. Like Joe, I suppose. I was hoping to have a break this weekend, but a last-minute VIP tour has come up on Saturday afternoon and they want me to talk about subjects I haven't covered for a while, so I need to refresh my memory. So while you're having a leisurely coffee with Mummy, I'll have my head in the books.'

I pretended to play a very tiny violin. Mark scowled at me, and then downed what was left of his beer.

35

It hadn't taken me long to succumb to the temptation of fish and chips, and anyway, I couldn't be bothered cooking.

'So, where's Bill tonight? Why are you not in the company of your handsome husband?'

Mark used his fork to point across the room.

'In the dining room. Lydia is having a wine tasting for one of her many retirement celebrations. One of the teachers has a cousin who is a sommelier and they're running it, they booked the dining room to hold it in.' That must have been why Emily was in the pub.

He looked at his watch. 'I can't imagine they'll be much longer, there must be only so much wine you can taste before you're just getting drunk and can't tell the difference.'

'Aren't they spitting it out?'

He gave me a pitying look. 'Have you met any teachers? I don't think there's a teacher in the country – on the planet, even – who would spit out wine, no matter how vile it was. In fact, he can tell you himself.'

Bill was walking across the room towards us. As he reached

the table, he stole a chip off my plate.

'Ooh, that looks good. Think I'll get my own.'

'Good idea,' said Mark. 'You need to soak up all that wine.'

'Did you spit?' I asked, grinning.

'Sophie Lockwood, don't blaspheme in my presence. Can I get anyone another drink?' I stared at my glass, trying to decide. 'That's a yes. Mark? Stupid question. I'll be back.'

I watched him stroll to the bar. He was a formidable presence, tall and broad. I had seen videos of him playing rugby back in the day and he was quite the sight. Less muscular these days, but still fit. I found it hard to imagine the children in his history class arguing with him, but I knew he faced the same behaviour issues as his colleagues.

I watched as he chatted to Emily and Lydia, who had appeared from the dining room, and pointed them in our direction. They walked over.

'Hi, Sophie.' Emily was as enthusiastic as ever.

Lydia smiled, looking lovely in a black and white striped dress. 'Hello, both. I wish I'd realised you were here, you could have joined us. There was plenty of wine.'

'Thank you,' I replied. 'I hope you've had a lovely evening. It's a fun idea, more interesting than sausage rolls and boxed wine.'

Lydia laughed. 'Yes indeed. One of my colleagues suggested it, they know I'm a bit of a wine buff.'

Emily put an arm around her mother's shoulder. 'She really is. She was able to identify two of the wines blindfolded.'

I was impressed. 'Have you worked in the wine industry?'

'Heavens no, it's just a hobby. I've been a teacher my whole life. Became a teacher, married a teacher and for a little while, was mother to a teacher.' She looked at Emily with an exaggerated sad expression.

'Mum!'

'I'm only kidding. I understand why you got out.'

A man holding an opened wine bottle and a couple of glasses approached the table.

'I thought you could drink this while you chat, we're over there.' He smiled at us all and left.

'That's Jacob, the sommelier. Do you mind?'

'No, no, please.'

The two women sat down and poured themselves a drink.

'Would you like some?' Lydia offered. I shook my head.

'Bill's on his way with a gin and tonic. So, you were a family of teachers.'

'We were. I met Geoff, Emily's dad, at teacher training college and we both taught in schools around here. Emily followed in our footsteps.'

'I think it was a legacy thing,' Emily explained. 'I wanted to carry on the work Dad was doing. Well, Mum too, but in Dad's memory. The reality is a bit different to the idea, though, even with Mum telling me about the cons as well as the pros of a teaching career in advance. You always think it's going to be different for you. In the end, I got tired of the focus on targets rather than what the children really needed. These days, it's less about inspiration and more about key performance indicators, so I left and decided to do what inspired *me* and went back to university. I've no idea what I'll do next, but I'll worry about that later.'

I watched as Lydia took a drink of the wine and closed her eyes. 'That's so good.'

'It sounds like you really enjoy your wine.'

Lydia laughed. 'Possibly a little too much. I didn't drink it at all for many years. Geoff never drank, he was allergic to alcohol, so I didn't bother either. Once he died, I started having the occasional glass and it just went from there. It's the history and people behind wine that fascinates me.'

Mark groaned. 'Sophie's like that with gin. I know more about the stuff than most and I don't even like it.'

By the time Bill returned with our drinks and a knife and fork tucked in his pocket, the two women had drained what was left of the wine.

'Thank you for joining us.' Lydia kissed Bill on the cheek. 'I'll see you tomorrow.' They said goodbye and went to join their group.

'You not heading over?' Mark asked Bill.

'No, I'll see them all tomorrow night at the big party. Are you sure you won't come?'

'Thanks, but I'll only end up smiling inanely while you all swap stories that mean nothing to me. After a while, all I'll be able to hear is *blah, blah, blah.* No, you go play with your friends. I'll be fine.'

A lad in a Black Swan Pub t-shirt put a plate in front of Bill and he tucked in. After discussing the merits of fish and chips in newspaper, which we all concluded was the best way to serve it, preferably eaten while sitting on a wall under thick cloud with rain threatening, Mark and I filled Bill in on our discoveries concerning Cora. Eventually, I started to flag and couldn't help but yawn.

'Something we said?' asked Mark. I shook my head as another yawn hit me. 'Another?' he asked as the ice cubes rattled in my empty glass.

'No, I should go. I promised Mum I'd meet her at ten tomorrow and at this rate, I'm going to sleep through my alarm.'

'Tell her hello from me, and that I'm still working on getting you a boyfriend.'

'I'll do no such thing,' I replied, as an image of Ryan Lavender crossed my mind, taking me by surprise. A thought I was not going to share with Mark or I'd never hear the end of it.

36

Mum and I had arranged to meet for coffee at her favourite café. I'd long since learnt not to be upset that it isn't one of the cafés I run, and to be honest, it's one of my favourites too.

The Sett Valley Café nestles next to the trail of the same name, an old railway line that has been converted into a very popular walking route that runs for 2.5 miles from the pretty town of Hayfield to New Mills. The café itself is small and quaint. The toilet walls are covered in framed photos of the owner's dogs and some of the canines who have visited the café, and the sound of birdsong can be heard once you lock the door. Outside, a large green canopy covers a number of picnic tables. It is incredibly popular with hikers, cyclists and horse riders, and it isn't uncommon to see the queue stretch well out of the door and onto the street. Its owner, Jo, is a bundle of energy who makes everyone feel like a friend.

It is a nice walk along the trail from Hayfield where Mum lives. She moved there a couple of years after Dad died. A neat little terraced cottage not unlike my own, her home is smaller than the house I grew up in, and Mum has kept active and made a new life for herself.

We found a seat at a table outside.

'So, are you going to tell me what you're thinking about? You're awfully quiet. Is everything alright at the House?'

'Oh yeah, fine. We're getting busier as the summer season kicks in, but everything's fine.'

'And Mark and Joyce?'

'As irritating as ever.' I grinned. She'd met them on a number of occasions.

'And bound to be causing trouble, with your help. So, go on, spit it out, whatever it is that's distracting you.'

I sighed. 'It's that murder in Castledale. We found the body and now I'm…'

'…trying to do the police's job for them. Why Joe puts up with you, I don't know.'

I was convinced she had hoped Joe and I would get together. I ignored her comment.

'There were people who didn't like her, but I don't know if any of them killed her. I veer between being convinced one of them did it and none of them did it. Right now, I'm in the messy middle of the spectrum, and I'm getting more and more confused.'

'Just because you found her, you don't have to work out who did it as well.' It didn't go unnoticed that she seemed utterly unperturbed by the fact that her daughter had found a murder victim.

Mum was reading the menu. 'Black Forest Velvet Hot Chocolate. Hmm, do you think it might be too sweet? Or perhaps the Choccy Orange Delight.'

I was only half listening to her.

'Hello, I've not seen you for ages.' I stood up and gave Jo a hug, trying not to crush the glasses that were hanging on a chain around her neck. 'When are you going to come and work for me?

We're not as grand as Charleton House, but if you ever fancy a change, I'll have an apron waiting for you.'

I laughed. 'If I ever decide to make a change, you'll be the first to know. You might have to get used to being called Duchess, though, old habits and all that.'

Jo looked thoughtful. 'I could live with that, I might ask my staff to start now. What can I get you?'

We ordered our drinks. As Jo walked back into the café, I heard another greeting.

'Morning, ladies.'

Mum and I looked up.

'Janet!' They clearly knew one another and Mum got up to give the newcomer a hug. 'Join us. This is my daughter, Sophie.'

'I'd have known who she was anywhere, she looks just like you, Christine.' As Janet sat down, her little black and white dog jumped up onto the bench beside her. Mum leant over the table and gave him a quick scratch behind the ears.

'Morning, Charlie, sausages for breakfast?'

'The little devil doesn't deserve them, he destroyed a new cushion last night. But God knows, I can't resist that face.'

Janet looked fit and healthy, and her outfit told me that she spent a lot of time walking. She wore a bright orange waterproof jacket and a turquoise scarf, which matched Charlie's turquoise collar. Joyce would have been proud. Janet was one of those lively older women that I hoped I would become – she had eyes that sparkled and skin that glowed. I admired people like that, while simultaneously hoping they'd fall face first in mud on one of their walks. Her short silver hair looked stylishly and effortlessly messy, the kind of look I was going for, only I usually ended up looking like I'd just got out of bed. I realised that between the three of us, and Jo, we were quite the silver-tops.

Jo reappeared from the café. 'Charlie my boy, have a treat.' As Jo fed the very pleased little dog a biscuit, she looked at me. 'I can't remember the owners' names, but I always remember the dogs. Although not in this case. Janet, you look well, retirement suits you.'

'Thank you. Although oddly, I find myself busier than ever.'

'Janet was a vicar,' Mum explained. The mention of her profession triggered a memory.

'Then you might be able to help me.'

'Sure, do you want a recommendation for somewhere to attend?'

Mum laughed. 'Don't suggest she goes to your old church. The place would get hit by lightning if Sophie darkened its door and I know you recently had the roof done.'

'*Muuum*,' I whined, realising I sounded like a child.

Janet laughed too. 'Okay, so what is it you're looking for?'

'Have you heard of St Lud's Church?' It was what had been written on a note in Cora's study. 'I was going to look it up online, but haven't had a chance yet.'

'Oh, Sophie!' exclaimed Mum. 'I know exactly where that is. You should have asked me.'

'I didn't have a chance, I could barely get a word in.'

Janet was continuing to grin at us. 'This is great entertainment, you should bring her more often, Christine. Lud's Church is just above Gradbach in Staffordshire, and it's not actually a church. Not in the way you're thinking, anyway. It's a natural chasm on the hillside in a forest. It was supposed to have been used as a meeting place by the Lollards during the early 15th century. They were followers of John Wycliffe, persecuted for their religious beliefs.'

'And who or what is Lud? Or does that come from the word Lollard?' I asked. Janet looked up and thanked Jo who had just put a bacon butty on the table, and a plate of sausages for Charlie.

'Two?' Janet exclaimed. 'You'll make him fat.' As she fed Charlie, she continued. 'Lud is thought to have come from Walter de Ludank who was captured there during one of their meetings. Is that helpful?'

'Maybe. Has anything significant happened there recently, do you know? Is there any scandal linked with the place? In modern times, I mean.'

Janet thought for a while, chewing on the generous serving of bacon in her butty.

'Not that I can think of. I can take you there, if you want. There's a nice three-mile circular walk.'

'I'm up for it,' said Mum, looking excited.

'Alright, that would be great, thank you.' I desperately tried to remember where my hiking boots were. I knew they were probably still coated in mud from my last hike in them, which had happened so long ago, I couldn't recall when or where it had been.

'Tomorrow?' asked Janet. 'The forecast is meant to be good and I wanted to take Charlie somewhere different this weekend.'

'I'd like that,' said Mum. I looked across at Charlie. He had a natural expression of curiosity, which got more intense when he cocked his head. A curious dog with a good sniffer could be a handy companion.

I told Janet it was a date.

I spent some of my Saturday night scrabbling around in cupboards and under the bed, trying to pull together my hiking gear. I found my crusty hiking boots, with hardened and cracked leather, in the garden shed. My two hiking socks didn't match, and my waterproof jacket was in a carrier bag in the boot of my car. The weather forecast was good, but you never went hiking without the right kit. That had been repeated to me throughout my childhood.

Pumpkin chased the laces that hung from the boots as I carried them from the garden to the front door. I decided to prolong the fun and took my boots on a couple of laps around the house and up and down the stairs. When I eventually stopped and put them on the rug by the front door, Pumpkin stayed with them and chewed the laces. There were days when I envied the simplicity of her life, and then I realised that she couldn't make her own coffee or butter a scone and decided I had the better deal.

When I had everything I needed, I called Mark. I'd convinced him to join me, but it wouldn't have surprised me if he'd changed his mind.

'I'm just making sure you've set your alarm for the morning. I'm not having you chickening out.'

'You know I don't own a pair of hiking boots.'

'It's not that strenuous a hike, you'll be fine in trainers.'

'I don't own trainers, or at least I don't think I do.' I heard a scuffling sound, and then Bill's voice.

'Hi, Sophie, he has a perfectly suitable pair of hiking boots. They've been stuck at the back of the wardrobe for so long, he's forgotten about them, so it's time they were exposed to the fresh air. He'll be there, I'm dropping him off. Just let me know where you're meeting.'

'Are you not coming?'

'Sadly not, I coach the school rugby team and they have a match tomorrow.'

'Excuses.' Mark had the phone again.

'It's only three miles,' I said. 'We'll be at the café for lunch before you know it.'

'Alright, that sounds acceptable. You're buying?'

'Yes, of course. Just promise me that you and Mum won't gang up on me.'

'I will promise no such thing, that's the main reason I'm coming. She understands the struggles and disappointments you present me with. OUCH!'

I laughed. I knew that Bill had hit him playfully.

'Soph, feel free to lose him while you're out.' It was Bill's voice again. 'Maybe some vultures will finish him off.'

37

It was one of those fresh sunny mornings that make you wonder why you don't get up early more often. Or at least, it made me wonder that, but snooze buttons had been invented for a reason. And how anyone functions without a cup of coffee in the morning, I have no idea, but a team of scientists should investigate what makes them tick before 10 am.

Mum and Janet were already waiting when I pulled into the layby at the side of the road. I got out of the car into a stiff breeze. I pulled a jacket on, knowing full well that once we got going, I'd probably want to take it off.

'Morning,' Janet called cheerily. She walked over and handed me a cup. 'Thought you might need a little extra coffee before we set off, so I brought a flask.' I accepted it gratefully.

Charlie was sitting by Mum's feet and staring at her intently. I guessed that she'd given him a treat and now he wasn't going to let her out of his sight. His scruffy black and white fur swirled in the wind and his ears flapped, which was very cute.

'Invigorating, isn't it?' Janet flung her hands in the air and took a deep breath.

'I'm surprised you're not at church on a Sunday morning,' I said.

'Look around, Sophie. I'm in the most beautiful church there is.' She turned back to her car. 'I've brought something for you.' She handed me a plastic bag which was clearly wrapped around a book. 'There are a number of chapters on Lud's Church in it, you might find it interesting.'

I thanked her and put it on the back seat of my car.

'Now, is that your friend?' Janet asked, looking down the road. I watched as Bill carefully parked his car behind mine. He got out and walked straight over to my mum, wrapping her in a hug.

'Christine, it's been ages, how are you?' I left them to catch up and for Mum to introduce him to Janet, while I opened the car door for Mark.

'Give me a hand.' I pulled him out. He wore a pair of hiking boots and lightweight cotton trousers.

'So you *do* own hiking gear.'

'Apparently so. I'd forgotten about these. I bought them years ago when we took that trip to America and Bill insisted we hike some trails in the Grand Canyon. They're not going to win any style awards, but I don't want to get anything else muddy and I'm very pleased I can still get into them.' There was barely an ounce of fat on the man. I'd never seen him naked, nor was it an ambition of mine, but I was pretty sure he could use his ribs like a xylophone. 'Now you promise me it's only three miles?'

'Well, 3.3, but near enough.'

'And we're going to a café afterwards?'

'We are, Jo has promised to keep some fresh sticky buns aside.'

Bill ran over, and gave Mark a kiss and me a quick hug.

'Got to go, I can't miss the coach.'

'Good luck,' I shouted after him.

As we set off, the wind settled down and the sun warmed our faces. Popcorn clouds drifted overhead and the patchwork landscape spread out endlessly. In August, the view before us would be covered with a carpet of heather, the pretty purple creating a scene that gave me another reason to return north from London when life had made me reluctant to stay in the city.

After squeezing through a narrow stile, we followed a rocky path into a forest. The path was well trodden and signposted, so there wasn't any chance of us getting lost; there was even a short stretch of boardwalk. We walked under the trees, the light glinting through the branches. It was cool beneath the canopy. Ferns framed the path and the air smelt clean and fresh.

Mark had found a fallen branch, which made the ideal walking stick. Combined with his moustache, it meant he looked a little like a Victorian explorer. All he needed was a net and a satchel, and if he tucked his trousers in his socks, it would have perfected the image.

'How are the boots?'

'Stiff. Bill told me I should have worn them in when I got them. I don't even remember buying them, and I'm sure I didn't actually wear them in America.'

'I'm honoured you joined us, I know this isn't how you'd typically spend a Sunday morning.'

'I'm here for the cake at the end of the walk. Do you really think that coming here will be useful?'

'No idea. If not, then we've had a nice walk.' I thought for a moment. 'We'll have to see what Janet tells us when we get to the church that isn't a church. There might even be a clue there.'

Mark didn't look convinced.

Lud's Church was clearly signposted. We followed some yellow markers to the end of the path and stopped. Ahead were a lot of bushes and what looked like a dark shadowy hole.

'Be careful,' Janet instructed. 'It's steep and rocky. It gets very slippy if it's been raining, but that shouldn't be a problem today.'

She led us towards the darkness and we started to descend carefully, clambering down into a deep chasm.

Ancient moss covered the rocks on either side of us, ferns sprouting wherever they were able to cling on. Looking up and seeing trees peering over the top was fascinating. It was like entering into a fairy-tale world. The natural walls loomed over us, closing us in and making the air cold and refreshing. We were the only ones in this secluded gully and I felt a million miles away from civilisation. It would have been incredible to come here as a child, a real fantasy world where anything was possible. In reality, it was only about 100 metres long, but if you stood still and looked in either direction, you'd feel as if it could have gone on forever, a forgotten land where pterodactyls flew overhead, or goblins skittered through the shadows.

Janet stopped and looked back at me. 'Pretty magical, eh?'

'I can't believe I didn't know about this. Mum, how could you keep it from me?' I joked.

'I have no idea why we didn't bring you. I can't even remember the last time I was here, it must be forty years ago. Maybe more, perhaps before you were born.'

'You can see how it was possible for people to meet here without being discovered.' I looked around as Janet spoke. 'It's said that Robin Hood and his Merry Men sheltered here. It's also associated with the legend of Sir Gawain and the Green Knight, where it's referred to as the Green Chapel. Of course, the Robin Hood story is rather doubtful, but there has been quite a lot of scholarly work that backs up the Green Knight idea.'

'And its role in religion?' I asked.

'Yes, followers of John Wycliffe used it during the 15th century, and as I said yesterday, it was likely named after Walter de Ludank, who was captured here during one of their meetings.'

I slowly wandered along the path and back, looking around on the ground and up the walls. There were lots of ledges and little nooks and crannies. I wondered what the possible link could be with Cora. From the *WHY?* written on the notepad, it seemed possible that Cora didn't know what the significance of Lud's Church was either. There was no doubt that it would make a fantastically atmospheric painting, but Hugh had said Cora hadn't had the time to do any painting for the last couple of years, and between the well dressing, the competition judging and her university work, I couldn't imagine that she had suddenly found the time recently.

Hold on, painting? Something tugged at the back of my memory. Was there a connection to a painting?

The thought did a rapid circuit of my brain and sped back into the depths of my subconscious before I could grasp it. So frustrating when that happens!

I wandered back and forth while Janet and Mum looked in detail at some of the plants that had made this their home. Mum's ability to rattle off the Latin names of almost every plant she came across was a skill I had never developed. I rooted around in gaps where something could have been hidden, I stared at the rocks in case there might be some sort of message or image formed by the natural colours. Nothing. Even Charlie didn't appear to pick up on any unusual scents.

To be honest, I would have been very shocked if there had been something for us to discover that gave us answers. It had been a long shot, but it had indeed been worth the walk, and I decided I would be back this way in the future. Now, though, it was time for cake.

38

The Sett Valley Café was busy and it took a while for us to get a table. A line of bicycles were propped up outside, their Lycra-clad owners enjoying full English breakfasts and lots of coffee. Various dogs welcomed everyone who walked past in the hope of a treat, and a couple of horses were tied up at the fence. This was the place to be if you liked fresh air, exercise and decent grub.

Eventually a family, the youngest members of which had chocolate smeared around their mouths, got up and we were able to nab their table. Once we were settled and Jo had made sure we all had coffee and cake, Janet asked the question that I knew had been bubbling away for most of the walk.

'So, do you mind telling me what all this is about? If you can.'

I gave her an overview of what had been happening in Castledale, and where I had seen Lud's Church written down.

'It might be nothing, but it was right there, staring at me, like it had very recently been noted down and left as a reminder of something important. Cora was also asking *why*, so there was something unusual about the location or instruction that she was acknowledging.'

'Good or bad unusual? That's the question,' said Mark. 'It would be a very odd place to go and meet someone, so that would require a *specific* unusual reason. Maybe it's something else.'

'You've said she was a painter, perhaps she planned on going there to paint the gorge?' Janet's idea wasn't unreasonable, and once again the elusive thought of earlier whizzed around my head. Something to do with a painting...

'True, or she might just have fancied a good walk,' suggested Mum. I mulled over those ideas. My feet were sore and I was tired from the most exercise I'd taken since I didn't know when. I was on my third coffee of the day and it wasn't doing the trick; I needed sugar.

I tucked into my cinnamon bun. It was so good – soft, sweet, still warm. I couldn't help but groan with pleasure. Mark turned to look at me with one eyebrow raised.

'Would you two like some time alone?'

'It's just amazing. Come on, try some.' He pulled back as I waved it in front of him. 'Not the centre, that's the best bit.'

'I won't, thanks. I wouldn't want to come between you, and I can hear your arteries shutting one by one.'

After some idle chatter, the conversation returned to the subject of Lud's Church and its possible link with Cora.

'Perhaps it represents something,' Mark was saying. 'It holds a link to someone or something. There could be someone in Cora's life with a similar name.'

I thought about the people I had spoken to, the artists and forgers I had heard of for the first time as I dug into Cora's work, but nothing and no one stuck out. Still, the time hadn't been wasted. It had been a glorious day for a walk and I had learnt something new about Derbyshire's history. It had also been nice to do something with Mark that hadn't involved books or the pub.

'Did you enjoy yourself, Mark?' Mum asked.

'I did, Christine. I think it helped that there was an educational aspect to the morning, I learnt a great deal.'

'You and Bill should do more hiking. Derbyshire is heaven for walkers and you don't see the half of it if you don't head out into the hills.'

Mark didn't look entirely convinced by this suggestion. 'Perhaps. The outdoor industry needs to pep up its fashion a little.' He looked down at his boots and dusty walking trousers. 'Hmm, I have some ideas, and actually this could be fun. And if the producers of my show decide that I need to present an episode from the top of a windswept hill, then I need to look the part. Perhaps they'll be interested in Lud's Church.'

'What's this about a show?'

Mark started to tell Mum and Janet his latest news and I turned back to my cinnamon bun. I was vaguely aware of him outlining his plans for each episode, but the sweetness and caffeine were working their magic.

'That's it!' I exclaimed, earning myself a glare from Mark as I interrupted him in the middle of a detailed description of his outfit for episode 1.

'That's what?' he grumbled.

'The connection between Cora and Lud's Church. Don't you remember when we went to visit Hugh?'

'Of course I remember. We took flowers. I chose...' As I interrupted him for the second time in as many minutes, Mark let out a growl uncannily similar to the sound a disgruntled Pumpkin would make if I didn't feed her fast enough for Her Ladyship's liking. Perhaps they were more similar than either would care to admit.

'There was a painting hanging in Hugh's kitchen,' I explained excitedly. 'Her father was the artist. It was wonderfully atmospheric... and unless I'm very much mistaken, it was of Lud's Church. Perhaps there was a reason why Cora's father chose that subject,' I insisted. 'Perhaps that's what Cora was trying to find out.'

'And that helps us how?' asked Mark. 'She's hardly going to tell us now, is she, and neither is the gorge.'

'Hugh might know…'

'And do you want to be the one to ask the poor grieving widower in his darkest hour? Anyway, I'm sure he'd have told the police by now if there was anything to tell and the killer would be locked away, and Joe and Harnby would be gloating at having solved the case before you, for once.'

Much as I hated to admit it, Mark was right. But I was going to keep that painting in mind, just in case. For now, though, I'd had a lovely morning, but I didn't feel as though I was any further ahead.

39

I had promised Mark a lift back to Charleton House on my way home and decided that I would pop in and see how my teams were doing. As I expected, the gardens were full with families making the most of the beautiful day. I strolled through the house, enjoying the chance to take in my magnificent surroundings at my own pace, rather than dashing between meetings.

Even so, it quickly became very clear that my pace did not match that of the public, who ambled slowly, coming to a sudden stop with no thought as to who might be behind them. Heads would turn in sync as the audio guides they followed told them to look at a particular painting or piece of furniture. I stopped to admire a collection of ceramics. A line of vessels of different sizes, it was a favourite of mine and a great example of the modern art that the Duke collected.

A wooden Roentgen desk from the 1800s that had been in the bedroom of the 5th Duke was filled with hidden compartments and fascinating internal mechanisms. I often wondered what sort of things he would hide in the little compartments. Letters from lovers? Documents with national secrets? A gun? Diaries that he later had to destroy because the contents were too scandalous to be discovered?

A satirical painting of a court scene where all the people had been replaced by dogs was getting a lot of attention from a couple who appeared to own dogs themselves. I guessed that from the amount of fur attached to their sweaters. I stopped to listen to a tour guide who didn't work for us, and I knew that what he was telling his group was wrong. I looked over at the visitor assistant who was standing in the corner of the room, ready to answer questions or stop children swinging on the curtains. She rolled her eyes at me, then shook her head. I laughed.

Some compulsion urged me to check out the Garden Café. I wasn't going to linger, I was hardly dressed for the beautiful room that had witnessed marriage proposals and extravagant parties. I nodded to the host who was standing at the lecture desk by the door as I slipped past and made for the kitchens.

'Sophie.'

I stopped and sighed. I really hadn't wanted to be seen in my grass-stained trousers, and immediately regretted not going straight home. Turning to see who was calling me, I came face to face with Ryan Lavender, looking very smart in a crisp white shirt, jeans and a tweed jacket that fitted him so perfectly, it had to have been tailored especially for his slim figure. My heart immediately fluttered at the sight of him, then sank at him getting to see me dressed like this. It had slipped my mind that he'd said he was visiting the Garden Café today. How could I have forgotten?

I noticed that a little dimple formed on the left side of his mouth when he smiled. Not the right, just the left.

Oh, for heaven's sake, I scolded myself. *Get a grip.* Then I remembered that he had talked about bringing someone here for afternoon tea, a female someone.

'I should let you get back to your friend,' I said, glancing across the room, wondering who his date was.

'Yes, well, nice to see you. Actually, do you have a minute?' He moved away and signalled for me to follow him. Oh God, all I needed was to be introduced to his gorgeous girlfriend when I was dressed like a slob. I knew that people liked to show off their connections to a place, especially somewhere like Charleton House, and I didn't normally mind. I enjoyed the opportunity to charm guests, tell them a few fascinating titbits about the history-soaked space they were dining in, but it usually happened when I was wearing a suit and my hair had at least had a brush waved in its general direction.

'Sophie, I'd like you to meet my mum. Mum, Sophie runs this restaurant, and the other cafés.' The smiling eyes of a woman who looked to be in her sixties peered at me over a small pair of wire-rimmed glasses. So, he had wanted to bring his mum, not a girlfriend. I smiled. Well, maybe I grinned.

'Your mum? Oh, right.' I realised I sounded a bit too surprised, and pleased.

'Lovely to meet you,' she said. 'This is a magical place, and you do a lovely afternoon tea.'

'Thank you, I'm glad you're enjoying it.'

'It's actually Sophie's day off, Mum. That's commitment for you.' I was so grateful to him for saying that. If nothing else, it explained my appearance.

'Well, enjoy your visit.' I didn't know what else to say. 'I should be off.'

'Oh yes,' Ryan's mum said. 'You should make the most of your time off, enjoy the sunshine.'

'I will, thank you. Good to see you, Ryan.'

'You too.'

I was on my way to the door when I heard him call my name. 'Sophie, sorry, I was just wondering, would you like to go for coffee sometime, or a drink? You probably get sick of coffee after a while, working in a café, or we could have lunch, but I suppose that's similar to your job, too, but you have to eat.' It was rather sweet to see him blustering his way through the question, and he couldn't have been more wrong about the coffee. Only after those thoughts did I realise that he was asking me on a date, or at least I thought he was. Wasn't he?

'Oh, um, yes. Yes, that would be great.'

'Great! I'll call you.'

'Yes, thanks, okay.' I had to leave, I was losing the ability to speak.

He smiled, and I could feel his eyes linger on me as I made an awkward exit. Glancing over my shoulder as I reached the door, I saw that he was still looking in my direction. I turned and gave an awkward little wave. I was definitely out of practice.

I was at a loose end. I thought about calling Joe and seeing if I could wheedle some information out of him, but between revising for his exams and investigating Cora's murder, he was probably low on patience and wouldn't put up with my ham-fisted attempts at finding out how close the police were to identifying the killer. I didn't want to go home, all I had there was a grumpy cat, a pile of laundry and a kitchen that needed cleaning.

I decided to pop into one of the gift shops and see Joyce. At least I could gloat about having the weekend off.

'She's not in,' a young sales assistant told me. 'She worked yesterday and took today off.' So much for gloating. 'I can get her to come and see you tomorrow.'

'No, it's okay, thanks.' As I turned away from the counter and dodged a couple of children who had started to fight using wooden swords, worryingly close to a glass display case, my phone beeped. It was a text message from Joyce.

'Send help (& wine) I'm trapped in a toilet at the village hall. Ginger

useless.' What did she expect me to do? Pass her glasses of wine under the door while she waited for a hunky fireman to come and rescue her? But I was up for the challenge.

40

Armed with a bottle of Pinot Grigio, I pulled into a parking space outside the Castledale village hall. There were no police cars or ambulances, and any hunky firefighters appeared to be off rescuing cats from trees. The front door to the hall was open and as I entered, I could hear a radio playing.

Barry was carrying a large black bag of – presumably – rubbish. He glanced my way, but didn't say anything. Lydia walked across the small stage at the far end of the room.

'Oh hello, you come to give a hand?'

'Possibly.' I paused, confused. 'Is Joyce here?'

'In the toilets with Ginger.' She tilted her head in the direction of a burgundy red door. Whatever was going on, no one else seemed to be panicking. Perhaps they were the ones who had trapped Joyce in the toilets. Perhaps she'd criticised someone's outfit.

I knocked on the door. I could hear voices and slowly pushed my way in, wondering if I should be prepared to use the bottle of wine as a weapon.

'Sophie love, you come to help?' Ginger was wielding a paintbrush and had a blob of white paint on her chin.

'I don't know. Where's Joyce?'

'Thank God you're here.' I turned round to see Joyce sitting on a toilet. The door to the cubicle was wide open. Fortunately, she wasn't actually using the toilet as anything other than a seat and her clothes remained exactly where they were meant to be. 'Have you brought glasses? No? There must be some mugs in the kitchen.'

'I thought there was an emergency.'

'There is. I'm spending my afternoon in the toilet of a poky village hall, watching Picasso here paint the place.'

'You didn't have to come,' said Ginger as she slapped some paint onto a wall.

'You told me you wanted help with your closet. I was tricked.'

'I said *water* closet. A water closet, and not *my* closet.'

'You did not say the word water, I didn't hear the word water. Who says *water closet* anymore?' Joyce spat the words out in disgust. 'Victoria is no longer on the throne, you know.'

'No, but you are.' Ginger guffawed at her own joke. I left them bickering and went to fetch three mugs. I was here now, I might as well join them.

When Joyce had a mug of wine in her hand and had stopped ranting about being poisoned by paint fumes, I told them about my morning at Lud's Church.

'It's a wonderful place,' said Ginger as she took a break from painting. 'I used to walk up that way a lot. So atmospheric.'

'Sounds gloomy and damp to me.'

'Far from it, Joyce.' I really wished there was a chance she would make the walk up there. 'It's like stepping back in time, I half expected a dinosaur to appear. You could be a million miles from anywhere.'

'You're not selling it to me, I just hope it was worth the walk. Find anything useful?'

'Nothing. Not even the history about John Wycliffe and the people who met there, I can't see what the link might have been with Cora. Mind you, it's a great place to meet someone and not be seen.'

'Ginger,' Lydia's head appeared around the door, 'the rest of us have done, here are the keys.' She looked at Joyce and me with a smile. 'We have more paintbrushes, you know.'

'Not in this outfit,' said Joyce, picking invisible fluff off her lime-green skirt. 'Ginger already knows that her life won't be worth living if any of the paint makes its way over here.'

'And I'm in charge of refreshments.' I raised my mug in the air. Lydia laughed and put the keys on a windowsill before leaving.

41

'Come on, let's go and watch.' Tina looked pleadingly at me.

'As much as I like the idea of standing behind the camera and pulling faces at him, it does seem a bit cruel. He's probably really nervous.'

Tina scoffed at that idea. 'Mark, nervous? He's probably demanding a Winnebago and jelly beans of a single colour.'

'I doubt the local channel can stretch to much more than a bottle of water and a stale ham sandwich.'

Mark was filming the first of his little historical segments. It was happening much sooner than expected and he had initially reacted with panic, and then gone unusually quiet. I had spent the last couple of days sending coffee and cake up to his office. Work had been too busy since the start of the week to spend much time thinking about Cora, and we'd reached Wednesday without Joe dropping by once, which meant that either the investigation was still in full flow, or his upcoming exams were dominating his life. Either way, life at Charleton House was unusually normal, or as normal as life round here could be. And if I was honest, I could do with a bit of entertainment.

'Oh, go on, then,' I finally agreed with Tina. 'But we need to keep out of the way and not throw him off. As much as I've been teasing him, this could be the start of something big for him.'

Her grin spread from ear to ear.

We watched from the far side of the courtyard as Mark was filmed walking across the cobbles, talking to camera. I knew he was used to being interviewed for television from time to time, but I wondered how he was coping with being the sole focus of a whole series. Actually, the history he was presenting was meant to be the focus, but this was Mark we were talking about.

We watched as the camera crew filmed the same walk again, then a third time as a group of schoolkids had decided to start skipping and waving behind him. Eventually, they appeared to have it 'in the can', as I seemed to recall a successful shoot being called, and Mark spotted us. He waved and we both gave him a thumbs up.

One of the crew turned in our direction, and then said something to Mark. I saw a look of uncertainly cross Mark's face, then he shook his head. Eventually, he walked towards us.

'Mark Boxer, is that really you, in the flesh?' Tina called out. 'Can I have an autograph?' She whipped a piece of paper and pen out of her pocket. 'Or maybe you'd sign my arm, I'd never wash again.'

'Sod off,' Mark said, a little grumpily. 'This is precisely why I told James I didn't want to ask you this.'

'Who's James?'

'The producer. We need a couple of people to be my audience, so to speak. They're going to film me talking about some records we have in the archives that have been put in a display case especially for this. They'd like me to be telling a couple of visitors rather than speaking to camera, and he wonders if you would both be the visitors. He thinks that because you work here, there's a better chance that you'll behave yourselves and we can get it done quickly. Which is clear evidence that he doesn't know you.'

I have never been someone to seek out the spotlight and the idea of being on camera made my stomach lurch. But despite his grumpy façade, I knew how much this meant to Mark, so I agreed. Tina was already nodding enthusiastically.

Mark turned back to James and gave him a thumbs up, with the most fake smile I had ever seen.

The Oak Room was closed to the public. An overflow library, occasional prayer room and sometimes used for smoking, it was a dark, cold space, even in the warmest of months. It wasn't used much these days and when the family did so, they needed to get the fire really going to make it inviting in any way.

Today, however, the wood-panelled walls started to glow with warmth as the crew set up the lights, although they were being focused on a large display case. Like a rectangular table with a glass top so you could peer down onto the valuable manuscripts within, it sat in the centre of the room.

'If you could both be stood on this side.' James shuffled Tina and me into position. 'Mark, you stay where you are.' A few more things were checked and double-checked, I have no idea what, and then Mark was explaining the importance of the very old, browning and brittle-looking document to us.

No sooner had Mark started talking than I felt a familiar sensation at the back of my nose. This was not the time to sneeze, especially as I was not known for little ladylike sneezes. Instead, I was known for the fact that I was unable to sneeze just the once. I smiled, hoping that wrinkling my face might help. It didn't. I tried holding my breath, but was worried I'd start to look as though I had a fuchsia-pink balloon balancing on my neck. There was nothing I could do to stop a window-shattering, raspberry-blowing spluttering sneeze from bursting out. Mark rolled his eyes. Then another followed, and another. I waited. Just the three? Great. No, two more.

After a pause, I had settled down.

'Okay, let's go again,' called James. Mark started talking, but I let out a sequence of five more sneezes. He muttered something under his breath.

'Is everyone ready?' asked James, once all was calm on the sneezing front, and had been for a minute or two. 'Okay, let's go again.'

A few minutes later, Mark was on a roll. I hadn't sneezed any more and there was no tickle in my nose, and Mark seemed very comfortable. Or he did, but now he had fallen silent.

I looked across at him to see he had an expression of horror on his face while staring at Tina. She was stifling a laugh and her shoulders were shaking.

'Sorry, I'm so sorry.' She burst into laughter. Mark let his head fall onto the glass of the display case. 'Sorry, I don't know what it is, I just couldn't help it.'

'It was all going so well.' Mark remained face down and his voice was muffled. 'Bring back those bloody schoolkids, all is forgiven.'

Tina sniffed, took a deep breath and flapped her arms around. 'I'm alright now, I promise, I'm alright.'

Mark pulled a yellow silk handkerchief out of his breast pocket and used it to wipe away the smear his forehead had left on the glass.

'Are you ready? Both of you? Are you sure?' We both nodded like scolded schoolchildren.

He was about three sentences in when I started to feel a small tickle in the back of my throat. It was the kind of thing I wouldn't notice usually, but at a time like this, I was super aware of everything. It grew and became all I could think about.

As Mark talked, he looked in my direction and horror once again dawned in his eyes. He said a few more lines, then stopped.

'For God's sake, what now?' I started coughing uncontrollably, trying to loosen whatever it was that wanted to hang out in the back of my throat. My eyes streamed. I glugged from the bottle of water that I was handed and watched as Tina started laughing again.

Mark shook his head and went to sit on the windowsill. 'Can't we do it without them?' he asked James.

'I'm fine, I'm fine,' I said, coughed again and cleared my throat loudly. 'I promise I'm fine.' Tina wiped the tears that had formed at the corners of her eyes and gave a thumbs up signal. She wasn't very convincing.

'Fifteen takes! Fifteen bloody takes, it took. I know you should never work with children or animals, but you can add you and Tina to that list now. It was so embarrassing.'

Joyce was smiling. 'Well done, Sophie, keep him on his toes.'

The three of us were sitting in her office. Mark had taken the spare chair next to her desk and I was on a pile of boxes. I didn't know what was in them, but they were doing a decent job of not collapsing. We had all finished work for the day, but none of us had the energy to actually drag ourselves out of Charleton House and go home.

'You should have given me a call,' Joyce went on. 'I can assure you I would have been every inch the professional.'

'It's your every inch I'd be worried about,' said Mark, waving his finger back and forth between her extremely short skirt and the height of her blonde bouffant, repeating the motion a couple more times to make his point very clear. 'They are showing this before the nine o'clock watershed, you'd give children nightmares.'

'I think you can do that all on your own. Talking of nightmares, what colour palette did you finally go for?'

'Navy blue and a muted yellow with a pair of brown brogues. I thought it all looked rather good. Sophie?'

'Extremely handsome,' I said, feeling like I'd made his life hard enough as it was. Anyway, he had looked very smart.

'I'm thinking of a tweed with a touch of turquoise next time.'

Joyce gave it some thought. 'Hmm, could work, but can I suggest that you show me first? It might be wise to have a second opinion.'

'It might be wise to wear a longer skirt too, but I don't see you following that advice.'

I groaned. 'Alright, children, I have had enough for the day. I'm going home. A fat, grumpy cat with claws sharp enough to draw blood sounds like a more appealing proposition than listening to you two sparring any longer. Mark, sorry I slowed things down today. Joyce, he's right, you're cutting it a bit fine with that skirt.'

I left before she could reply.

42

I hadn't spoken to Mark and Joyce all day. It seemed that Thursday was the new Friday as far as coffee was concerned and we'd been busy with staff needing sustenance and escaping their offices most of the day. Then there were the front-line staff – the visitor assistants, retail staff and ticketing teams who had set breaks and all needed to get their drinks and snacks in a rush so they had time to enjoy them before their break was over.

I felt for them. I knew what it was like to have your schedule controlled by others, right down to when you could go to the loo or have a drink. When I'd started out in hospitality, that was what my life had been like. Now I was management, I could control my own day much more, hide away in my office if I didn't wish to be disturbed, have as much coffee as I wanted when I wanted, and sneak off to solve the occasional murder or two.

By the time I was ready to leave work, what had started as a chilly grey day had warmed up, and I decided to take the long way home and enjoy some of Derbyshire's winding roads with the window open. It was without any planning at all that I found myself driving through Castledale. A couple of people were sitting outside the Bull's Head pub, dogs dozing under their table.

I turned down Swallow Lane, another instinctive action. It was a little while since I had driven down here and I slowed as I reached the well. Many of the flowers were looking tired and really needed disposing of, but who wants to be the person to remove the acts of kindness that mark the location of someone's murder? I imagined it would get left to the local council to come and clear it at some point. I thought about getting out and reading some of the cards in case the killer had left a cryptic clue in one of them, but it had rained a couple of times since Cora's death and I could see from the car that all the writing had been obliterated and turned into a swirly blue or black pattern that would be indecipherable.

A car passed me and I watched as it turned. I couldn't see Hugh's driveway from here, but I could tell that was where the driver was going. I followed slowly and idled opposite the gates.

There were a number of cars in the driveway – another business dinner, perhaps? But that seemed a bit soon after his wife's death. Hugh was talking to the occupant of the car that had just pulled in, but I hadn't spotted him registering my presence, so it was a surprise when he gave me a wave and started to walk in my direction. Rats! What was I going to say? I couldn't be doing anything other than spying on him.

'Sophie? It is Sophie, isn't it?'

'Yes, I was just passing. There are so many flowers at the well. It's lovely.'

'It is.' His stern features broke into the beginnings of a smile and a warmth crept into his eyes. 'Some of Cora's students have come over for a drink, they wanted to pay their respects and I like talking about her. Why don't you join us?'

'Thank you, but I wouldn't want to intrude.'

'I insist. You didn't know her when she was alive, so you

might as well get to know a bit about her, especially as you were the one who... who... well, you know.'

It was a kind offer and I did like the idea of finding out more about her. The students might reveal something that would help identify her killer. I pulled into the last available space in the driveway and followed Hugh through the house and into the garden.

Sitting in the evening warmth were about ten people. Hugh introduced me to the group as 'a friend', which I supposed avoided the awkward revelation of how he knew me, and went to get me a glass of wine. He seemed much more at ease than when I had last seen him.

'This is very nice of you,' I said to the students. 'Very thoughtful to come round and see Hugh.'

'We've met him a couple of times,' explained a young woman with waist-length blonde hair and a pretty floral summer dress. 'Cora would have her students over for a Christmas drink and a summer garden party. He always made a real effort to talk to us and make us feel welcome. We phoned him and said we would be getting together to remember her, and he suggested we come over here. To be honest, I think he wants the company. He travelled quite a lot for work, but when he was here, there was Cora. Now the house is empty.'

'I'd heard that Cora didn't socialise with her students too much.'

'Not down the pub, not really,' said a young man who was wearing a shirt and bow tie. Mark would have been impressed. 'Some lecturers can get a bit too pally, but she always kept an appropriate distance. When she held her parties here, she was very much the host and we respected that.'

'I believe she joined you for a drink a couple of days before she died.' I wanted my questions to sound as natural as possible, and they had just given me a great way in.

'Yeah. She joined us for one, and then left.'

'What sort of things did you talk about?' I asked.

'This and that. How our work was going, what it had been like for her as a student.' He broke into a smile and looked at the others, who smiled back. They seemed to know where this was heading. 'We got talking about teachers who had inspired us, and then we talked about memories of school. Turned out she had a bit of a wild streak in her youth.'

The girl with the blonde hair laughed. 'I thought I'd been naughty, but apparently Cora had put vodka in a teacher's coffee and he got progressively more drunk as the lesson went on. She was one of those people who hadn't done brilliantly at school, but found their feet later on.'

That was putting it mildly, I thought. Her past behaviour had certainly had a lingering impact on Barry and Fiona, who had remembered it well enough. I was beginning to wonder if that was the key element in all of this. Art forgery seemed like a good angle, but one suspect was dead and the other involved an elderly lady climbing walls and running over fields. Which reminded me, I needed to talk to Fiona about her grandfather. I'd let that slip my mind.

I chatted to the students for a little longer. They were a bright, kind group who seemed genuinely fond of Cora. It was quite refreshing to spend time with people who thought highly of her and talked about the hole her loss would leave in their lives. She was actually going to leave behind a positive legacy, which was a reminder to look a bit deeper at someone and the impact they made. Very few people were entirely bad.

After a while, it became clear that I wasn't going to find out anything new about Cora and I went to find Hugh to say goodbye. He was laughing with a student as he cut more cheese and laid out crackers on a plate. Laughter transformed him and I could see the handsome man that Cora had fallen for.

The student left and Hugh looked over at me.

'Having a nice time, Sophie? If that's not a strange thing to ask.'

'I am, thank you for inviting me. It's been lovely to hear about Cora and how much the students liked her.'

Hugh nodded. 'I agree. I've had so many conversations about her that no husband should experience, it's nice to be surrounded by youth and positivity and people who just want to talk about how much they liked her. I know she wasn't an angel, none of us are. Heaven knows, I have a bit of a temper.'

'I did hear that she was a bit of a... a bit of a handful at school.'

He laughed. 'That's an understatement. She was a nightmare, she said it herself. She was expelled from one school and seemed to spend an inordinate amount of time in detention.' A serious expression crossed his face. 'It got quite serious for a while. She felt bad about it. I think that being so good with the students was her way of paying something back, making sure others had a really good education after disrupting things for her schoolmates. She had talked about becoming a governor on the board of her old school, but she was very conflicted about whether or not it was appropriate.'

'Which school did she go to?'

'Stanton Hall School.'

'Sounds very grand.'

'Not at all, just a grand name. Personally, I think she made for a very good example. Never give up on the bad kids.'

I thanked him once more and said goodbye. As I left, I realised that I was starting to like Cora again. The students had spoken so positively of her and she had clearly made a strong impact on them, so that was what people should be remembering about her. Not what she got up to at school all those years ago. Even if there were people who disliked her for other reasons – the way she had written about them in articles, or because she had voted against them going further in an art competition – there was an area of her life where she had done only good.

Now I had an even stronger urge to find out who had killed her. Despite hunger starting to gnaw at me, I felt it was time to go and talk to Fiona.

43

I doubted that Fiona would still be at Betty's working, so I made a quick phone call to Ginger, who seemed to know everything about Castledale life and was able to tell me where she lived. Fiona's home was a small modern house, the kind of building that looks like it could have been constructed from a flat pack and you can only hope that the occupant has been able to inject some personality into the interior.

Fiona was cleaning her car as I pulled up. It was a reminder that I ought to do mine. I hadn't done it for at least two years, but I figured it rained often enough that nature would take care of it. She looked up as I got out. I could tell she was trying to figure out how to respond to my arrival. Betty must have told her that I knew about Anthony.

'Hi, Fiona, fancy doing mine while you're at it?' I grinned, but she didn't seem to find it funny.

'Are you here to accuse me of killing Cora?'

'What? Er, no, I...'

'I didn't, just so you know. Yes, she was going to be talking about my grandfather in one of her articles, but she had spoken to Betty and me already. She wanted to ask her about him, find out more about his side of the story, so we knew it was coming. We were angry, but we'd also had time to calm down about it. It was old news, and if we'd wanted to kill her, why would we have waited until now? We could have done it when she came to Betty's house, and then got rid of the body. There was no need to leave her in the street to be found by a passer-by.'

It sounded like a fair point.

'That was pretty decent of her, to come and talk to you first.'

'She was still going to write about him, she wasn't that decent.'

He had committed a crime, I wanted to say, but kept that thought to myself. It was a shame, Fiona and I had got on well until now, and in another life we could have been friends. In this life, however, it looked as though that ship could have sailed. So I might as well ask the question that had been nagging away at me for a while.

'Could you tell me, Fiona, what your connection is with Hugh?'

'*What?*' The word exploded out of her. I was reminded for a second of an irate Betty, despite the fact the two weren't related by blood. 'What connection? What are you on about now?'

I took a deep breath. 'You went to visit him, didn't you, about a week ago?'

'How…' Fiona looked to be holding her temper in check with a tremendous effort. 'How do you know who I've visited? Have you been following me?'

Put like that, it seemed a pretty crass thing to have done. I reminded myself that the woman in front of me could be a murderer, and ploughed on.

'That once, I did happen to follow you into Castledale, yes.' I held up my hand to stop the tirade that looked about to come my way. 'Please, let me finish. I was just wondering how you knew him, as you and his wife weren't exactly friendly.'

'Are you suggesting I was sleeping with Cora's husband?'

'No, no, not at all,' I said hastily. 'It's been suggested that you may have been going to cover for his usual cleaner while she's on holiday.'

Fiona gave a mirthless laugh.

'When Cora came to visit us, neither Betty nor I held back. I won't go into detail, suffice to say we used a few choice words to describe her plans, and her personally. I have no doubt she told her husband all about it, so why do you think he would then employ me and give me the run of his house?'

Fiona glared at me. I gazed back. Sometimes, silence has more effect than questions. This was one of those times.

'It's quite simple,' Fiona said eventually. She seemed to have got her anger under control, as the words came out more evenly and in less of a snarl than earlier. 'I just wanted to know if he'd be publishing anything Cora may have written about Grandad.'

'And?'

'And he was very polite, actually, said he had no interest in publishing anything, so I could put my mind at rest. Nice man. Deserved better than her.'

I nodded, more at the 'nice man' bit than the opinion on Cora.

'I've just come from his house, actually, met some of Cora's students from the university. They really liked her. She made a positive impact somewhere.'

'Good, she has – had – a lot to make up for. There are plenty of students, and teachers, from years back who won't feel the same way.'

I wondered if this was all defensive bluster, excuse making, if Fiona *was* actually the one who had killed Cora. She seemed very calm. It was possible that she'd killed her more for Betty than for any anger she still held on to. There was something she had said, though, which brought a question to mind.

'You said teachers were also subject to Cora's bullying. Did Lydia teach at your school?' If Lydia had suffered at the hands of a nightmare teenager, then perhaps that gave her a motive, but Fiona shook her head.

'No, she taught at St Michael's, a good few miles away.'

'And Emily?'

'She would have been very young when Cora was at school, but I don't think so. I'm pretty sure she went to her mum's school.'

Here was another possible avenue that looked fruitless. The school link was the thing that kept coming up, though, and even if Lydia didn't teach Cora, she might know of someone who did or where I should look for more information.

Another quick call to Ginger and I had Lydia's address. I really was hungry, but if I was lucky, I might get offered a biscuit, which would see me through until I got home.

Lydia's house was very much like my own, a small worker's cottage in a snug row of identical buildings. There was a real charm to them that was added to by different coloured doors and window boxes.

I was about to knock on the door when it opened. I steadied myself so as not to land in a heap in the hallway.

'Oh, sorry, Sophie.' Emily had a bag over her shoulder and car keys in her hand. 'I'm just on my way out, is everything alright?'

'I wanted a quick word with your mum, is she in?'

Emily shook her head. 'Bridge night. She's usually out quite late, so can I help or pass on a message?'

'I wanted to find out more about Cora's schooldays and I know your mum was a teacher around then. I have a feeling that Cora made the teachers' lives just as miserable as the students'. I know your mum didn't teach at Stanton Hall, but I thought maybe she'd heard something on the grapevine. Has she ever said anything to you?'

'No. She's always been very good about not telling me things I shouldn't know, safeguarding people's privacy. That changed as I got older, of course, when I taught for a while, but back when I was a kid, no. It was hard enough having your mum teach in your school as it was, I really didn't want to know about her day. I'm so sorry, but I'm running late.'

She pulled the door closed behind her and I walked to her car with her.

'Do you fancy coming over for lunch on Sunday?' Emily asked as she unlocked the car. 'Mum makes a fantastic roast.'

'I'd love to, but I'll be working.'

'No problem, we'll have it in the evening.'

'I can't have you change your dinner plans for me.'

Emily kept talking as she got in the car. 'It's really no problem, we often have our meal in the evening. I insist, we'd love to have you over.' Just the thought of a Sunday roast with all the trimmings made my stomach rumble. 'Mum also does the best apple crumble in Derbyshire…'

'I can't say no to that. I can be done by six and head straight over, if that works for you?'

'Perfect, can't wait.'

Emily drove off and I thought about Yorkshire puddings drowning in rich, thick gravy. Drowning? That was an unfortunate word to use. Okay, overflowing.

I was done, I had to go home. My stomach was about to start eating itself.

44

After an evening of talking to Hugh, the students and Fiona, I had eaten like a horse and slept well, which was good as Friday had been busy. It hadn't really felt like a Friday as I was working all weekend, and I certainly hadn't been able to take it easy as I had been overseeing the catering for a lunch the Duchess was hosting for a local branch of the Women's Institute. Now you might think that it was nerve-racking feeding a duchess, but it was nothing compared to catering for the WI. That gave me sleepless nights.

Once I got home, I didn't turn the radio on, deciding instead to enjoy the peace for a little while. I picked the post up off the mat, went into the kitchen and hunted through the larder shelves. I hardly had anything in, certainly nothing that appealed, but I went through the cupboard again, on the basis that if I looked hard enough and often enough, something would miraculously appear.

It didn't work.

I sighed. Emergency baked beans on toast, then. I actually loved this simple meal so, as much as the cans of beans were kept as back-ups for situations just like this, it was also a treat that I would really enjoy.

There was no sign of Pumpkin. She was either outside terrorising the local mouse population or sleeping soundly on my bed. I kicked off my shoes, poured myself a gin and tonic, and sat down at the table. I'd get round to eating eventually. I went through my mail – bills, bills and more bills. That seemed to be all that ever dropped through my letterbox these days. I guess I really am a grown-up.

One letter stood out, though. The envelope was handwritten and the postmark was local. A fundraising letter from the Brownie group, perhaps, or someone who considered themselves the Neighbourhood Watch? We had a few of those on this road.

As I opened it, I simultaneously felt a shove against my leg. Pumpkin had surfaced and wanted attention, and she had one heck of a headbutt. I gave her a scratch behind her ears as I read the letter.

Pumpkin meowed angrily. I'd stopped sooner than she would have liked, but the content of the letter was most definitely not a fundraising appeal.

> *We need to talk.*
> *Lud's Church,*
> *Saturday 7pm.*

The handwriting was scruffy, like someone had held the pen in their non-dominant hand in an attempt to disguise who the author was. The jagged, childlike writing gave it a serial-killer feel. I felt Pumpkin bat my hand with a paw.

'Sorry, girl.' I picked her up and she rubbed her head against my chin. Her hefty, soft body was comforting and she purred as I held her close and stroked her. Perhaps it was because I'd spent so much time thinking about murder over the last few years, but I felt surprisingly calm about the strange invitation.

I knew immediately that I would be going.

45

'You need to tell the police, tell Joe at the very least.' Bill had a worried look on his face, but I shook my head.

'It might be a prank and I don't want to waste his time, he has his exams coming up.'

'That's a ridiculous reason not to tell him, but still, I agree with you,' said Mark as he poured me a gin and tonic. 'For the shock.'

'What shock? I'm fine.'

'Just in case of any future shock, then. Besides which, five o'clock has been and gone, so you're a drink behind.'

'Sophie, I'm serious. Don't listen to my ridiculous husband.'

Mark stood upright and sucked in air. 'Who are you calling ridiculous?'

'Look at you.' Bill had a point. Mark was wearing a smoking jacket of black and purple velvet. 'You don't even smoke, and contrary to popular opinion, mainly yours, you are not the reincarnation of Oscar Wilde. Are you trying to get our friend killed?'

'Of course not, I just think we should be cautious and not start jumping to conclusions.'

'She's had an anonymous spidery note delivered to her home, telling her to be at a location you can only walk to which provides the definition for words like *hidden, concealed* and *very, very dangerous when you are there on your own at the behest of a killer.*' Bill screwed up his face in frustration. 'Soph, don't turn into one of those irritating amateur sleuths who do stupid things and cause readers to scream at a book.'

'How about this?' said Mark. 'We will go with her. We'll all go in Sophie's car. That way, whoever wrote the note – who, by the way, we don't yet know is the killer – will think Sophie is on her own. Then, as we head to Lud's Church, we'll call Joe. If there is any kind of problem when we get there, we'll know the police are on the way.'

'That's a great idea,' said Bill, his tone dripping with sarcasm. 'Unless the killer's intention is to whack Sophie the minute she turns up.'

'We don't know it's the killer…'

'It probably is the killer,' I interrupted.

'I'm trying to help you here, Sophie. We don't *know* it's the killer, and if it is, Bill and I will protect you.'

'What are you going to do, strangle them with your dressing gown cord?' asked Bill.

'It's not a dressing gown, it's a smoking jacket, and you should know, you bought it for me.'

'Against my better judgement.' Bill looked back and forth between the two of us. 'Alright, but I am calling Joe the minute we leave the roadside.'

It didn't take much for them to convince me to stay for dinner. Shepherd's pie served in front of the TV, the perfect Friday night.

Mark sat in an armchair with his feet on an ottoman, Bill and I were at either end of the sofa, our feet on the coffee table.

I looked at Mark and grinned. 'So, this is what I'm missing out on. And they say romance is dead.'

Bill turned to face me. 'Hey, I made you dinner, didn't I?'

'Talking of relationships that turn into marriage that turn into wild Friday nights in front of the TV,' said Mark, 'has Ryan asked you out yet?'

'What's this?' Bill nearly dropped a forkful of mashed potato onto his lap.

'It's been suggested that the two of us go for coffee.'

'By whom? With whom? Pray tell.' Bill put his fork down on his plate with a clunk. 'And why haven't either of you told me about this?'

Mark shrugged.

'Ryan Lavender,' I answered.

'*The* Ryan Lavender? My God, Sophie, when are you meeting him?'

'I don't know, he hasn't called yet and I doubt he will. He was probably just being polite.'

'When he does, and I'm sure he will, I want to hear all about it. I can't trust Mark to remember a thing.'

'Oh, don't worry,' said Mark, sounding very confident. 'We'll be going on a double date. I'm hoping that he'll want to co-present a series with me.'

'Your first series hasn't aired yet,' I reminded him. 'You haven't finished filming. In fact, you've barely started, so it's weeks away yet, isn't it?'

'Alright, alright, drag a man down, why don't you? But it's coming. It won't be long and you'll be sat in front of the television at this precise time, waiting for me to appear.' He gestured dramatically towards the screen.

'Hey, turn the volume up,' I instructed Bill. 'This is about the art competition that Cora was judging and Betty was mad about.'

'This year's competition is being presented in memory of Cora Parrish, one of the hard-working judges, who so tragically died two weeks ago. Here are the finalists...'

Music started to play and the first of the finalists' work filled the screen, their name at the bottom. One by one, all the finalists' paintings were shown. We gave our own opinions, some considered and constructive, some not so much so. Typically, they were Derbyshire landscapes, but one had me speechless.

It was a painting of what could only be Lud's Church. Light shone through the deep greens of leaves and moss, the stone as richly textured as the real thing. I shivered. I wasn't sure whether it was because of the realism of the painting or the name of the artist that appeared on the screen.

Fiona Hardcastle.

'Looks like we know who you're meeting tomorrow,' said Mark.

'I had no idea she was an artist too!' I exclaimed. 'But I suppose it never came up, we were always talking about Cora or Betty and Anthony. Dammit, I should have dug deeper. I didn't think of looking at who the successful entrants to the art competition were, I would never have assumed that any of them had an axe to grind. After all, they've got through.'

'Do you know why she might have killed Cora?' asked Bill after turning off the TV.

'Might?' responded Mark. 'I think it's pretty clear she did it.'

'I did wonder if she was having an affair with Hugh, but other than seeing her go round to his house the once, I had no evidence for that. She might've been trying to prevent Cora from talking about her grandfather, Anthony. But that was years ago. As she herself said, his guilt is old news. Anyone could have found out about it if they tried.'

'But no one did,' pointed out Mark. 'Whether that was sheer coincidence or because Betty did a great job of suppressing the information, we don't know, but she'd managed to stop it leaking out all these years.'

'Perhaps Fiona wasn't protecting Anthony, maybe it was Betty she was worried about. This was an act of desperation to protect an old lady, despite it possibly being fruitless.' I was thinking out loud, grasping at straws, but after what we had seen, I was also certain that we would be meeting Fiona up at Lud's Church. But I didn't really understand why.

'Betty does not need protecting,' said Mark. 'From what you've said, everyone else needs protecting from her.'

He was right, and I really wasn't clear on Fiona's motive. There were a few to choose from. As far as I knew, she'd had the opportunity. I'd never asked where she was on the Friday night Cora died, although I knew she was unlikely to have been seen on any local cameras. She looked fit enough to be able to restrain Cora, and then hold her down as she drowned in the well.

There were still so many questions, but presumably I'd get some answers tomorrow night.

46

My little car was a mess, inside and out. I always intended to clean it, then it would rain and it seemed pointless. The back seat was covered with junk and I needed to clear it out before I drove Bill and Mark to Lud's Church, unless one of them wanted to travel in the boot, although it was just as disgraceful in there. Shopping bags, egg cartons, glass milk bottles I meant to drop off at my favourite farm shop, empty takeout coffee cups that I'd thrown back there when I needed to clear the footwell of the passenger seat. There were even cardboard boxes that I'd taken from work weeks ago and could no longer recall for what purpose.

I piled everything up on the pavement next to the car as I tried to sort it out. Hidden amongst all the clutter was the book that Janet had loaned me, still wrapped in a carrier bag. I'd forgotten all about it.

I sat in the passenger seat with the door open and started to flick through it. Perhaps there was something in there which might throw further light onto what Fiona had done. I was assuming that this evening she was going to confess to killing Cora, but even after sleeping on it, I wasn't entirely convinced she was the culprit and I was even more determined not to tell Joe yet for fear of looking more stupid than usual.

The book talked about the myths of Derbyshire, not just Lud's Church. There were the Bakewell Witches and tales about the ghosts of two lovers who supposedly haunt Winnats Pass, which I knew a little about. I read the section on Lud's Church, but didn't learn anything new. If anything, I felt that I had a better sense of the place from having actually visited it than this book could ever have given me. It was still very thoughtful of Janet, though.

I closed the book and put it on my lap. Perhaps the note had been a prank and there wasn't going to be anyone up at the gorge. Maybe my reputation for getting caught up in murders had travelled and some local kids were seeing if they could make me run around fruitlessly.

I looked down at the book. The name of the author was familiar. I turned to the back and looked at the photograph. His face was looking back at me, smiling. He appeared to be in his forties, had a tidy beard and looked warm and friendly.

As I thought about the name, I looked over at the pile of stuff I had created on the pavement. *Shadow Hills Wine* was written on one of the boxes. Who loved their wine? More to the point, which wine lover had a husband who had been allergic to alcohol? Whose *husband* had experienced the young Cora Parrish?

I looked down at the face of the author. The face of Geoff Dockery, geography teacher at Stanton Hall School and author of a number of books about Derbyshire.

Fiona hadn't killed Cora. The killer was Lydia Dockery.

'Do you know what happened to her husband? How did he die?' asked Mark as I drove.

'I've no idea. But I'm going to guess it was related to Cora in some way. Lydia mentioned that he was allergic to alcohol and those students said that she had added vodka to a teacher's drink. It can't have killed him, otherwise that would have been manslaughter or something, so I don't know. But I wonder if it had a lasting effect.'

'I know a lot of teachers who quit because of stress,' said Bill. 'Long-term stress and sickness. It's a hard job and if there is someone making your life a misery, it doesn't matter if it's a pupil, parent or colleague. Perhaps there were other things going on too, but Cora became the focus of the anger?'

I could see Mark nodding next to me. 'Mind you, people always assume that vodka is tasteless, but if someone puts it in your coffee, you're likely to know about it.'

I thought before answering. 'If Geoff was allergic, then he wouldn't have drunk alcohol regularly, if at all. So he wouldn't know what was causing it to taste different. Maybe he just thought there was something wrong with the coffee, but kept drinking because he needed the caffeine.'

'Remind you of anyone?' asked Bill, staring at me in the mirror. I smiled back.

'True, I've drunk some godawful stuff over the years because it was all I could find.'

I pulled into the side of the road, at the same spot that I had met Mum and Janet almost a week ago. I pulled on a jumper. There was a very slight chill in the air, and I knew it would be cold in Lud's Church, especially in the evening. I made sure I had Geoff Dockery's book with me; I didn't need it for any practical purpose, but I felt as if it was evidence of some kind.

My heart rate started to race as my eyes followed the line of the path into the trees. I'd been so calm about this until now, oddly calm. I had kept a lookout for other cars during our drive, but hadn't seen any, so I had no idea how Cora's killer would have got up here. But then, she could have left her car tucked away in a number of places. She might even have cycled, although I found that unlikely.

'I'm calling Joe now, in case I lose signal,' said Bill.

'Do you have to?' I asked. 'I feel like this is all a hoax. Why would Lydia leave a note? She knows she'd get caught. We're just going to look stupid if Joe calls out the cavalry.'

'Perhaps she wants to get caught.'

I let Bill's comment sink in as I walked. The ex-sportsman's strong legs powered him along as he waited for Joe to pick up.

'Hi, Joe, sorry to disturb you on a Saturday night, but I thought you should know where we are…'

I listened as Bill explained to Joe what was going on. Even though the phone wasn't on speaker, I could hear the loud shout from the other end and Bill pulled it away from his ear.

'I think you should talk to him, Sophie, I've just gone deaf.'

'Hi,' I said cautiously.

'What the hell are you thinking, Sophie? I want you all to stay right where you are. No, don't stay there, stay at your car, at least. Where are you? Are you there yet? My God, woman, you're going to have me in an early grave. Just don't go to Lud's Church, are you there yet?'

I could hear rustling and he cursed from time to time. I could imagine him trying to pull his shoes on with one hand and heading for the door.

'I'm going to call Harnby and we'll be right there, just stay put.' He paused and I could hear the slam of a car door. 'What am I saying? Of course you're going to do your own thing, damn it. I'm coming.'

I handed the phone back to Bill. 'I don't think I'll be getting a Christmas card off him this year.'

'We're not doing as he says, then?' Mark sounded a little disappointed. 'Ignore me, that was a stupid question. But do we want to put together an actual plan or are we going to stumble in and hope that Lydia is just sat there, waiting for us?'

I stopped and looked at them both.

'I want you to wait at the entrance to the gorge. I don't believe for one minute that I am at risk. I think Lydia is a woman who wants to hand herself in. My guess is she's known that Cora had something to do with her husband's death for a very long time and she snapped. Either that, or since Cora came back into her life she's been thinking about getting some kind of revenge, and on that night, she just saw an opportunity and took it. She's not out to get me, she's not going to try and silence me. I think that she feels close to her husband up at Lud's Church, that's why she's there. Maybe she wants to explain it all to someone.'

As I spoke, I felt increasingly sorry for Lydia. Cora returning to the area couldn't have been easy for her, all the happy memories she'd had with her husband here being overshadowed by Cora's presence.

After retracing our steps from our previous visit, Mark and I stood with Bill at the entrance to the gorge. From here, the shadows looked darker, the rocks more impenetrable. It looked like the entrance to another world.

'You're not going alone.' Mark's height was particularly noticeable when he had a serious expression on his face and was looming over me.

'You'll both stay right here,' I instructed them. 'She just wants someone to talk to. You can meet Joe when he gets here.'

Mark shook his head and looked at the heavens.

'Bloody stubborn woman.' I'd have hit him, but I had other things on my mind. 'Shout if there's a problem, we'll be right here.'

I nodded. 'Tell Joe to go easy when he gets here.'

47

None of the evening sunshine had reached into the gorge and I knew my arms were covered in goosebumps. If I was honest, that was also because I was quickly being drained of the confidence and bravado I had been feeling up until this point. I wasn't sure where Lydia would be, but I was still convinced that she wasn't going to leap out at me from behind a rock and try to kill me. Or at least, I was pretty sure.

I looked up. The pale sky was visible between the rock walls, the trees were leaning over, watching me. It was quiet and still, easy for her to tuck herself out of sight.

'Lydia, I'm here,' I called. Not too loud, I was 99% certain I was safe. Maybe 95%. I heard the crunch of stones underfoot, but not under my foot. A shadow up ahead moved.

I was 90% certain I was safe.

'Lydia, do you want to talk? I know that Cora made a lot of people's lives hell, your husband's included. It must have been hard seeing her almost every day, and then to have her come and start running the well-dressing group. I don't know how you did that. I'm not sure I could have coped. Why don't you tell me what happened?'

I stood, surrounded by the cold silence. A goblin could have popped out from between the crevices, or an axe-wielding Neanderthal. It was the kind of place where anything could happen. Was she round a corner? Up above? Was she here at all? Maybe this whole set-up was simply a warning: *stop asking questions or something could happen to you too*. Now I was just getting paranoid.

A trickle of small stones skittered down the rock face somewhere. I walked a little further forward.

'Lydia?'

'You think it was my mum who killed Cora?'

I spun around to face Emily. She was standing in the centre of the path, looking shocked.

'Mum? Mum wouldn't hurt a fly. I never understood why she didn't hate Cora as much as I did, after what she put my father through, after she killed him.'

I'd been wrong twice. It hadn't been Fiona and it wasn't Lydia, either.

I thought fast. 'You overheard Cora and the students in the bar in Sheffield, and when she said she had been a difficult pupil, you realised your dad had been the teacher whose coffee she put alcohol in. Did it make him very ill?'

'He was off work for a couple of days, but that wasn't the only thing she did. She let down the tyres on his car day after day, his work would go missing, essays that he had marked for pupils. She was disruptive in lessons. She seemed to choose my dad as the teacher she was going to target the most.

'Eventually, she said he had made a pass at her. It was ridiculous and he was cleared, but the investigation took its toll on him and he just got so tired, he lost his spark. My dad loved teaching, any child was lucky to have him, but the stress of the job got too much. He ended up taking early retirement and without teaching, he became the shadow of the man he was.

'The way Mum told it, it was Cora who started it all. She marked the beginning of him getting ill all the time, falling out of love with the job. When he died, it broke Mum's heart. That's why we moved. She wasn't sure she could stay here, but moving away made it even harder. Years later, once she got stronger, she made the move back.'

'And you followed her.'

Emily smiled. 'I grew up here, I wanted to come home too.'

'But then Cora returned to the area.'

'She was a constant reminder of what Dad had been through. I tried talking to her about it once, I thought that maybe she would be sorry for what happened, but she wasn't, not at all. Called it childish games.'

'And then you heard her laughing about her behaviour with some students.'

'I wanted to march right up, tell the students everything she had done, but I managed to hold it together. The next time I saw her was when I was out the back of the village hall. I spotted her walking home. She was already late for the Duchess, but I guessed she wanted to go home and change. I couldn't help it, I just felt this rage. I took her by surprise, jumping over the wall like that.' This was the first time that Emily had smiled; she appeared amused by the memory of what had happened.

'She was *very* surprised, but I think she knew as soon as I had hold of her what was happening, why I was so mad at her. She tried to defend herself, calm me down, tell me she was sorry, but I didn't want to hear it. It was too late.'

'Did you tell her to meet you here?' Emily looked momentarily confused. 'There was a note on Cora's desk that said Lud's Church, but it looked like she didn't know what it was about.'

'Oh that, yeah. I left her a message on her phone, telling her to meet me here. She rang me back and told me she wasn't coming all the way out here when we could talk at the village hall.' Emily stopped speaking for a moment and looked around. 'This was Dad's favourite place, it was what sparked his interest in Derbyshire's myths and legends. He often brought us here. I wanted her to find out more about the kind of man he was, thought that perhaps she'd feel a greater sense of regret if she came here, somewhere that meant so much to him. But she refused. It was still all about her, and what was good for her.'

So Mark had been right, the painting of Lud's Church hanging in Cora's kitchen had no relevance at all to her murder. And I was right not to feel any kind of fear. Emily wasn't going to hurt me, she just seemed relieved to talk.

'Cora was a child when it all happened.'

'She was fifteen, old enough to know better. And anyway, she was an adult when we came back here. She could have apologised.'

'Why me? Did you want me to see the place your dad loved too?'

'I did. I like you, Sophie. I meant it when I said I wanted us to spend time together, I really thought that we could become friends. That's why I'm telling you all this, and here. I needed to see it one last time, too.'

She stopped talking and looked around the gorge. For a moment, I could see the child she had been, running around, trying to climb up the rock face, finding places to hide. I felt desperately sorry for her.

'One last time?' I asked.

Emily's gaze lifted from me and she smiled at something over my shoulder. At the same time, I heard footsteps.

'I thought you would call the police, whoever you thought you were meeting. I hoped so. I would have handed myself in eventually, but I'm grateful you saved me that call.'

'I'll take it from here, Sophie.' Detective Sergeant Harnby did not look happy, and I wasn't sure who she was more furious at, me or Emily.

48

Pumpkin had made herself at home on Bill's lap and she was looking at him with a fondness I rarely saw.

'I see you,' I said to Bill, 'feeding her cheese. The next time she jumps on my bed, the legs are going to give way.' I could have sworn she glared at me. If she could speak, I think she would have said something very rude. Then she went back to nuzzling Bill's chin.

The front door crashed open and Joyce backed in, carrying a cardboard box.

'No, no, it's fine, I don't need any help, you all just stay where you are.' She turned and saw Mark, who was sitting in the armchair with an amused look on his face. 'Mark, I don't care if you are appearing on TV tonight, you can get up and help.'

'You said you were fine.'

'Mark…'

'And if I don't?' He immediately regretted his response. I couldn't see Joyce's face, but his expression went from one of smug *tonight's all about me* to abject fear.

'You often call me a witch, tonight you might just discover how far my powers extend.'

Mark shot out of his seat, grabbed the box from her arms and dashed towards the kitchen. I could have sworn he bobbed his head as a display of subservience with every step. He was accompanied by the sounds of clinking bottles – the liquid refreshments had arrived.

'Bring one back through, will you?' she called after him. 'I'm going to need a drink to get through this.'

'His slot is only ten minutes long,' I reminded her.

'That's ten minutes *too* long in my book,' she grumbled, before sitting in the armchair.

'Oi!' said Mark as he returned with a bottle of champagne and a number of glasses. 'That's my seat.'

'Are you going to pour me a glass?' Joyce asked haughtily.

'I thought *I* was meant to be the centre of attention,' Mark grumbled amiably as he popped open the bottle.

'Ginger won't be long,' said Joyce as she raised the glass to watch the bubbles float in rapidly moving lines to the surface. 'I think she's actually interested in what you have to say.'

'And Joe?' I asked, looking at Bill.

'Said he'd be here. I think he gets his results today, so we might have to tread carefully.'

'I heard that,' Joe called down the hall. 'So you assumed I'd fail.'

'I saw you pull up,' said Bill, laughing. 'So? Any news?'

Ellie, Joe's girlfriend, was behind him, and from the look on her face we could tell it was good news. Joyce got up and threw her arms around Joe, planting a big kiss on his cheek.

'Congratulations, Detective Sergeant,' said Mark, handing him a glass of champagne.

'Not yet, I've got to actually apply for a sergeant's vacancy, but hopefully it won't be long.'

'Well, I'm going to be calling you Sergeant from now on regardless. Bill, you're not going to shake your brother's hand?'

Bill looked down at Pumpkin. 'Maybe later.'

'Very wise, she holds a grudge,' I informed him. Joe laughed.

'Sorry, sorry, am I late?' Ginger bustled in. There were only eight of us including Pumpkin in the room, but my small house was starting to feel rather crowded. 'I brought a cake. You didn't bake one, did you, Sophie?' I looked at the floor, feeling guilty. 'Well, you won't find one down there, so it's a good job I did.'

The coffee table had become an explosion of crisps, cheese, olives, sausage rolls and other party snacks. Now Ginger added a chocolate cake to the mix, the words *Can I have your autograph Mark?* iced in wobbly writing on the top.

'I was a bit rushed when I added the final touches,' Ginger explained.

Ellie took over the champagne-pouring duties and Joyce reluctantly returned the armchair to Mark.

'How's Lydia?' I asked Ginger, who shook her head in response.

'Not seen her for a while, but apparently Betty has been popping around. Never thought I'd see her become the Good Samaritan of the village, but I believe they've been spending quite a lot of time together. I'm sure Lydia is grateful for the company. I don't know if she'll be involved in the well-dressing festival next year, though, it's all very sad. Emily was only just in her teens when her dad died, I guess she never got over it. Always blamed Cora. Apparently, Hugh has been to visit Lydia too, took flowers. I guess not everyone bears a grudge in the same way.'

I thought about Emily and felt a stab of sorrow. I had liked her. It had crossed my mind that she had only befriended me as a way of discovering what I was learning about the case – she had no doubt heard about my reputation. But I wanted to think better of her than that.

'What are you two whispering about?' shouted Joyce.

'You've got the subtlety of a sledgehammer, Joyce Brocklehurst,' retorted Ginger in response.

'Hey, Sophie, look. It's your boyfriend,' said Joyce, confirming that sledgehammer was indeed the right word. Ryan Lavender's face appeared on the muted TV in an advert for a new history series.

'He's not my boyfriend,' I replied, aware that I was starting to turn red.

'Don't give me that.' Joyce peered at me over the bright yellow glasses that she had just put on. 'A little birdie tells me that you're going out for dinner next week.'

A collective and rather childish 'Oooohh!' filled the room as everyone responded to the news.

'Leave the poor girl alone.' Ginger pulled me down between her and Bill on the sofa.

'Shhhh, shhhhh. It's next, I'm next. It's me…' called Mark. Everyone found a seat, Joe on the floor. Joyce perched on the cushioned arm of Mark's chair, her legs crossed delicately at the ankles. I turned up the volume on the TV. Ellie topped up everyone's champagne before joining Joe on the floor as the evening news host introduced the new segment, describing Mark as an expert on local history. The theme music started and everyone whooped and cheered as various shots of Mark in historic locations faded in and out. Glasses were raised, and eventually we descended into silence as the music came to an end and Mark, looking every inch the expert historian, walked into view.

I watched as Joyce put a hand on his shoulder and gave it a gentle squeeze.

'Excellent wardrobe choice, Mark. I couldn't have done better myself.'

Keep reading for some bonus short stories

A VILLAGE AFFAIR

Marion stood at the kitchen window, her hands resting in soapy suds. The warmth of the water was comforting and she'd lost track of how long she'd been standing there. She was watching. She often watched. Marion had a healthy interest in the activities of her small village, and the kitchen sink was a perfect vantage point.

At this precise moment she was watching her neighbour, Ginger Salt. Ginger was repairing the wall of her small garden across the road. She was hardly a delicate woman, Ginger. Rather rough around the edges, was how Marion would describe her.

She must have skin like leather, all the time she spends outside, and I bet there's plenty of muck under those fingernails, Marion thought as she watched Ginger handle the blocks of stone with ease in the afternoon sun. She scolded herself for thinking so unkindly. She knew that she was supposed to like Ginger, everyone liked Ginger. But Marion had her reasons for resenting Ginger's ever helpful nature, her remarkable skill with a sewing machine, her ability to repair her own car and the loud, cheerful *hellos* she called to whoever was nearby as she walked down the street. Marion used to have the same view as everyone else – Ginger was good for a laugh, and always kind and generous. But Marion was no longer so keen on her.

It had all started when Frank got involved with the well-dressing group at the village hall. Every May they made the dressings, a centuries-old tradition that gave thanks for a reliable water source. Large boards, decorated with natural objects such as twigs, petals and leaves to form pictures, were displayed next to the village's wells. Frank was one of only two men involved, and Marion had been surprised that he was interested, but after he retired he'd found himself with too much time on his hands and had gone in search of a new hobby. Marion hadn't minded, then. She'd thought it an odd choice, but if he enjoyed it, so be it, and it wasn't a year-long thing. It wasn't as if she'd become a golf widow who rarely saw her fella when it was a dry day.

Last year had been his first with the group, and after the well dressing, Frank had started to socialise with some of them. The nights he spent down the pub were fine; she quite liked watching her soap operas without him making disparaging jokes, and she could put her feet up and work her way through a bag of chocolate Revels without having to share. At first, he would regale her with tales of what everyone had been up to, but over time, it became what *Ginger* had been up to. And more than once, Marion had popped out to the village shop and seen the two of them sitting at a table outside the pub. Just Frank and Ginger, no one else.

It hadn't bothered her, until it did. Until she felt as though they were sharing a private joke over the garden wall, or talking too enthusiastically about the next year's well dressing whenever she came by, as though they had suddenly changed the subject upon seeing her. Marion didn't think of herself as the paranoid sort, but as winter turned to spring and this year's festival edged ever closer, it seemed to her as if they were always together.

Marion and Frank had been a couple for twenty years, but they had never exchanged vows. It wasn't that they were anti-marriage, it had just never happened. Both had experienced painful divorces, so it simply hadn't been at the forefront of their minds when they'd first got together, and their life had continued happily without it.

But Marion had started to think she might quite like to marry Frank. She had, until recently, thought their relationship was as strong as ever, stronger even, so she liked the idea of calling Frank her husband and putting their relationship on a formal footing. But perhaps she had left it too late. Over the last few months, it had seemed as though he was losing interest, and that blasted Ginger Salt had caught his eye.

Everyone knew Ginger was one of those lesbian types. No one really talked about it, it was just something that they all knew. Marion had never seen her with someone who could have been classed as a girlfriend, although Ginger spent a lot of time in the company of a woman who worked up at nearby Charleton House, the magnificent stately home nestling in the stunning setting of the Derbyshire hills. Janet, was that it? Judy? No, Joyce. She certainly didn't look as though she might choose Ginger as a girlfriend – if anything, Marion would have thought that Joyce would be the one Frank was distracted by, all blonde hair and cleavage. But for some reason, it was Ginger he couldn't stay away from.

The well-dressing festival was fast approaching, and Frank had been out most of the week. When he did actually make it home for meals, all he could talk about was what they'd been up to at the village hall. He spoke about working on the boards, which sounded a bit like *treading the boards* to Marion the first time she heard it, and she'd got confused and thought he was rehearsing for a play. Instead, as she soon found out, he'd been repairing the big wooden frames that the well dressings would be displayed on. She'd heard everything about the group members puddling the clay, which meant getting it just wet enough that once it was spread out on the boards, the decorations would stick to it. She'd heard more than she felt necessary about the process of pricking – marking out the design in the clay with a pointed tool – and she'd told him off when he took her packet of cocktail sticks to use. She was sure he'd only need the one, but the rest of them never made it back home. They didn't cost much, and she knew it was petty of her, but the whole situation was putting her on edge and she had exploded at him when he said he couldn't find the leftovers back at the hall.

As the weekend got closer, Frank became more and more jittery. Whenever Marion asked what was wrong, he'd say it was nothing more than nerves about the event, that he wanted it to go smoothly It was very unlike him – he'd always been remarkably, sometimes frustratingly, laid back. It was so unusual that Marion was starting to think that maybe he was unwell.

Then another possible reason for the change in his behaviour formed in her mind, and she became convinced it was true when she popped into the village shop to get another bag of Revels and some bread. Jack, the owner of the chip shop, was in there talking to Helen, the shopkeeper, as she rang his items through the till. They hadn't spotted Marion as she walked through the open door and made her way to the bakery section that was out of sight at the back of the small store.

'We were all a bit surprised when he told us over a pint the other day. Didn't think he was the type, but I reckon he's making the right decision.'

'Oh aye, reckon there'll be some tears, though,' said Helen.

'Oh, I dunno, I've never seen Marion as the emotional type.'

'Still, it'll be a shock, who knows how she'll respond?'

Marion crept back out, thinking she'd drive to Asda instead. She was more anonymous there and no one would be discussing her private business, which it seemed the villagers knew more about than she did.

. . .

The car needed a good clean. It always needed a good clean. But at least it wasn't full of junk like Gillian's little runaround. Every time she gave Marion a lift to their Knit and Natter group, Marion found herself having to move magazines, empty shopping bags, and egg boxes off the seat. Gillian lived on her own and didn't often have anyone else in the car with her, and it showed. At least Marion took any rubbish into the house, and if she had an egg box to return, return it she did.

So it came as a surprise to hear a clunk from the boot as Marion started to pull away from the kerb. She stopped and the clunk repeated itself. There was something rolling around back there, and it was going to annoy her if she didn't secure it. She tried to think what it might be; it was weeks since she had used the car, so it wasn't anything *she'd* left behind, she was sure of it.

Marion hoisted herself out of the car and walked round to open the boot. A bottle of champagne was rolling around freely. She picked it up and read the label – Moët and Chandon. It was expensive stuff, the price sticker was still on it and she could tell it had been bought at the village shop. There was dust on the shoulders of the bottle and Marion recalled that Helen had a small selection of wine behind the counter, and a dusty bottle of champagne had been amongst it. Hardly the height of romance, a dirty bottle from a little village shop. Marion took a moment of pleasure that Ginger was going to find herself having to pretend that the drink she was being wooed with didn't taste like vinegar.

Serves her right, thought Marion. *If she thinks she's getting a romantic man about town who knows his Chardonnay from his Chablis, she's about to be disappointed.*

Marion wedged the bottle in the box containing the foot pump, spare oil and a couple of other emergency items. Strictly speaking, there wasn't room for it, but she gave it a good shove and forced it in. Frank would be lucky if he could get it out.

Marion climbed back in the car, trying to remember the last time she and Frank had shared a bottle of champagne. Her mind was a blank. There had been plenty of bottles of wine, and a lot of laughter over the years. She remembered a trip to France a number of summers back. They'd spent it driving around the countryside, tasting wine at little farms, and came home with a car full of the stuff. Some of the bottles had handwritten labels and had been so cheap, they'd handed over loose change to pay for them. But it was the best wine she'd ever tasted.

She smiled as she recalled them drinking so much in the company of the wine maker at one farm, he and his wife had invited them to stay over so they didn't have to drive anywhere. They still exchanged Christmas cards. Claudette and Henry, they were their names. He had a missing front tooth, and she would giggle at the smallest thing, which in turn set Marion off.

It was a long time since she and Frank had been abroad. Maybe they should do that again. She corrected herself. Maybe *she* should do that again.

Marion drove down the main street of Castledale, past the village hall where Frank would most likely be working side by side with Ginger. She passed Jack, who'd stopped to chat to someone outside the Bull's Head pub.

Probably talking about me, the old gossip, she thought.

Two doors down, past the village shop and the butcher's, which had somehow survived despite the obscenely huge supermarket that had opened three miles away, was Susan's the florist. This shop had met the horticultural needs of every birthday, marriage, death and any other event you cared to think of in the area for the last ten years. Marion had slowed down. Old Mr Jefferson was taking his time to cross the road with his equally doddery Jack Russell, imaginatively named *Dog*. As she waited, hoping he wouldn't fall flat on his face, Marion spotted a familiar face coming out of the florist's. Frank was carrying the most enormous bouquet of red roses under one arm, and pink roses under the other. He looked like a mobile entrant for the Chelsea Flower Show.

They must have cost him a bloody fortune, she thought and started to do the maths in her head. She stopped the mental gymnastics when an even more important question popped into her brain.

Who the hell are they for?

In their early years as a couple, Frank had brought her flowers most weeks, then it had been once a month, then just on her birthday. She hadn't minded, cut flowers were a waste and she'd rather have a pot plant. But this extravagant floral purchase clearly indicated that someone had Frank feeling all romantic.

She watched as he crossed the road without checking for traffic. *He'll get 'imself knocked over one of these days*, she grumbled to herself, wondering briefly if that might not be a bad idea. He strode towards the village hall, but instead of heading for the door, which would have given him the excuse that he'd bought them for the well dressing he was working on, he walked straight past the building.

The driver behind Marion beeped their car horn. Old Mr Jefferson had made it over the road and was now disappearing into the Bull's Head. Marion wanted to see where Frank was going, but he was heading down a narrow alleyway that was closed off to cars, and Marion had no choice but to continue her planned journey. She slowed a little as she passed him; he looked as if he was deep in thought.

Marion stamped the accelerator pedal to the floor with frustration, and shot out of the village so fast she almost gave herself whiplash. *Sod him*, she thought. *He can go without his favourite butter this week, and if he reckons I'm picking 'im up a couple of cans of his stout, he can go whistle.*

. . .

The evening's Knit and Natter get-together was being held in the Bull's Head. Marion didn't really feel like going. Castledale was a small village and if the gossip was out about Frank and Ginger, then everyone in the pub would know. But she refused to be beaten. She would walk in with her head held high and focus on finishing the sleeve of the jumper she was knitting for Frank.

Marion paused as she put her knitting in the yellow sunflower bag that she had made herself. The old fool didn't deserve a new jumper. That was easy enough to sort out, she'd give it to charity. Someone who really deserved it would get it. Frank deserved nothing more than a good poke with her knitting needles. She wondered if it was possible to murder someone with a knitting needle. She was sure it was, if you could be accurate enough to hit something essential. She could wait until he was asleep, and then with a quick *knit one, pearl one*, old Romeo would be unable to share that champagne with his frumpy Juliet.

No, that was a horrible thought.

She briefly considered what it would be like to sleep alone. Frank was a snorer, and over the years, she'd got used to the sound of the giant whistling bumble bee that lay next to her. On the rare occasion that one of them had been away for the night, she found herself struggling to sleep without the familiar sound. She'd always considered herself lucky – he could have sounded like a congested walrus and she was grateful for that small mercy. Maybe she'd play whale noises to fill the silence if he was going to leave.

The knitter-and-natterers had made themselves comfortable at a large round table in a corner of the pub. Balls of wool mingled with glasses of wine, and the sounds of knitting needles and chatter were interspersed with *bugger* and *bother it* and occasionally something a bit more colourful as the number of dropped stitches increased in direct proportion to the amount of wine that had been consumed.

The woman sitting across from Marion drained the final

drops from the wine bottle into her glass and stuck it back in the ice bucket, upside down.

'It's my turn,' said Marion as she put her knitting down. 'I'll get a white and a red.' There were mutterings of thanks as everyone kept an eye on their needles.

Marion stood at the corner of the bar. Beyond was a dartboard, and a couple of old blokes were watching a game, their backs to Marion.

'I didn't think she was interested in that sort of thing,' said the man with a grey beard. "Ow do you know, any road?'

'He told us the other night, but he better be careful, Marion is bound to find out. Gossip travels like wildfire round here.' Marion felt a cold shiver pass through her body. She wanted to walk away – run away, even, if her knees would hold out, but she couldn't make her legs move.

'Why did he tell people if he didn't want Marion to find out?'

'I don't know. Maybe so he couldn't back out, or to counter his own disbelief that it was all happening. Maybe telling people made it feel more real.'

'Well, all credit to him, he's a braver man than me.' The two men laughed. Marion's throat had gone dry, and her voice was hoarse and scratchy as she asked the barman for two bottles of wine. Damn that bloody Frank Holder. She was tempted to grab one of the bottles and just glug the whole thing down, but no, she needed a steady hand if she was going to stab him with her knitting needles.

Saturday was dry and bright, the perfect day to start the well dressing celebrations. Frank had left early to help position the boards. He'd left so quietly, Marion hadn't been aware of his departure and woke to an empty bed.

She lay there, staring at the blue sky through the break in the curtains, planning her morning. It had always irritated her, the way Frank never closed the curtains properly, but today it didn't seem to matter so much. In fact, she rather liked the ray of light that striped the bedroom.

Marion lay in bed, thinking. She decided not to plot his death, and not to hunt him down with a knitting needle, nor was she going to let him make a fool of himself. She was going to fight for him. She was going to stride through the village and find Ginger Salt, tell her to keep her hands off her man. She hadn't spent the last twenty years building a comfortable life with Frank just to have Ginger swoop in and steal him over a load of clay and rose petals.

Frank was a kind, gentle man and had probably been momentarily captured by the charms – if you could call them that – of their neighbour. Marion just needed to give him a good shake, tell him what's what and they could go back to the way things were. He could find a new hobby, maybe something they could do together.

She would have to deal with Ginger, though. Ginger needed a good talking-to, a real stern warning, and Marion didn't care if she delivered it with an audience. The rest of the village already knew what was going on.

After a quick shower in a bathroom that smelt overwhelmingly of Frank's musty aftershave, something he only ever doused himself in for special occasions, Marion chose a pale yellow sundress that brushed gently against her curves, and her favourite floppy straw hat to keep the sun out of her eyes. She hung a white handbag over her shoulder and set out. In previous years, she had participated in the blessing of the wells. But today she couldn't remain quiet or calm long enough to get through the service, let alone the perambulation from dressing to dressing as each was blessed by the vicar of St Edmund's.

The station car park was full, every side street bumper to bumper. The field next to the church had been turned into a temporary car park, and volunteers in bright vests were directing drivers into neat rows.

'Mornin', Marion luv,' boomed Jack as he stood outside the chippy. He looked rather pleased with himself, thought Marion. Probably laughing at her. Helen was tidying a display of postcards outside the door of her shop. She waved at Marion.

'Beautiful day,' she called out. Marion grunted to herself and strode on. She passed the Children's Well and Sheepwash Well without a second look at the wonderful displays that had taken hours of work. She didn't stop to take photographs or coo over the skill or design alongside those currently admiring them. The roads in the centre of the village had been closed to traffic, and Marion strode purposefully along the middle of them. She didn't even stop to pet Dog, who was used to receiving a treat from Marion most days and watched her progress down the road with confusion and a hungry look in his eyes.

Marion was heading for the Top Pump Well. That was the dressing Frank had told her he was working on with Ginger, an image of a rainbow and a pair of hands holding the world, or something like that. Frank had seemed oddly vague. Marion could see the side street that she would need to turn down. She was getting close.

She pulled her shoulders back and slowed her pace. She didn't want to appear flustered, she was in control. She knew what she wanted, and she was going to get it.

'Marion! Marion! Over here.' Marion glanced towards the source of the voice. It sounded like Ginger. 'Marion, love. Lovely dress, perfect for a day like today, it's going to be a scorcher.' It *was* Ginger and she looked very pleased with herself.

'Ginger, I want to have a word with you.'

'Do you, love? Perfect, cos I want to have a word with you, too. Why don't we head over here out of the road?'

'Here is just fine,' Marion said as calmly as she could, her voice on the edge of wobbling. She'd practised what she was going to say to Ginger, and to Frank, but now she was face to face with the woman, she'd forgotten the first sentence.

'Er, well, I need to sort something out. I was just on my way to do something important. Come with me, we can talk when we get there.' Ginger started to walk off.

Bloody woman, thought Marion. *Reckons she's in charge. Well alright, I'll follow, but she'll be in for a surprise when we do talk.* The delay would give Marion the time to try to remember that blinder of an opening sentence she'd planned on hurling at Ginger.

Ginger was leading them through a growing crowd of people. There was a low hum in the air, and they appeared to be waiting for something. Marion couldn't see the board in question, it was probably tucked out of sight next to the garage they were approaching. There was a grass bank just beyond that glowed with a carpet of daffodils every spring. She couldn't recall a well being there, but then she wasn't thinking straight, she had more important things on her mind.

'Ginger, I would like to…'

'Hang on, luv. Can you just wait here?' Ginger left her in front of a pair of blue wooden garage doors. The paint was peeling off and Marion was disappointed that the owner couldn't be bothered to give them a fresh coat if they knew there would be a well dressing just round the corner.

'Ginger, I want a word and I want it now…'

'Aye, of course, I'll just be a minute, wait right here, don't move.' Ginger scuttled off towards a regular door set in the near side of the garage. Marion sighed with frustration. The hum of the crowd had settled down and it was only then that she noticed they were all focused on the garage doors. Maybe she had been right and there wasn't a well round the corner. So, what on earth were they all waiting for?

She wished Ginger would hurry up; whatever she was up to, Marion was not interested. She was keeping an eye out for Frank, she'd rather hoped he'd be around when she laid down the law to Ginger. That way she wouldn't have to repeat herself.

There was the sound of scratching and rattling metal, and the garage doors shook. They slowly opened with a dreadful harsh dragging noise as they were forced across the top of the tarmac. Marion turned to look up the road. Where was that bloody man of hers? And hers he was and hers he'd bloody remain.

She spotted Helen, who was doing what Marion assumed was her version of running, a funny little skip that wasn't much faster than a quick walk. She looked very undignified. Marion was startled by a collective gasp from the crowd. What in heaven's name had Ginger done now? She was always the centre of attention and Marion had had enough. It was now or never.

She turned and made to step towards the door that Ginger had walked through, but she didn't get any further. The garage doors were now wide open and Marion was at the front of the crowd with the best view of what lay beyond. Just inside, in the full light of the sun, was a large well dressing.

An odd place for it, thought Marion. *Just like Ginger to try and do something different.* It was made up of pinks, reds and whites. *A bit feminine for Ginger, and very unlike Frank, if this is what he was working on.*

Then she saw him. Frank stepped out from behind the dressing with an expression on his face that Marion couldn't read.

'What the hell are you...' Marion stopped as the words on the well dressing registered in her mind. Spelt out in rich red rose petals was:

Marion
Will you marry me?

The crowd was now silent and she knew that all eyes were on her. Frank shuffled forward and pulled the cap from his head.

'What do you reckon, girl? I figured it was time we made things formal. I should have done this a long time ago. It were Ginger 'ere who helped me see how lucky I am and I'd be honoured if you'd, well, you know...' He looked down at the cap in his hands, which he was nervously turning round and round. 'Well, will ya?'

So this was what the daft sod had been doing. Marion looked at the dressing, and the rose petals that she'd first seen in the bouquet in Frank's arms. It must have taken hours of painstaking work. The petals were laid in immaculate rows, coffee beans creating a crisp outline around each word. Leaves in different shades of green formed a gentle swirling pattern behind the rose petals, catkins and tree bark a border around the whole piece.

The sneaky devil! He started to get down on one knee, but Marion grabbed his arm before he had a chance to sink to the ground.

'Don't do that, you'll never get back up. Of course I will, ya daft bugger.' There was laughter from the crowd and a round of applause as he leaned forward and kissed her. As their lips parted, Marion stepped back, feeling suddenly shy and a little bit silly. Ginger moved out from behind the dressing, carrying a tray with a bottle of champagne and two glasses.

'Now, get this down you. Frank, will you do the honours?' He took the bottle and filled the glasses a little unsteadily as hands slapped his back and words of congratulation were called out. Marion took a glass from him gratefully and looked at a beaming Ginger.

She's not all that bad, thought Marion. *I might even need her help encouraging him to set a date.* She took a sip of the perfectly chilled liquid, enjoying the bubbles on her tongue. It didn't taste so bad after all.

She looked from Frank to the bright well dressing. *Maybe I'll have a go at this malarkey myself*, she thought. *I reckon it'd be fun to do together.*

WELL DRESSED TO DIE

THE LETTER OF THE LAW

Detective Constable Joe Greene brought his motorcycle to a stop outside a smart semi-detached house and removed his helmet. Leaning against the garden wall was a rather scruffy-looking man; his t-shirt advertised a beer festival that had taken place fifteen years ago, and it stretched over a belly which provided further evidence of the owner's love of the calorific 'bread in a glass'. Curly hair flopped over his ears and hung in his eyes.

'Alright, Father. Sorry I'm late,' said Joe as he climbed off the bike.

'No worries. Figured I'd wait for you out here so she doesn't have to repeat herself.'

'Lead on. When we're done, we can go and have a pint.' Joe had, technically, clocked off from work, but when a call had come through to the station that Father Craig Mortimer, an occasional drinking buddy of his, wanted a chat, he was happy to agree to meet him on the way home.

'Is she very upset?' asked Joe as they approached the door.

'She was earlier; she might have calmed down by now. I'm not surprised, though; it's a horrible thing to have happen and she doesn't deserve it.' Craig knocked on the door before pushing it open. 'Jean, It's Father Craig. Can we come in?'

A friendly looking woman with dark hair containing a few streaks of grey, a red cardigan over her shoulders and drying her hands on a towel, appeared at the end of the hall. She looked to be somewhere in her sixties.

'Of course. You must be the police,' she said as she looked over Craig's shoulder at Joe. 'Oh, off duty?'

'Just, yes. I'm on my way home – excuse my appearance.' Joe ran his fingers through his hair as though that would improve things and make up for his ancient bike kit. He wished he hadn't chosen to wear his oldest, most severely scuffed and oil-stained leather trousers to ride to work. The jacket was bearable, if you ignored the way the colour had faded unevenly over the years. 'I'll just take my boots off.'

'There's no need. So long as they're not caked in mud, you're fine, really. I've put the kettle on.'

Jean led them into her sitting room, then left them there while she answered the summons of the whistling kettle. It was a comfortable space; the furniture was quite old and well used, but looked welcoming rather than tatty.

After Jean had returned from making the tea and poured them both a cup, Joe asked to see the letter.

'It was delivered by hand this morning. I was out shopping and it was waiting for me when I got back.' The letter, which had been made by cutting words out of a newspaper, was short and to the point, describing Jean as an overweight old woman whom nobody liked. It also said she was a dreadful minister and should resign. Joe examined the letter and its envelope. The latter was self-sealing, so there wouldn't be any DNA on it.

Looking up, Joe could see tears welling in Jean's eyes. 'You have no idea who is behind this?' She shook her head.

'Jean is incredibly hard working,' Craig explained. 'She's done a huge amount for the churches under her watch. She's very well thought of by everyone who works with her. This just doesn't make any sense.' He turned to Jean. 'You're the last person I would expect to be getting hate mail.'

She smiled weakly at him.

'And outside the church?' Joe asked between bites of a Jammy Dodger. He was ready for his dinner, but a couple of biscuits would tide him over. Jean shook her head.

Joe looked at the letter again. He hated to admit it, but no crime had been committed at this point.

'Is there anyone at all you can think of who might have reason to be … frustrated with you?' He was trying to keep his language subtle; he didn't think *'Have you annoyed anyone to the point of hate mail?'* would be helpful. Jean was quiet for a moment, then looked at Joe; she seemed hesitant to speak.

'Well, there is the lad next door. His parents are away and he's been playing his music very loud. I went to talk to him, ask him to turn it down; that was yesterday afternoon.'

'How did he react?'

'As you'd expect from a sixteen-year-old boy. He grunted and told me where to go, in none too delicate tones.'

Joe and Craig looked at one another. This was a valid route to explore.

'I'll have a chat with our young music lover, but I'm afraid at this stage, it's all I can do. Let's hope it's a one off and they've got things off their chest, but please, call me or Craig if you get anything else.'

Jean smiled. 'Thank you, Detective. To be honest, it's just a relief to know that I have people on my side who will take this seriously. I've never really minded living on my own; I'm used to it now, but it's hard at times like this. You're both very kind.'

. . .

Craig had gone on ahead to the pub to get the drinks in, but Joe had hung back, knocking on the door of the house next to Jean's. He knocked again, then a third time. It was six o'clock and he found it hard to imagine that even the laziest of teenagers would be in bed at this time. He couldn't hear any music, though.

Eventually the door opened and a tall, gangly youth with heavy eyebrows glared at him. The smell of stale take-out food wafted out of the door.

'Yeah?'

Joe introduced himself. 'I believe that the lady next door has had a word with you about the volume of your music.'

The lad rolled his eyes. 'I turned it down, alright? I can't turn it down any more, I won't be able to hear it, miserable old…'

'Alright, none of that. Were you keen to get your own back?'

The teenager looked at him blankly. 'Wha'dya mean? She doesn't play music, not that I can hear. How can I tell her to turn it down?'

'I didn't mean that. Did you drop a letter through her door? Maybe in a moment of anger?'

'What letter? Why would I do that? I don't understand.' The boy really didn't, Joe was sure. This lad would probably have cursed at Jean, thought he was tough to do so, but Joe doubted he would even have thought of cutting out words to compose the spiteful letter he'd seen. In fact, Joe wasn't sure he knew how to read and write. No, that was unfair, but still, Joe was sure the boy didn't have it in him.

'If it turns out you're in the midst of a bout of amnesia, just stop it, alright?'

'I told you, I didn't do anything.'

Joe attempted to give him the look of a worldly elder, and then walked off. It was time for that pint.

. . .

Craig had found them a table in the corner of the Black Swan, a pub that belonged either in a cosy TV murder mystery or on a Christmas card, with its open fire and big wooden ceiling beams. Craig didn't look anything like a member of the clergy, but everyone knew who he was and it had taken him ten minutes to get from the bar to the table as at least half of the pub regulars wanted to stop him and say hello. Working at Charleton House, a glorious display of baroque opulence that had been standing for over 500 years, Craig was responsible for the chapel within the magnificent building. What had once been a private place of worship for the Duke and Duchess of Ravensbury and their family was now open for the local community, and Craig was kept busy.

Joe sat down next to him and Craig slid a glass over.

'One pint of faux beer. You could always leave your bike here and crash at mine for the night.'

'Thanks, but I'll pass. Next time.' Joe glugged down half the amber liquid and sat back. 'I needed that.'

'Long day?'

'Aren't they all?'

'Yeah, I've noticed that,' said Craig. 'The days seem longer as I get older, and at the same time, they go by quicker, and before I know it, I'm at the end of the month and behind, on everything.'

'Age, mate, and I don't think God can stop that happening. He might have a place saved for you upstairs, but down here, you're getting on in years.'

Craig grimaced and nodded.

After a conversation about the recent winning streak of Craig's favourite local football team, The She Devils, a squad of women who were sponsored by the Black Swan and known for not taking prisoners, they moved on to the reason for their get together.

'So, what do you think?' asked Craig.

'About the letter? Let's just hope that's the end of it; that whoever sent it wants to make a point, and they've moved on. It's probably some sad bugger who spends their evenings shouting at the TV and they'll be distracted by something else come the morning. It would be nice to send a message to them, though, stop them doing it altogether, but it's never that simple. Do you know Jean well?'

Craig shook his head. 'We met at an annual conference and kept in touch when we realised how close we live to one another, but I've never had any reason to go to St Luke's parish.'

'She has a good reputation?'

'Stella, but not a goody two shoes, know what I mean?'

Joe did; he hadn't detected any kind of sickly-sweet too-good-to-be-true essence about Jean.

He quickly emptied his glass. 'I should get going; I promised Ellie I'd take her for a curry and I'm already late.'

'When am I going to hear wedding bells?' asked Craig. 'I'm assuming I'll get asked to do the deed.'

'Give us a chance, it's not much over a year.'

'We all thought you'd end up with Sophie from the café up at the house, but Ellie seems like a nice lass.'

'She is, and who's "we"?'

'Everyone. All of us. Each and every one of us who has ever spent time in a room with the two of you.'

'Nah, she's more like a sister is Sophie. I did think about it, but after a while, it got a bit weird. We're still good friends, though.'

'Glad to hear it, she can do the catering for the wedding.' Craig grinned and Joe punched him on the shoulder.

'Let me know if Jean hears any more,' Joe called as he walked away.

Joe didn't have to wait long. Only two days had passed before another letter was hand delivered to Jean, accompanied that evening by a phone call with nothing but silence on the other end. The letter made it clear what the sender thought about female ministers and compared her to Satan.

Joe knew that it was now a case of harassment. It didn't take him long to find out that the call had come from a pay-as-you-go phone, the sim card bought locally. He was convinced this was the work of someone with a vendetta.

He sat across from Jean in her kitchen, this time in a smart suit and officially on duty. Joe had a boyish look to him and there was little that showed signs of ageing, something he found useful when talking to witnesses. Those who concluded he was young and inexperienced often found themselves saying more than they intended to, so not always being taken seriously could have its advantages. On this occasion, even though Jean was the one Joe was trying to help, she revealed some things that he suspected she'd rather have kept to herself.

'My contract at St Luke's is coming to an end,' she explained. 'I had a three-year contract and it's now up for renewal. I had thought that it would be smooth sailing, but at the last parochial church council meeting, two of the churchwardens withdrew their support for me. One of them, Frank Porter, was particularly vociferous. He claimed that I was difficult to work with and not a team player. I was so surprised, he hadn't complained before. It was an open meeting so a lot of people heard. I was mortified.'

Joe could tell that the criticism had stung and it still upset her all these weeks later. He passed her a tissue from a box on the coffee table. While she blew her nose, a black and white cat rubbed itself against his leg, leaving a layer of fur on his smart trousers.

'You held on to the post, though?'

'Oh yes, it was only the two who voted against me. Frank resigned, though.' She looked up at Joe; they seemed to be thinking the same thing.

. . .

'So, when is the sting operation?'

Joe, who had made a visit to Craig in his vestry at Charleton House, looked confused.

'What sting?'

'You know, lie in wait in an unmarked van around the corner from Frank's house on bin day, then when he puts his recycling out, you dash round, scoop it up and go through the paper and find the newspapers with all the words missing.'

'That would certainly add an air – a pretty pungent air – of sneakiness to our investigation, but it would also be illegal. I need a warrant to go through his stuff and we haven't got enough evidence for that. Plus, he might not be much of a recycler; he doesn't sound like the kind of bloke who'd give a stuff about the environment.'

'So, what are you going to do?'

'Not a lot at this stage, I'm afraid. I'm really hoping it's going to tail off into nothing and Jean will be left in peace.'

'You said that last time, look what happened.' Craig had a point, but he knew Joe's hands were tied, so he changed the subject. 'You coming to the pub quiz tomorrow? The Black Swan has just started it up. Course, a load of staff from here have formed teams and they're all history buffs and have PhDs and the like, so you'll need to be a member of Mensa to stand a chance.'

'I wouldn't be much use, then.'

'Can't disagree with you, but you could bring Mark. If he's married into the family, you may as well make use of him.' Mark, Joe's brother-in-law, was a tour guide at Charleton House and his brain was like a sponge for historical facts, absorbing odds and ends that would be of no use anywhere other than a pub quiz.

'I'll ask. In the meantime, you need to improve the quality of your coffee, or I'll be arresting you for attempting to poison a police officer.'

'Keep complaining about the refreshments I serve,' Craig said with an exaggerated air of mystery to his voice, 'and you might find it's more than just an attempt.'

The following evening, Mark was filling in their pub quiz team form while Craig updated Joe on what was happening with Jean.

'She had another one this morning. Same style of lettering, same self-sealing envelope. Called her a Satan worshiper and compared her sexual habits to Mary Magdalene, which makes him look like rather an idiot and not as devout as he likes to make out cos nowhere in the bible does it suggest she was a prostitute.'

'She's lucky that he hasn't threatened to mess with her food.' Mark was still scribbling as he spoke. Joe and Craig remained silent; they knew he'd get to the point in a moment. 'Abraham Lincoln received rather a lot of hate mail – I suppose people in positions of power do – and one of his threatened to put a spider in his dumpling.' There was another pause. 'I once received hate mail.' He looked up. 'OK, I'm ready. When are they going to get this show on the road?' He linked his fingers together and stretched his arms out in front of him as though he was preparing for physical exertion.

'Go on, then,' Craig encouraged him, 'you can't stop there. Tell us about the hate mail, unless it's too difficult to talk about.' He rested his hand on Mark's shoulder and displayed an expression of concern that held a hint of mockery.

'Oh, that. It was from an ex-boyfriend; he hoped that I would be killed by kittens with laser eyes.'

'You poor thing,' said Craig, with definite mockery in his voice. 'I'll go and get us another round of drinks; I think you need something for the obvious lingering shock.'

After losing the quiz by one point, because none of them could be sure of the names of all the Spice Girls and their last-ditch guess of Flirty Spice was received with loud and prolonged laughter from much of the room, the three men settled down for a final drink before heading home.

'So, what do you make of this Jean woman?' Mark asked. 'Is she likely to get someone's back up to such an extent that they'd rather spend the night cutting up newspapers than enjoying a good book?'

'Let's put it this way,' replied Craig. 'I spoke to another member of the PCC committee, after Joe had told me what had happened with Frank, and it seems that when Jean's appointment was put to a vote at an open meeting, dozens of the congregation turned up to show their support. She is hugely popular, so no, I don't think she is.'

'Poor woman,' Mark muttered, shaking his head.

'I know, but there's not a lot else we can do at this point.' Joe was genuinely disappointed. He hated the idea of Jean suffering as much as the others did, but whoever had it in for her knew what they were doing.

Over the next couple of months, the letters kept coming; every week or so, another would arrive, the contents getting more and more personal. Forensic test results always came back blank.

Then there were the silent calls, all from the same mobile phone. Now they were coming in the early hours of the morning, so Jean was both upset and utterly exhausted, but she refused to ignore the phone for fear that it was one of her congregation who needed her. Both Craig and Joe made a point of checking in on her, making sure she was OK and trying to deal with the fact that amongst the church community, there was a building resentment towards the police for their lack of progress. Joe was always dreading the next call to say there had been another letter, or worse, and he was as frustrated as anyone. He enjoyed Jean's company; her unexpected love of motor racing was something he shared and it gave them plenty to talk about each time he popped round.

The dreaded next call came when he was on a night shift. It was 3 am on a Thursday when he drove over. The lights were on throughout the house and a little white car was parked on Jean's driveway. He was let into the house by a woman who looked about 120 if she was a day, and she was furious.

'Right, young man, this is getting ridiculous. What are you going to do about it? That's what I want to know.'

'It's alright, Betty, let him through. He's doing his best.' Jean's shout was followed up by a loud sniff and Joe found her sitting on the sofa, being comforted by another woman who looked only a year or two younger than the gatekeeper who had opened the door to him.

'This is Betty and Marion: they were kind enough to stay over for the night and listen out for the phone so I could get some sleep without missing any possible calls from someone who genuinely needs me. I'm afraid I woke when one of the calls came through.'

'That was my fault,' said Betty, looking a little sheepish. 'I had this with me.' She held up a whistle. 'Wanted to deafen the bugger, only I blew it a bit hard down the phone and woke Jean. Sorry, love.'

'Oh, you're alright, I like the idea of you bursting his eardrums. Well, I came down, and… well, he called again straight away. He's just not stopping.'

'Couldn't believe it,' said Marion. 'Barely minutes had gone by and he was at it again. The whistle hadn't put him off; it seems nothing does.'

Joe looked at the three women before him. He was slightly afraid of them; he just wished that Jean's harasser was too.

. . .

Joe wheeled his chair from one side of the office to the other and brought it to a halt next to the desk of Detective Sergeant Colette Harnby, who was trying to dab a coffee stain off her jacket with a look of annoyance. Joe had just got off the phone after a call from Jean. He looked frazzled, and his hair, which needed a brush at the best of times, was definitely out of control. DS Harnby opted not to say anything about his hair; she realised from the look on his face it wouldn't go down well, which was saying something about a man who was so mild mannered.

'D'ya reckon we could get CCTV installed outside Jean's?'

'We'd need a very good reason – has something else happened?'

'It has.' He sighed. 'She got a parcel delivered this morning, by hand. It contained dog sh… I mean dog excrement. Distressing enough as that is, it also means that they're still comfortable enough to make a visit to her house and don't plan on slowing down. If anything, things are ramping up.'

Permission was granted.

It was two days later that there seemed to be a ray of hope. Another letter had arrived, once again with a self-adhesive stamp and self-sealing envelope. As Joe stood before Harnby's desk reading it out to her, he found it hard to hide the excited grin that kept trying to push its way on to his face.

'*…and you're not a team player…* recognise it?'

'Not off hand and you better tell me quick. I'm afraid you're going to leave a puddle on the floor at this rate.'

'Those are carbon copies of the words that Frank used at the open meeting. We've got him – this gives me a solid reason to bring him in.'

Harnby smiled; she looked as relieved as he felt.

'Go on, get the warrant, and we'll search his house. It's about time we had some good news.'

Joe grabbed his jacket and practically skipped out of the room.

The search of Frank's house found nothing. He did read the same newspaper that had been used to form the words of the letters, but his copies were intact. And anyway, with a readership of over 300,000 across the UK, his daily paper alone was hardly going to stand up in court as evidence of his guilt.

He looked concerned as he was interviewed.

'I don't like Jean; I never have and I make no secret of it. We've butted heads since the day she joined us. I've done my best not to rock the boat, but I had to speak out when it came to the continuation of her contract. I don't believe I'm the only one who feels this way, so it was important the matter was brought to a vote. All this is public knowledge.'

'So you deny sending the letters.'

'Of course I do. It's a blooming stupid thing to do, and as for late-night phone calls, I haven't got the time or energy. It's childish; well, it would be if it didn't cause so much distress, and I don't want to cause that. I've always used the official channels available to me.'

He had a point: he'd been open and honest about his feelings from the very beginning. Joe's heart was sinking when he was faced by Frank's calm self-assurance; he knew the man was innocent, which left him precisely nowhere.

A week later, the police removed the CCTV that had been installed. There was nothing on the tape of any use, and Jean and her OAP bodyguards had been updating their community on the current state of affairs, including telling them that there was a camera positioned outside the house, so there was no point keeping it there. But, in the hope that they would also update their friends and associates about its removal, Joe had replaced it with a covert camera and not said a word.

Joe lived in a converted chicken barn at the end of his parents' garden. The small stone building was upside down: you entered into a double bedroom with an en-suite shower room, and then climbed an ornate iron spiral staircase to get to the lounge-cum-kitchen. The Tardis-like building was surprisingly light and airy and gave him the best of both worlds: the privacy of his own place with his parents' kitchen and utility room only a hundred yards away. Some weeks, his own kitchen wasn't used at all, his mother taking pity on him and leaving him a plate of dinner in his fridge (and if she was in a particularly generous mood, she'd take his laundry with her, although she always insisted he come and collect it so she could try to wheedle any local gossip out of him).

Joe had his feet up and was watching clips of old TT races on his laptop, a mug of tea and a half-eaten packet of Hobnobs next to him, when Jean called him. He didn't mind being disturbed on his day off; he wasn't up to much. Jean was clearly distraught and, when he'd managed to calm her down, she told him the disturbing news that she'd received a delivery: a dreadful, upsetting delivery which made Joe so angry, he wanted to punch something. The parcel contained a dead gerbil, and a note informing Jean that she was soon to be just as dead.

Joe called Craig and asked him to go round to Jean's. He then called the station, asking for an officer to be dispatched to collect the animal. From one perspective, this rather macabre delivery was good news.

A short while later, two officers were sitting in front of a computer screen at the police station. DS Harnby hadn't minded Joe coming in on his day off, either; she was just annoyed that he hadn't brought coffee and pastries from somewhere more interesting than the station canteen. His inability to juggle coffee on a motorbike was, in her opinion, a weak argument.

Once he'd promised to go and fetch snacks after they'd done, he pulled up the footage from the covert camera. Jean had been pretty clear on the period of time that the parcel must have been dropped off on her doorstep because she'd gone out shopping between 10am and 1pm and it had been waiting for her on her return. Joe was hunched over, staring at the screen. He and Harnby watched the three hours of footage on fast forward, pausing it from time to time, then they went over it again. Jean's front door was blocked by a large bush, but the entry to her driveway was clear and gave them a great view of any comings and goings.

'Get any closer and you're going to get sucked in.' Harnby grabbed Joe's shoulder and pulled him back into his seat. 'I can't see.'

They watched in silence. After watching and re-watching, forwarding and rewinding, they had to admit it was clear no one had walked down that driveway. Not the postman, not a paperboy; not even a neighbourhood cat.

Neither of them wanted to be the first to speak, putting what they now knew into words. Joe pulled on his coat and together they walked to the station car park. This was going to be the strangest and most uncomfortable couple of hours he had ever experienced.

Craig and Mark stared at Joe with open mouths.

'It was Jean all along? She sent all those things to herself?' Mark said with incredulity in his voice.

Craig looked baffled. 'I don't know what to think. I don't know if I should be as mad as hell or upset at how she played me… us. What did she say?'

'Nothing. She didn't say a word, not at first,' Joe replied. He thought back to the smile and look of relief on Jean's face as she had opened the front door, which had turned to confusion, and then an expression devoid of emotion as she spotted the impeccably dressed and stern-faced DS Harnby, and the uniformed officer standing behind her. As they searched Jean's house, they had found, tucked in a desk drawer, newspapers which had been cut up, words missing. A simple, inexpensive mobile phone was in another drawer, and Joe would have staked a lot of money on it being the phone that was used to call her landline. That, he realised, meant that when the supportive old women had stayed over, Jean had been calling the landline from upstairs. When another call had come through as the three of them stood by the phone, she had likely pressed redial on the mobile in her dressing-gown pocket.

He didn't like to think about where she had got the gerbil from.

Once they were back at the station and her solicitor had arrived, Jean started to speak, but only to say that if she were them, she'd be thinking the same thing: that she'd done it all herself. Later, she repeatedly said that the whole thing stank; that whoever had set her up had done a brilliant job.

The three men took long drinks from their pint glasses.

'Was she lonely?' asked Mark as he wiped foam from his moustache.

'No, she was very busy with the parish, always planning or attending events. Everyone... well, most people liked her,' Craig explained, and then turned to Joe. 'Have you any idea why she did it?'

'Nope, and we might never find out.'

'What will she be charged with?'

'It could be wasting police time, maybe perverting the course of justice. She'll certainly have her day in court.'

Craig nodded sadly and, after taking another drink from his glass, said, 'Well, I'm glad it's all over, but that's the only positive thing I can find in all of this. Mark, you look deep in thought.'

Mark nodded. 'I'd just remembered. A couple of years ago, I

got some nasty letters. I'd got the chance to work with an archaeologist at Charleton House, but he tried to blackmail me.' He sounded deadly serious.

'Why? What happened?' asked Joe.

Mark glanced up at his two friends, then replied, 'It turned out he had a lot of dirt on me.'

There was a long pause, then Joe and Craig gave a simultaneous groan.

'After that,' said Joe, rolling his eyes at his brother-in-law, 'the next round is on you.'

KEY TO A KILLER

1

'I can't believe that we get to do this.'

Mark took hold of the staff pass that was hanging round his neck and waved it. 'Perks of the job, and in your case, of being related to a Charleton House tour guide. Come over here, we have a couple of Dickens first editions.'

The library at Charleton House was a bookworm's dream. It was all dark wood, large leather sofas and a collection of books to make the most ardent bibliophile exclaim in wonder. Mark watched as his guest walked slowly along the shelves, stopping occasionally to cautiously examine a spine. He paused next to a sliding ladder and glanced at Mark with a mischievous look in his eye.

'We could have some fun on this.'

Mark laughed. 'We'd need to oil it first.' His guest continued to examine the books, leaning forward to read the spines, his hands clasped behind his back as though he was forcing himself not to reach out.

'It's quite alright, you can touch them.'

Mark spun round and his companion jumped upright. An

elegant, regal-looking woman had entered the room and she smiled at the two men.

'Karl, this is the Duchess of Ravensbury,' said Mark. 'Your Grace, this is Karl Drinkwater, my cousin.'

The striking woman strode across the room and shook Karl's hand. Evelyn Fitzwilliam Scott, the 12th Duchess of Ravensbury, was a woman who exuded authority – tall, with perfect posture and sharp features that were softened by a gentle look in her eye.

'How lovely to meet a member of Mark's family. I can see the similarity.' Mark's height was matched by that of his cousin, although Karl was heavier set and didn't sport facial hair of any kind, let alone any that could compete with Mark's magnificent handlebar moustache. 'So, you're getting the tour.' The Duchess smiled warmly at Karl. 'Do you live locally?'

'No, Edinburgh. I'm here for a week.'

'Edinburgh is such a delightful city, a visit is long overdue. Speaking of which, that's a rather magnificent bowtie, Mark. Your family's tartan?'

'Yes, or at least I have distant links to the Robertson clan.' As he instinctively reached up to straighten the dark green, blue and red tie, Mark saw Karl contain a smirk. His cousin had teased him about it over breakfast, asking if it spun round or squirted water.

Karl turned, his eye caught by an object on a shelf. 'Is that a 1937 Imperial Number 1 typewriter, a Good Companion model?'

'It is, do you like typewriters?' said the Duchess, sounding impressed that Karl had identified it.

'Yes, it's what I do – I repair and restore them. That's a rather nice example, may I have a look?'

'Of course.' The Duchess removed it from the shelf and placed it on a large wooden desk next to a window that overlooked a courtyard. She turned on a beautiful Tiffany lamp to provide additional light.

'I don't think it's been used for decades, it's purely for display.

It will get dusted from time to time, but we haven't been looking after it, I'm afraid.'

'May I?' Karl's fingers hovered above the machine.

'Be my guest.'

Karl tried a few keys and the return bar. 'It needs some TLC and a thorough clean, but no more than that. I would be happy to take care of it for you.'

The Duchess rested a hand on Karl's arm. 'Would you? I would, of course, pay for your work.'

'And I wouldn't accept, Mark's tour is payment enough. I can probably do it before I head back to Scotland. Has it always been in the family?'

'Oh yes.' The Duchess was searching through a cupboard and pulling out the case. 'It does have rather a sad story behind it, I'm afraid.'

Mark could feel his heart beat a little faster. He loved a good story, and if it was about the Fitzwilliam-Scott family, then all the better.

'It belonged to a cousin of my father, James Grey-Lyons. He was tragically murdered when he was only twenty-five – on his birthday, in fact. I'm afraid the killer was never caught. This typewriter was in the room where he was murdered. He had just been presented with it, a gift from a friend who was badly injured in the attack.'

Karl had frozen with his hand resting on the typewriter. He pulled it away quickly as the Duchess finished speaking.

'Did it happen here?' he asked.

'No, no, at Berwick Hall, a few miles from here. James's family home.'

Mark knew the hall well. Like Charleton House, it was open to the public and he knew many of the staff. He had collaborated with a number of the Berwick Hall tour guides on joint projects, and although he knew that James Grey-Lyons had died young, he had not been aware of the circumstances.

'They kept that quiet,' he said, unsurprised that the Berwick staff had tried to keep the murder under wraps. Probably all too painful for the family.

'Yes, his mother was devastated, and as the years went by and the killing remained a mystery, she refused to discuss it. She didn't want her son's memory to be clouded by speculation and gossip, especially as it was so unusual.' The Duchess had found the case and lifted the typewriter carefully into it.

'In what way?' asked Mark, desperate to know more.

'When his body was found... please, sit down.' The Duchess led the two men to a couple of the large sofas before continuing. 'When the victims were found, the room in which they had been attacked was locked, from the inside, and the key was still in the lock. No one could understand how the killer had escaped.'

'A window?' suggested Mark.

'Yes, but it was shut and the catch secured firmly from the inside. There was no way someone could secure it from the outside.'

Mark doubted that, but kept his thoughts to himself. If you could break into a locked car with a coat hanger, then you could figure out how to secure the catch on a window of a historic house that was bound to be full of cracks from hundreds of years of wear and tear from nature.

'And his friend, didn't he see his attacker?'

'No, Mark, sadly not. Charles received a very severe blow to the head and was unconscious when found.'

The two men glanced at one another, intrigued.

'And you say this was a gift from one to the other?' Karl asked, looking at the typewriter on the other side of the room.

'Yes, James was quite a talented writer. He already had a typewriter, of course, but he had mentioned this particular model in passing to Charles, who then bought it as a gift. They were very close. Charles was devastated, as you can imagine, blamed himself for not being able to save James and later ended his own life. Then there was Sylvia, James's fiancée. She left the country and went to live in Italy. They had been a devoted couple. The whole thing was tragic.'

They all sat in silence for a few moments.

'Well, I really must be going. The Duke and I are having a high court judge for lunch.' She raised an eyebrow and Karl looked momentarily surprised that she would make such an obviously jocular gesture. 'Thank you, Karl, I do appreciate you looking at the typewriter for me. I'm not really sure what I will do with it, but I don't like the idea of it just sitting there, rusty and unloved.'

'I will do my best to return it to you as good as new.'

The two men stood as the Duchess left.

'So much for a holiday,' said Mark as Karl picked up the case.

'Give it a rest. I'll never forget the trip you made to Edinburgh last summer. After you learnt about the wizard who said the Devil had given him a magical staff, you spent the rest of the day doing research on him and you talked of nothing else all week.'

Mark grinned. 'Guilty as charged. Come on, I'll show you more of the house, and then I'll take you to the café. They have really good coffee.'

2

'I think you've got some competition, Bill.' There was a teasing overtone to Karl's voice. 'You should have seen the way Mark looked at the Duchess, like a puppy dog.'

Mark's husband laughed. 'Oh don't worry, I know he'd ditch me for her in a heartbeat.'

'What are you on about?' Mark's attention was firmly on the laptop in front of him.

'Hey, get any closer to that and you'll get sucked in. You don't need glasses, do you?'

'I do not.' Mark sat back at Bill's comment, but his eyes didn't leave the screen.

'What's so important that you need to ignore our guest?'

'Karl isn't a guest, he's family. It's not the same. Well, it's not the same when it comes to him anyway, especially after he finished the last of the Tunnock's teacakes. They were meant to be a gift, but he emptied the packet.'

Karl laughed. He had brought the fluffy chocolate-covered biscuit and marshmallow treats with him from Edinburgh, knowing Mark loved them, but he also couldn't resist them.

Anyway, he had another packet secreted in his luggage and would surprise Mark with it later.

'I still want to know what's so important.' Bill rested a hand on Mark's shoulder and looked at the screen. 'Who is James Grey-Lyons?'

'Relative of the Duchess, he died in rather curious circumstances. The story had been relegated to the mists of time, but I've been able to find an old newspaper article that talks about it. It seems the family tried to cover it up and the details have been kept rather hazy – intentionally, I'm sure. I thought I'd give Ananya a call, she'll be able to tell me more.'

'She is?' asked Bill.

'Ananya Shah, a tour guide at Berwick Hall where it happened. She can show us the room as well – maybe we can work it out, solve the mystery.' Mark looked across at Karl who had sunk into a soft armchair with a glass of wine. 'Imagine that, you come south of the border and solve a murder that the Sassenachs couldn't figure out.'

'Whoa, wind the tape back, please.' Bill looked confused. 'Murder?'

Mark closed the laptop and poured himself a glass of wine with a dramatic flourish, allowing the liquid to trickle out of the bottle from a height. He then turned his chair to face the two men; he loved to tell a good story.

'If we're all comfortable, I shall begin...' Mark chose to ignore the roll of Bill's eyes.

3

'It's always been something the family preferred not to talk about. They don't deny it happened and these days they're not going to great lengths to cover it up, it was just such an upsetting time that they don't discuss it.'

Ananya led Mark and Karl down a long gallery with a high ceiling and oriel and bay windows. 'This became the Earl's bedroom in the late 1600s, a smoking room in the 20th century and it's now used as a dining room by the current family from time to time. This…' Ananya had reached a wooden door at the far end of the room with a chair in front of it '…is now storage, having been a dressing room. During the period of time we're talking about, it became a sort of small sitting-room-cum-smoking-room that offered more privacy. It was a favourite of the men in the family. After 1958, when James died, the family didn't want it to be used for anything else, although they didn't go as far as turning it into a shrine.'

Ananya moved the chair aside and searched through a bunch of keys, eventually finding the one she was looking for.

'Apparently, James often met his friends in here, it was a sanctuary of sorts for him. He liked to come here to read and write, and I imagine it was very cosy, especially in the winter with the fire roaring away.'

The door opened with a loud creak. The group were faced with stacks of metal-framed chairs, their red velvet seats and backs indicating that they were used for events. The room felt cold. It was an unusual shape and most of the walls had been plastered and painted a pale blue-grey shade. A stone fireplace filled one corner, dust-covered boxes were stacked against the walls, and the small window was so dirty that the light struggled to find a way in.

'It doesn't look much, I know, but you have to imagine two big leather armchairs, a rug, the fire blazing away. There was a chest below the window, about the size of that one, but the original has long gone…' Ananya pointed to the right of the fireplace, '…and a small desk with a chair against that wall. I'm not sure about anything else. There might have been more furniture, but I doubt there was much.'

Mark stepped carefully around the stacks of chairs, trying to make sure that he didn't rub against anything and get dust on his outfit.

'I believe the police couldn't work out how the killer got in. May I?' He indicated towards the Tudor casement window.

'Go ahead. It will probably stick, but it does open.'

Mark pulled a silk handkerchief out of his waistcoat pocket and used it to protect his hand from the dust and dirt on the window catch. It was definitely stuck. He gave it a couple of shoves, then a final hard push and the window opened slowly and with some difficulty. He peered out, calling to the others over his shoulder.

'We're on the first floor, but someone could have climbed up. There's a drainpipe here and that climbing plant thingy looks pretty robust. The killer could have climbed that.'

Ananya shook her head. 'The gardens have changed since then. Plus the window was firmly closed and latched from the inside. That was the first thing the police noticed, after the door being locked from the inside. The key was still in the lock on this side.'

Mark pulled the window closed and started fiddling with the catch. Karl joined him and watched.

'What are you doing?'

'Trying to see if there is any way to manipulate the catch from outside. Some way you can lever it open and secure it again.' He ran his finger around the edge of the frame. There were no obvious holes or cracks. He closed the window and wiped his fingers on the handkerchief, folded it neatly and put it in his pocket. 'No, nothing.'

'What about the fireplace?' Karl walked over and tried to peer up the chimney.

'Too narrow,' said Ananya. 'I suppose a child might get down there.'

'Or Santa,' said Karl, his voice dampened by the dark hole as he examined it. 'Despite all the mince pies he eats, he somehow manages to get down every chimney. Now if there's a man who would be able to get away with murder, it would be him. He has the best reason in the world to break into everyone's house.' Karl stood up and grinned at Mark.

'I'll put it to the family,' said Ananya, smiling. 'You may have cracked the case. Why are you interested anyway? If you want to talk about it to the public, Mark, we really ought to speak to the family first.'

Mark shook his head. 'Nothing like that. Personal curiosity.'

'He wants to impress the boss,' said Karl.

'I have no doubt the Duchess would like to know what happened to her relative, but she wouldn't want me to go upsetting the rest of the family.'

'Then you should talk to Andrew Sales. He was a police officer at the time – young lad and his first dead body, apparently. He was in here the other week and I took his details. We're going to interview him for a memory project.'

Mark knew what Ananya was talking about, the conservation staff had done the same thing at Charleton House. People connected with the place were recorded talking about their memories, ensuring the history of the house and family remained for posterity.

'How about it?' Mark looked at his cousin. 'You up for a bit of sleuthing?'

Karl nodded. Now that he'd had a look at the scene of the crime, and how apparently impossible it was for someone to get in, his curiosity had been piqued.

'Let's go and see this Andrew bloke now. I'm only here for the week, the clock is ticking.'

4

Retired police officer Andrew Sales was a large, jovial-looking man. Mark pictured him in uniform, the British bobby hat perched on his round head, rosy cheeked, calling small children scamps and sending them on their way after a paternal ticking off for being naughty. He and Karl were led into Andrew's back garden where they sat in the warmth of the afternoon sun under a large umbrella.

'Of course I remember the case, how could I forget it? Not only was it me first dead body, but it was one of the Grey-Lyons family and bloomin' weird too. We never solved it.' Andrew shook his head. 'What is it you want to know?'

'Everything,' said Karl eagerly. Andrew settled back into his chair and folded his arms.

'Alright then. Well, I was on patrol in Bakewell when the call came out. I was closest so I went straight to the house. All I knew was there had been a disturbance, so I wasn't ready for what I saw. I was led through the house to a small room by a funny little man, I don't remember his name. The house wasn't open to the public back then, so it was all quiet. I could see that the door had been forced open from yards away – there was splinters of wood all around and it had a big crack in it. I thought that was why I'd been called, someone had tried to break into the room.

'There was a young lad, worked in the gardens. He was outside the door, sat on a chair, looking very pale. I had quite the shock when I walked into the room. There was one chap sat in an armchair – looked like he was asleep, but he was at a bit of an odd angle – and another fella on the floor in front of the fireplace. I could see straight away that his head was a mess, the blood 'n stuff in his hair. I have to admit I was a bit shocked.

'It was the sound of the Countess running down the corridor shouting about her James that woke me out of it. The young gardener managed to shake himself from the state he'd been in and had the good sense to stop her entering. I was checking the fella in the armchair to see if there was a pulse when I heard moaning behind me. The other one, on the floor, he was coming around. It was clear that the one in the armchair – James Grey-Lyons – was dead, so I went to deal with… Charles. That was his name, Charles. Well, he'd had one hell of a bang on the head. I tried to make him comfortable until the ambulance took him off to hospital.'

Andrew stared off into the distance. Neither Mark nor Karl wanted to interrupt his thoughts. Mark's own mind was working furiously, trying to grasp at the significance of something Andrew had said. What was it?

Eventually, Andrew turned back to them and interrupted Mark's attempts to bring the elusive thread to the fore. Frustrated, Mark paid attention to what the elderly man was saying.

'I have to confess, I felt a bit useless. I'd not been in the force for long and I was still very green, and it being my first dead one, so I just waited until the DI turned up.'

'What did you think had happened?' Mark was keen to get Andrew's first impressions.

'Well, once I realised that the door had been broken down by the young gardener, I checked the lock on that. The key was still in it, on the inside, so no one had left that way. I looked at the window. The catch was firmly closed and it was only a small fireplace, so I couldn't imagine anyone getting in and out that way.'

Mark's mind cleared and the elusive thread came forward in all its glory. 'You say the gardener broke the door down,' he said eagerly to Andrew. 'Could he not have slipped the key back into the lock after doing that, and then made out that it had been there all along?'

'He could,' said Andrew, smiling wryly, 'had there not been half the household standing by to witness the act. He was a junior member of staff, so he wasn't going to be breaking no doors down before fetching the head gardener, the butler, the chief cook and bottle washer, Uncle Tom Cobley and all to give him the go ahead. And every single person – about ten of 'em in all – said the same thing. The window latch was secure and that key was in the door *before* it was broken down.'

Mark deflated. He'd been so sure he was on the right track. 'What about the murder weapon?' he asked.

'No idea! He'd been stabbed, James. It was clearly a very narrow blade, like *really* narrow. I wondered whether he felt it, to be honest. There wasn't much blood, just a little on his shirt. We couldn't find anything in the room that could have done that, so we had to assume the killer had taken the weapon with him. It must have been very distinctive.

'As for Charles, well, that was easier to work out. A stone had come loose from the fireplace, and it was lying next to him, with plenty of blood on it. The killer must have been surprised to find someone in the room with James and whacked him with it instinctively. James's death seemed to be very planned, so discovering the other man there must really have thrown him, or her.'

'What about a shard of glass, as the weapon used to kill James?' suggested Karl. 'That would be difficult to spot.'

'Or a corkscrew?' added Mark.

'We didn't find anything, although we scoured the place

multiple times. There was a corkscrew, but it wouldn't have matched the wound, and besides which, it had a cork on its end.' Andrew looked at them both with a thoughtful expression. 'So, why the interest?'

Mark and Karl glanced at one another.

'History,' said Mark after a moment's thought. 'Working out the puzzles of the past, and this is a real puzzle.'

Andrew nodded, apparently satisfied with the response. 'It would be grand if you worked it out. It might give Sylvia some peace too.'

'Sylvia?' Mark hadn't expected that. 'She's still alive?'

'She certainly is. Moved back over from Italy after her husband died.'

Mark's ears pricked up. 'She married someone else?' He exchanged a glance with Karl, who raised his eyebrows.

Andrew frowned. 'She did indeed, but don't go thinking there was any hanky-panky going on while James was still alive. It was a good two years later that she married an Italian chap. But now she lives Matlock way. She wanted to be near her children who all decided to live over here. Makes sense, she's getting on now.'

Mark wondered if there were other reasons, too: looking to the past; wanting to be close to James. A guilty conscience, maybe. Who knew, but it certainly wouldn't surprise him.

5

*S*ylvia, Mark observed, was a small yet rather determined-looking old woman, with sharp clear eyes and a demeanour that left you with the belief that she knew what you were thinking, and had equally clear eyes in the back of her head. Sylvia's daughter had opened the door – the two men had phoned ahead and were expected. She'd led them to Sylvia's sitting room and left them with her mother, who had remained seated in a well-worn armchair as they entered.

'So, you want to talk about James, do you?' Sylvia sounded pleasant and welcoming, but Mark had decided that was just a way of disarming them. 'What do you want to know?' Beside her was a small table that seemed to hold all of her essentials: a book, glasses, tea cup and saucer, television guide, TV remote, a small diary and pen. If there was someone to bring her food, then she could sit there all day.

She looked at the two men intently, and Mark could see Karl shifting nervously in his seat. Mark had been concerned about quizzing an old lady about her murdered sweetheart, but not anymore. Sylvia looked like she could handle it.

'I... I mean we only found out about James's death a couple of days ago and we are intrigued, we'd like to know more. Everyone says it was impossible, and yet it happened. We want to find out how the impossible was achieved.'

'Many have tried and all have wasted their time,' said Sylvia. 'We kept the manner of his death quiet for as long as we could – we didn't want the attention it would no doubt have garnered, and we wanted to be left alone to grieve. The police investigation meant that a certain amount of information did start to leak out. Every now and again, someone crawls out of the woodwork and decides they know the answer.' She locked eyes with Mark as she said this. 'Of course, they never do. The way the killer carried out the act is as much of a mystery as *why* they did it.'

'I was going to ask about that, it might be a good place to start. Was there really no motive that you could think of?' Mark pulled out a notepad, his pen poised.

'No, none at all. James was the third of three sons, so he was unlikely to inherit the family wealth. He was a kind, sweet man who, as far as I know, never insulted anyone in his life. He was a writer, but he didn't pen anything that could be considered offensive. He didn't gamble, so he had no debts. Yes, he drank from time to time, but nothing that would cause concern, and I can say hand on heart that I believe he was utterly faithful to me. We were due to be married the following spring and we had never even seen a bump in the road, much less had to navigate one. So, as you can see, there was no motive that I can think of. I would say this was a senseless killing, but it occurred in his home in a locked room, not on a street corner, so that does not make an ounce of sense. Unless someone did it merely to see if they could.'

'What about Charles?' It was Karl's turn to ask a question. 'Could he have been the intended target?'

'We considered that,' Sylvia replied with a sigh of frustration. 'But no. Very few people knew he was there that night, and although he was a little more outspoken than James, he was well-respected and not a single enemy was identified. Certainly not one who felt so strongly that they wanted to kill him.'

There was something about Sylvia that Mark instinctively liked. She looked and sounded utterly fearsome, and spoke about the murder of her fiancé with a matter-of-factness that suggested she had spent a long time coming to terms with his death and was at some kind of peace with what had happened. She did not sound bitter or angry. Equally, she didn't seem to cling on to any hope that his killer would be found. Sylvia was a woman who did not carry hatred in her heart, she had taken control of her life.

Karl was now on the edge of his seat, listening intently. 'About Charles – we were told that he later died by suicide,' he said.

'Yes, it was so tragic. I don't think any of us were aware of just how hard the whole event had hit him. He was so concerned for everyone else. He was a great support to James's mother and he looked after me so well.' Sylvia smiled fondly. 'He even asked me to marry him, said James had asked him to take care of me if anything happened to him. It was so sweet of him, but he was only doing it to be kind. Handsome chap, Charles was always the one who attracted the ladies. In fact, when I first met the two of them, it was Charles, not James who caught my fancy.' The old lady's eyes twinkled for a second, then clouded with sadness again. 'But then I got to know James – gentle, kind James – and after that, I knew he was the man for me.

'Anyway, it was clear that Charles blamed himself for not being able to save James's life, despite the fact that he was unconscious and unable to help, especially as his father was a surgeon. Although Charles had not followed in his footsteps, he did have quite a lot of knowledge which, had he been conscious, might have been of use.

'We all hoped that he would eventually be able to move on. None of us blamed him. After all, there was nothing he could have done and he was very lucky to survive himself. Survivor's guilt, I believe that's what it's called. It was... oh, some two years after James died that I was told that Charles was gone too. He was close to his family, he had a lot of friends, he had me. There were so many people who could have helped, but he did a very good job of hiding just how much he was hurting.'

Sylvia was starting to slow down, and the two men didn't want to overstay their welcome. Mark glanced across at Karl, who took the hint and stood up.

'Thank you so much for your time.'

She started to call for her daughter, but Mark stopped her.

'It's quite alright, we'll find our own way out.'

They weren't quite at the door when Sylvia spoke.

'I didn't ask why you are interested in what happened sixty-five years ago and it probably won't make any difference. But if you are able to find out what happened, I would like to know.'

Mark promised they would tell her whatever they found out, and then the two men left the house, none the wiser than when they had entered it.

6

'So, you've got the bug, eh?' Andrew laughed as he took Mark and Karl back out to his garden. 'I wondered if I'd see you both again. You've got that look in your eyes, like a dog with a bone. I take it you went to see Sylvia?'

'We did,' replied Mark. 'She is quite the woman.'

'She's that alright, marvellous, she is. Been through a lot, but she just stands up straight and keeps on going. Was she helpful?'

Mark looked thoughtful. 'I'm not sure. She didn't say anything particularly new, but it was helpful to get more of a picture of the two men and the circumstances.'

Andrew nodded. 'Always important, the character and the background, when you're looking at something like this. But I doubt you're here to discuss methodology, so what can I do for you?'

Mark glanced down at his notes. 'What else was in the room? Anything that could have helped the killer get in? Anything unusual?'

Andrew scratched his chin as he thought. 'There was nothing that stood out, and there wasn't a whole lot in there in the way of furniture or stuff. There were a couple of pictures on the walls, sketches of the building in gold frames. A wooden chest, but it wasn't big enough for anyone to hide in. I thought of that. The table was fairly simple…'

'Was it a table or a desk?' Mark interrupted.

'Table, one of those with fold-out leaves. It was against the wall with one leaf out. Do you think that makes a difference?'

'I doubt it. I can't see how, I just want to make sure we don't miss anything.' Andrew nodded thoughtfully. 'And the floor,' said Mark. 'I believe there was a rug on the wooden floorboards?'

'That's right.'

'Were any of the floorboards loose? Was there a way in from the room below?'

Andrew shook his head firmly. 'Not a chance, that building is solid as anything. It wasn't built as any kind of fortress, but the walls are right thick and the floors too. I don't even recall noticing a squeaking floorboard.'

Karl and Mark exchanged a quizzical look. They were both stumped.

'Did the men have anything on them?' asked Karl. 'Maybe they had something the killer wanted that would give us a clue, or he or she put something in one of the men's pocket to make it look like he had brought it in with him and it hadn't been used by the killer to gain access to the room.'

'My, my, I hadn't thought of that, no one did. Maybe you two should sign up with the Derbyshire Police. I can't be one hundred per cent sure because it was a while ago. James was wearing a shirt, no jacket. There wasn't anything in his trouser pockets that I remember, but then he was home and didn't need to carry anything around with him. It was different with Charles as he was visiting. He was smartly dressed, but his hat had rolled across the floor. I know he had a handkerchief because I noticed it had his initials sewn in. A wallet. He had a rather nice fountain pen that I have to admit I took a fancy to, but would likely cost a month's wages to the likes of me. The cork from the wine, and of course, he had brought the typewriter with him, but that was on the table ready to be used.'

'And no one was behaving oddly? No one had been spotted in the garden? Unusual visitors who could have secreted themselves away and everyone thought they had left?'

Andrew smiled at Mark. 'You really are thinking of everything, but no. Nothing unusual.'

After a minute or two's silence as they were all immersed in their thoughts, Karl spoke. 'I can't think of anything else. Maybe we should go back to Berwick Hall, Mark, take another look.' His cousin nodded.

'I was thinking the same thing. There must be something in there that can tell us what happened.'

'Well, good luck, lads. We couldn't find a single thing in there that could help us out, but if you can solve it, well, you deserve a medal, that's what I say.' Andrew stood up and shook their hands firmly before walking them to the garden gate. 'I imagine you'll bring a lot of peace to Sylvia as well if you work out what happened.'

7

The two men sat in Karl's car reflecting on Andrew's words.

'I don't think he believes we can do it, do you?' Karl said, with amusement in his voice.

'Nope, not a chance. He reckons we're wasting our time, I'm sure of it, and maybe we are, but I do like the challenge.'

'It's like when I'm trying to work out what's stopping a typewriter from working. I've had a few where I just can't explain it and it's been a real head scratcher. The house could be on fire and I wouldn't notice, I get that caught up in it, but cracking it is the best feeling.'

'You're a nerd, do you know that?'

'Takes one to know one.'

Mark laughed. 'Touche. Back to Berwick Hall, then?'

'Yep, then we should go home. I want to do some more work on the typewriter, see if I can get it cleaned up for the Duchess before I go.'

. . .

'My instinct is it's something to do with the windows, so I want to take a closer look.' Mark was leading the way past members of the public who were examining the information boards in the Earl's Apartment. He nodded a greeting to some of the Berwick Hall staff who recognised him. 'Or maybe it was an inside job and the door lock had been fixed so that it could be unlocked with the key still in place on the inside.'

'Hmm.' Karl was deep in thought and nearly stumbled over a small child. 'The killer can't have hidden inside the room because there would have been a lot of activity and they would have been spotted if they had crawled out from under a floorboard. I know Andrew said the floorboards weren't an option, but he might have been wrong.'

'Perhaps, but if they could hide, they might have stayed there for a while, if they had supplies. They could have climbed out in the night and no one would be any the wiser. It would have been easy then for them to escape from the house.'

Ananya was waiting for them outside the heavy wooden door with the same large bunch of keys. She let them in with an amused look on her face; she knew how much of a blood hound Mark could become from her previous encounters with him. Karl immediately started knocking on the wooden panelling surrounding the door, the only panelled part of the room.

'You're wasting your time,' said Mark, coming over to him. 'Look, it's basically a screen. Unless the killer was no more than about four inches wide, or thin, or whatever, they couldn't have been in there.'

Karl grunted. He knew that from their last visit, but he was desperate for answers. Next, he moved aside a painting. It depicted a large, muscular angel with wings and a beard who was holding a baby at arm's length as if he didn't know what to do with it and wished it would stop crying. Karl tapped the wall – nothing. It was solid.

Mark lifted the lid of the chest.

'You'd be lucky if you could get both your boots in that, let alone the rest of you,' said Karl, peering over his shoulder.

'Can we move this?' Mark asked Ananya.

'Be my guest.'

The two men took an end of the chest each and lifted it away from the window. Mark bent down, trying not to kneel on the dusty floor for fear of spoiling his trousers, and started examining the floorboards.

'If the chest had a false bottom, someone could climb into it, then straight into a hole in the floor. The closed chest would hide any change to the wooden boards and the chances are that back then, the police wouldn't have done much more than open the lid and take a quick look for the murder weapon.'

Ananya looked amused.

After poking around the boards for any sign that they'd been tampered with, stamping on them to see if the sound changed and simply getting as close to them as possible and trying to see any inconsistencies, Mark stood slowly, groaning as he straightened up.

'Don't tell me you've reached that stage,' teased Karl.

'What stage?'

'The groaning when you stand up, sit down, lift something…'

'Sadly, yes, I'm an old man.'

'You're only six months older than me.'

'I know, so it won't be long and you'll be creaking too.'

Karl bent over and touched his toes with well-practised ease.

'Yoga. You should give it a go.'

'The killer would have needed to do more than yoga to get in a chest this size. You said the original was the same size as this?' Mark looked quizzically at Ananya, who nodded. 'There's nothing to indicate a hole below it in the floor and only a toddler could hide in this.'

'Maybe a toddler was the killer, convinced to carry out the murder on behalf of someone who offered them a year's supply of chocolate and a pair of roller-skates.' Surprisingly, Karl looked serious.

'You don't spend much time with children, do you?' Mark twisted one end of his moustache. He had another look at the catches on the window, but having given them a thorough going over the first time he and Karl had examined the room, he made a rather half-hearted attempt.

'I'm stumped, blooming stumped. The killer was some kind of magician.' He walked slowly to the door, followed by Karl and Ananya.

'I wouldn't feel too bad, Mark, you're not the first to be flummoxed. It seems that no one can figure it out. It will remain a mystery. Maybe it's better that way, the identity of the killer could cause a lot of heartache.'

'Maybe,' mumbled Mark, who was still deep in thought as he led the way out of the room.

8

With the table cleared from their dinner of homemade lasagne and garlic bread, Bill laid out the marking he needed to do for the following day: piles of pupils' exercise books, some covered in bright stickers, some doodled all over, one or two carefully wrapped in paper to make a colourful cover of stripes or rainbows. Karl stationed himself at the opposite end, having placed the typewriter squarely in front of him on top of an old tea towel and laid a small number of tools out in a perfectly neat row.

'Are typewriter emergencies common? I assume they are if you travel with your tool kit,' teased Bill.

'Constantly, you'd be amazed. I'm always asked to attend the scene of a typewriter catastrophe when I'm on the road.' He glanced up at Bill and smiled. 'These aren't my usual tools, these are things Mark helped me gather up – a few pieces from a glasses repair kit, a screwdriver from a tool box in your garage that looks like it hasn't seen any action since 1982 or thereabouts. It depends how bad things are in here.' He peered into the typewriter with the torch on his phone. 'I might be able to sort it, otherwise I'll need to take it home.'

'And I'll have to come and fetch it on behalf of the Duchess, all expenses paid,' called Mark from the other side of the open doors that divided the house in two, the dining room on one side, the sitting room on the other. 'I could stay at the Balmoral Hotel, champagne served with every meal.'

'I'm going to guess that it's more likely you'll be sleeping in my spare room, if you can find the bed under all the clutter, and drinking cheap bottled beer from the supermarket up the road. The typewriter repair business doesn't lend itself to me having a wine cellar,' said Karl.

The two men at the table worked in silence, the sound of the TV in the background. There was a comfortable ease and peace about the evening. No one needed to speak; they were all engrossed in their work or entertainment, easy enough in one another's company that they didn't have to work at being together. Mark's attention had drifted from the TV programme and he was making notes, a spider graph appearing on the page of his notebook as he tried to link together everything he knew about the murder at Berwick Hall, and it wasn't much. In the end, the graph wasn't very web like.

Mark got up to pour a glass of wine for everyone. He leaned over Karl's shoulder as he placed them on the table.

'Does it work?'

'You can find out if you like. You got some paper?' Bill passed a couple of sheets across without looking up from his work. 'I still need a bit more time with it,' said Karl, 'and it needs a really good clean, but it should work OK. The keys will be a bit sticky and I doubt there'll be much or any ink on the ribbon, but we'll find out.' Karl stood up, wine glass in hand, and Mark took his place at the table. He fed the paper in, turning the knob carefully. After straightening the paper, he placed his fingers gently on the keys.

He felt a kind of reverence. This might have been the last thing that James had touched. Andrew hadn't mentioned there being a piece of paper in the machine, any typed final words, so perhaps Mark would be the first to use it since Charles purchased it for his friend. The joy of receiving this might have been the last thing the young man felt before being murdered.

Mark had no idea what to write. He couldn't think of any words worthy of a moment like this. The keys were smooth beneath his fingers and for a brief moment, he started to doubt whether he should type anything at all. Maybe he should let the final touch be that of James.

'Hang on, put the paper rest up.' Karl pressed a small button, then he pressed it again. 'I'll have to add this to my list of jobs, I need to…' He poked around at the back of the machine for a moment before a slim metal arm swung up behind the floppy piece of paper. It caught the paper awkwardly rather than supporting it squarely. 'Bugger, sorry. Hang on.' As Karl retrieved the paper, then made sure the rest was upright, he yelped. 'Ow! That's not right, may I take a closer look?'

Mark stood up and once again the two men changed places. Karl spun the typewriter around so the back of it was facing him.

'This has been altered. The arm should be a blunt, narrow, straight piece of metal with a rounded tip.' He sat in silence, until his cousin spoke from behind him.

'Are you thinking what I'm thinking?'

'I'd normally say *I hope not*, but on this occasion…'

'Karl, tell me if I'm losing my mind…'

'You're losing…'

'Shut up. Tell me if I'm wrong, but does that metal arm look like a blade? A very small, narrow blade that could fit the description of the type of weapon that might have killed James?'

9

The leather sofa creaked as Karl made himself comfortable in the Charleton House library. He still couldn't quite believe that he was sitting down for coffee with a member of one of the country's most significant aristocratic families. Not only that, but the Duchess was pouring.

'I have to confess, I didn't think for one minute that you would solve the murder. I really thought you would just clean up the typewriter and return it to me, but then I should have known better.' She looked at Mark and smiled warmly. 'Your cousin has a marvellous ability to discover all sorts of wonders amongst our collections and stores.'

'You have a true treasure trove, Duchess, it makes my job extremely easy,' Mark replied, bathing in her compliment.

'So, I am dying to know what you discovered… sugar? Milk?'

'Oh, er, yes, just milk.' Now the Duchess was offering to add milk and sugar, Karl was staggered. 'Right, well, we, er… Mark, do you want to start?'

Mark, at ease in the company of the Duchess, sat back into the sofa with his cup of coffee in his hands.

'To be entirely honest, it was sheer chance. We checked every aspect of the room – the windows, door, floor and ceiling. It seemed impossible for anyone to get in from the outside, so everyone said it was an impossible murder. James dead, Charles injured and unconscious. No way in, no way out. There was nowhere anyone could hide.'

Mark stopped and took a sip of his coffee. He was enjoying telling the story, although it wasn't actually a story. It was a disturbing, sad and upsetting reality. Before he could continue, Karl, having found some confidence, stepped in.

'Charles and James had been close friends for a very long time. Charles had been an advocate of James's writing and expressed a keenness to support him. He surprised James with a typewriter he was particularly fond of for his birthday. A beautiful and thoughtful gift, I must say. I would be very happy if someone gave me one of those.' He eyed Mark and the Duchess laughed.

'You'd better make a note of that, Mark.'

'Charles arrived for the boys' night in, dressed as smartly as ever, and wearing a hat.' Mark had been nodding along as Karl spoke and now took over again. 'But Charles had an extra surprise, and not the pleasant kind that you would expect on your birthday. You see, he had tampered with the paper rest at the back of the typewriter and turned it into an extremely sharp little blade. It was only about 10cm long and less than 1cm wide. A blade like that is too small to get a good hold of, plus Charles would have ripped his hand to shreds trying, but he had planned ahead and brought with him a cork from a bottle of wine. The police did find a second cork in the room, but either got confused and forgot there was already one on the end of the corkscrew, or dismissed it as being from a previous occasion that Charles opened a bottle of wine. Either way they didn't view it as significant. With the blunt end of the blade inserted into the cork, Charles could get just enough purchase to stab his friend. Add to this the knowledge he had picked up from his surgeon father, and he would have known exactly where he needed to insert the blade in order to have the desired result – death.'

The Duchess shook her head slowly as she considered what she had been told.

'But what about Charles's injuries? He had been badly attacked.'

'It was self-inflicted,' said Karl. 'It would have taken a heck of a lot of determination, but he was able to give himself a bash on the back of the head. He was wearing a hat when he arrived at Berwick Hall, which would have hidden the injury, and once he had killed James, he hit himself with a stone that had come loose from the fireplace – or more likely, he had loosened it on a previous visit – to reopen the wound. Then he just had to lie down on the floor, pretend to be unconscious when the police entered, and then come round...' Karl made little air quotes as he said *come round* '...with some moaning and groaning, feign shock at the death of his friend and claim to have seen nothing, knowing that the chances of them finding the blade in the typewriter were remote, and he was right. It might be that he thought about trying to retrieve the typewriter, but felt it might draw attention to it.'

There was silence for a few moments as they all considered the circumstances that had been described. It had been cold-blooded murder, carried out by a man James considered a friend.

'But why?' asked the Duchess. 'From everything I've been told, they were each devoted to the other on an equal footing. They had been for many years.'

'Another devotion got caught up in the mix,' said Karl, getting carried away by telling the story as he poured himself more coffee, an amused Mark watching. 'James fell head over heels in love with Sylvia and fortunately, Charles appeared to approve of the match. He was perfectly happy for Sylvia to spend a lot of time with him and James, and there was no sign of Charles feeling like a gooseberry and getting annoyed at the new situation. In reality, despite having no trouble attracting female attention with his good looks, Charles was also very much in love with Sylvia. The bottom line is he wanted her for himself. It must have been excruciating for him to watch Sylvia and James's relationship blossom, when all the while he was falling further and further in love with her, believing that he would never be able to have her.

'Eventually he concluded that he had to have her no matter what and took action. Once James had died and, I presume, he believed an appropriate amount of time had passed, Charles proposed to Sylvia himself, couching it as being about taking care of her and something that James would have wanted. Sylvia thought he was just being thoughtful and looking out for the fiancée of his best friend, but marrying her had actually been his intention all along. She turned him down.

'When she went on to marry an Italian man, Charles was devastated. He had killed his dearest friend for nothing, and so in a fit of remorse, or maybe despair, he killed himself. The dates fit – Sylvia's marriage and Charles's suicide happened within weeks of each other – so we're sure this is the reason behind the crime.'

Silence descended once again while they all considered the events of the past. A large clock gave a low, rumbling, masculine chime, the perfect sound for the room, but none of them registered it.

Eventually, the Duchess spoke softly.

'Have you told Sylvia?'

'No,' answered Mark. 'I didn't feel that we were the right people to do that.'

'I'll do it,' she replied without hesitation. 'I know her a little – enough that, along with my family connection to James, it wouldn't seem strange for me to visit and break the news to her.' She looked at the two men intently. 'You are sure that was what happened? It does make sense, but if I am about to tell an elderly woman that a friend she loved and trusted killed her fiancé, then I need to be sure.'

Mark and Karl glanced at each other. They were absolutely certain.

'The police haven't confirmed it one way or the other. When we gave Joe the typewriter, he said it would be handed to some kind of cold-case team. He was convinced by our theory, but it's not official, not yet.'

'Well, perhaps I can couch it as preparing her for the likely outcome, not wanting her to be shocked if it comes to light that Charles was indeed the killer. Sylvia is a very strong woman, but she was heartbroken when James died. I was once told by another cousin that Luca was never her true love. He was a good man and they were very happy, but James was the only man she ever really loved.'

EPILOGUE

'So, I'm related to a celebrity. Will you still acknowledge me when we're out in public?'

Mark laughed. He'd just finished telling his cousin about his latest project, a ten-minute slot on a weekly TV news programme where he would be talking about local history.

'For now, but I might have to reconsider if I get my own series. You can carry my bags.'

Mark had his feet up after a long day of delivering tours at Charleton House. His bright orange socks stood out like little traffic cones against the dark fabric of the sofa, his orange tie had been loosened and hung skew-whiff around his neck. A phone was wedged between his ear and the sofa.

'Well, I have my own celebrity news,' declared Karl. 'Some of my typewriters are going to be starring in a new World War Two film. It's set at that training college for spies that was based at Arisaig House in Inverness-shire. I'm providing three in total. It's a nice little sideline I'm developing, supplying period typewriters to film and TV companies. I don't know why I didn't think about it before.'

Mark could hear the sound of a bottle being opened. 'You on the cheap supermarket beer?'

'No, celebrating with some locally brewed stuff. A gift from a happy customer.'

'Speaking of which, a happy customer is what I'm calling about. The Duchess was very pleased with the typewriter you sent down, she couldn't tell the difference between yours and the Good Companion that Charles gave James.'

'Any idea what the police are planning to do with the original?'

'Not a clue. Even Joe doesn't know, but he doesn't work in that department, he just handed it over.' Mark swirled the red wine in his glass.

'What good is a brother-in-law in the police if he's not going to give you inside information?' Karl's tone made it clear he was joking. He'd met Joe many times and liked him. 'What's the Duchess planning for it, then?'

Mark thought back to the meeting he'd had with the Duchess the previous week. 'A small display in the library, so it won't be seen by general visitors, just those on special tours where we'll talk specifically about James's writing. It's more of a prop for us to use as a talking point than a display that people will look at on their own. We're not going to discuss his death, but she wants to make sure that his writing is enjoyed by a much wider audience. The typewriter will be paired with a photograph of him and a few examples of his work. She'd like to publish a book of his essays and poems, but that's a bigger piece of work and only in the very early planning stages.'

'You should tell her that if she ever gets James's typewriter back, I'll happily continue to work on it.'

'You won't find handling it rather gruesome, especially the blade itself?' Mark waited for a response while Karl took a drink of beer. He could hear loud gulps.

'Nah. It doesn't look gory, it's just a typewriter that needs cleaning and a new paper rest fitting. It happens to have a rather fascinating story behind it, and we both love a good story, don't we.'

Mark smiled and took a sip of wine.

'We certainly do.'

Make sure you find out when the next Charleton House Mystery is released by signing up to Kate's newsletters at www.katepadams.com

READ A FREE CHARLETON HOUSE MYSTERY

Building a relationship with my readers is one of the best things about writing. I occasionally send newsletters with details on new releases, special offers, interviews and articles relating to The Charleton House Mysteries.

Sign up to my mailing list and you'll also receive the very first Charleton House Mystery, *A Stately Murder*.

Head to my website for your free copy and find out what happens when Sophie stumbles across the victim of the first murder Charleton House has ever known.

www.katepadams.com

ABOUT THE AUTHOR

After 25 years working in some of England's finest buildings, Kate P. Adams has turned to murder.

Kate grew up in Derbyshire, the setting for many of her books, and went on to work in theatres around the country, the Natural History Museum - London, the University of Oxford and Hampton Court Palace. Every day she explored darkened corridors and rooms full of history behind doors the public never get to enter. Kate spent years in these beautiful buildings listening to fantastic tales, wondering where the bodies were hidden, and hoping that she'd run into a ghost or two.

Kate has an unhealthy obsession with finding the perfect cup of coffee, enjoys a gin and tonic, and is managed by Pumpkin, a domineering tabby cat who is a little on the large side. Now that she lives in the USA, writing The Charleton House Mysteries allows Kate to go home to her beloved Derbyshire everyday, in her head at least.

ACKNOWLEDGEMENTS

Many thanks to my advance readers; your support and feedback means a great deal to me.

I am extremely grateful to Rosanna Summers whose insightful comments made the book so much better that it would otherwise have been.

Thank you to Glyn Williams who taught me the ins and outs of well dressing.

I'm extremely grateful to Richard Mason, my police advisor who guides me on procedure and makes sure I am, largely, within the law. When I break the rules, that's all me!

My talented editor Alison Jack, and Julia Gibbs, my eagle-eyed proofreader. It is always a pleasure to work with them, and this time they really pulled out the stops to help me complete this book during a difficult time.

Printed in Great Britain
by Amazon